DIVIDED
LOYALTIES

*For Colleen —
Enjoy the journey*

Mary K. Tilghman

WHAT READERS SAY ABOUT
DIVIDED LOYALTIES

"This is a charming story of compelling characters set against the backdrop of the Civil War. The author does a wonderful job capturing historic details and realities of life in Maryland at that time. A romance is woven amidst the war story, making for a delightful read."

"Well researched and an engaging story. Recommended to all lovers of historical fiction."

"This book brilliantly captures a young woman's modern day resilience during a time when our nation was at the breaking point."

"A balanced approach to the complexity of the time. You gave reality to the abstract through the lens of your characters."

DIVIDED LOYALTIES

Mary K. Tilghman

Foxhall books
Baltimore

Second edition 2019

This is a work of fiction. Names, characters, businesses, places, events and incidents are either the products of the author's imagination or used in a fictitious manner. Any resemblance to actual persons living or dead, or actual events is purely coincidental.

ISBN: 978-1-7338792-0-0

Published 2019 by Foxhall Books, Baltimore
Originally published by Black Rose Writing

www.maryktilghmanwrites.com
Printed in the United States of America
DIVIDED LOYALTIES is printed in Baskerville.

Dedicated
to the strong women who nurture us all—
mothers and grandmothers, aunts and sisters,
nurses, teachers and so many others.
In particular, I dedicate this work to
my mother Patricia Tilghman,
my mother-in-law Angela Truitt
and my grandmothers Regina Gill and Catherine Tilghman

Chapter 1
MARCH OF SOLDIERS

The pounding steps of soldiers echoed through the valley. These troops were the first Maureen and Joe saw marching by their farm. Maureen usually loved the sound of visitors outside her door. These men, marching from parts unknown, were strangers, and they brought fear—fear and the specter of war at their doorstep.

She couldn't help watching them as she and her brother Joe fixed the fence near the road. Most marched in neatly-formed columns, a model of military discipline, looking neither right nor left as they passed.

Maureen looked at her brother as his brown hawk-like eyes followed the troops until they marched out of sight. She knew his heart and spirit were with them. He wanted to join the fight.

"Something's brewing." Joe turned away from the road. "When I was in Sharpsburg this morning, there was talk of a Confederate occupation. It's not gonna happen, but you know how people are. It's all they talked about. Some were packing up and going farther north."

While he was talking, more troops passed by, this a rag tag band of men who stopped for a sip of water from the nearby creek, laughing and shouting to one another. Maureen bristled at their coarse language.

"Don't pay them any attention, Moe," Joe whispered, and returned his attention to his work. "They're just showing off."

"They're the scruffiest lot of soldiers I ever saw," Maureen muttered. "Confederates! What are Confederates doing here?"

She frowned and crossed her arms. When one of them grinned at her and winked, she scowled at him and looked away. He was not the sort she'd want to run into on her way to town. He was cocky, and with a gun he would be downright dangerous.

1

The thought made her shiver.

"They want to provoke us, Moe. Ignore them." His dark eyes slid away from his work to the soldiers as they continued on their way. He set his jaw as he shoved the last rail firmly into place and then he climbed to sit on the mended fence.

"It all seems so familiar, doesn't it, Joe?" Maureen rested her arms on the fence and looked up at her brother. Joe nodded, his focus fixed on the now quiet road. Maureen wasn't sure he was listening.

"Like the British soldiers we saw in Galway," he finally answered. "I was thinking of that, too. I'll never forget Old Man Murphy. He'shouted every time a soldier walked past his house."

"The men at the pub used to get so angry at them." Maureen remembered how, night after night, the townsmen gathered for a pint in the small pub her parents kept on the road to Galway. As the peat fire grew smokier, the conversation usually grew louder. Always, they ended the night complaining about the British soldiers.

"It seemed like more and more marched through town as time went by," she said.

Joe shoved his hands in his pockets and shook his head. "They said the British Army was an occupying force. But this is different. This country is at war with itself."

Maureen knew Joe was anxious to enlist. He begged his father for permission for months though Father wouldn't hear of it. After their father was injured in a fall earlier that summer, Joe took on running the farm. All the while, Maureen knew Joe never gave up his intentions to enlist.

The two of them, born only a year apart, had been inseparable for as long as they could remember. Maureen couldn't imagine life without her strong-willed brother.

It was clear he was determined to go, and soon, now that Father was nearly well. She only wished she knew how she could serve her adopted country, too.

"No use thinking about it now," Joe said. "You better go see that the chickens aren't out. One of those soldiers might decide to liberate them." He jumped from the fence and stomped off toward the orchard, anger evident in his wiry frame.

Maureen rushed to the hen house in the back yard. With relief, she saw her favorite, a black hen with a white diamond on her chest, leading the rest toward Maureen, cackling non-stop.

"Here you go." Maureen spread feed on the dusty ground. She hadn't thought about hungry soldiers stealing her chickens. She'd have to keep an eye on them.

She relished the peaceful moment as the chickens pecked away at their food. Both she and Joe worked hard to keep the farm running these past few months. Besides her farm chores, she helped her mother care for her father—not an easy task when her father grumbled every waking moment.

She understood his pain and frustration. Summer hardly had a chance to begin when he fell through the shed roof. Now the season was in full bloom and the corn stalks in the fields stood taller than Joe. She knew how disappointed Father was that he was missing it all.

"Nice to have nothing to do."

Maureen turned to see her brother's friend Patrick sauntering up to the henhouse from the road. She held her tongue, much as she wanted to tell him all she did that very morning.

She'd tended to her chickens, drawn water, lit the fire, made the coffee and the oatmeal, re-bandaged her father's wound, brought him his breakfast and listened to him go on about her incompetence yet again. She'd helped Joe in the cornfield and spent the last hour with him repairing the fence.

Instead, she greeted Patrick with an unimpressed sigh.

"Hello, Patrick." She crossed her arms. "Joe's not here. I saw him head toward the orchard a while ago."

Patrick's pale baby face turned deep red. "What makes you think I was looking for Joe?"

"Why else would you be here?" She wasn't in the mood for his tiresome flirting. He flirted with every girl. Though Maureen longed for a beau of her own, she knew his flirtations were meaningless.

"You're right, of course. I was looking for Joe. We were going to see about joining the army today."

Maureen stood up straight, the chickens forgotten.

3

"Today! Before Father's recovered?"

"We're not leaving today. We just wanted to find out what we have to do to enlist. I wouldn't leave without saying goodbye to you." Patrick's eyes twinkled and she knew he was teasing her again.

"Go on with your blathering, you eejit." She put her hand on her hip and frowned. She found her brother's friend a little annoying. "You're all ready to leave?"

"Yes, I am. I figure I'm enlisting no matter what Joe decides. I don't want to miss the war. The people in town are saying it might not last until the end of the year," he told her.

Maureen was figuring out how to respond when she saw her friend Eliza duck under an apple tree branch and skip down the well-worn path between their two farms. Usually neat as a pin, she had bits of grass in her hair and mud on her white muslin skirt. Maureen smiled with relief when she saw her, a welcome distraction to Joe's tiresome friend.

"Where have you been?" Maureen reached over and pulled a strand of grass out of her best friend's long blonde braid.

Eliza laughed. "I was…helping mother in the garden. I guess I look a mess."

"Indeed, you do," Maureen said.

Even dirty, Eliza couldn't help but be pretty. With her golden skin, long yellow tresses and perfectly oval face, she was the opposite of Maureen.

Her mother always said Maureen and her brother were Black Irish like their father. Maureen's eyes, dark as night, glowed in her square face. Although her unruly curly hair was nearly black, her skin was so pale it sunburned the moment she walked outside. She barely reached five feet while her willowy friend was a head taller.

Though Eliza and Maureen called each other cousins, their connection was only by marriage. Uncle Raymond, a distant relation to Maureen's father, had come to the States long ago, met and married Priscilla Riley and adopted her two children Robert and Eliza.

"How did you escape your father's sick room?" Eliza asked.

"Doctor Lee was here this morning. He told Father to get out of

4

bed, and you know Father. He started one of his tirades. When he decided to go on about my inadequacies, Mother—bless her heart—sent me out to help Joe."

She stopped a minute when she heard her father's growling filtering through the back door. She listened until she heard her mother answer his call.

"So, Patrick says he's signing up today," Maureen continued. "I wish there was something I could do to serve. I'd go in a heartbeat."

Eliza laughed. "A girl in the army—" She stopped when she saw Maureen's face darken. "You're serious, aren't you?"

"Right ye be," Maureen replied. "I'm not saying I want to take up arms, but there must be some way I can serve. This country welcomed us when we were forced to leave Ireland. It was scary at first. So many strangers who didn't talk like us. Then one night I lay in my bed and listened to the crickets. It was then I realized I was home. Here there was peace, freedom and a whole new family to love. No more soldiers on patrol. No more angry men dreaming of independence. This country is my home now."

Her friends stood silently for a moment. Then Patrick had to interrupt.

"But it's a man's job to protect it. That's why we're taking up arms." Although his frown looked serious, Maureen couldn't miss the twinkle in his eye as he added his last jab. "You womenfolk stay behind to keep the home fires burning."

"Really now, Patrick Toohey? Is that our job?" Maureen glowered at Patrick. "The cheek of ya."

Joe sauntered toward them from the front of the house, a half-eaten apple in his hand.

"Moe's spouting off again, isn't she? I heard ya. She can be right gabby when she wants to be."

Maureen threw her hands up in exasperation. "Don't you be siding with Patrick!"

Joe laughed. He elbowed his friend in the ribs. "Been catching a little heat from my sister?" When he caught sight of Eliza, he dropped his apple as he blushed. "Hello, Miss Brennan! How are ya?" He bowed with an awkward flourish.

Maureen shook her head at them all. "I've had just about enough from all of ya." She wiped the dust off her hands and started back toward the house.

"Come on, Maureen," Patrick said, a sly smile crossing his face. "Can't you take a little teasing? We don't mean no harm."

"Don't mind her. The soldiers have set her off," Joe said and clapped his friend on the shoulder. "You all ready to go, Pat?"

Patrick nodded solemnly.

"My brother already left," Eliza said. "Amy begged him not to go—they've barely been married a year. You know how conscientious Robert is. He told her he was duty-bound to enlist. Then he brought her to stay with us while he's gone. She's done nothing but mope about the house, poor thing."

"You heard about Zack and Tom?" Patrick asked.

Joe shook his head. "What eejits. Gone and joined the Confederate Army."

"Their pa's a Southern sympathizer. The Hendersons have lots of family in Virginia," Patrick explained.

"Doesn't make it right," Joe muttered.

"They're following their hearts just like you," Maureen offered. She knew soft-hearted Tom well enough. She was sweet on him for the longest time though he never noticed.

"Are they now?" Joe's eyes were full of scorn.

"What about you, Joe?" Patrick asked. "Ready to go?"

Maureen saw a look of alarm pass over Eliza's face. Maureen knew without Eliza telling her that she had developed quite an attachment to Joe.

"I hafta talk to Father one more time. If he says no… I'm not sure what I'll do."

Maureen understood the despair in her brother's voice. He loved his new country the way a convert loves his new church. He was fervent in his love for America. When Uncle Raymond used to tell stories of General Washington's celebration of St. Patrick's Day during the Revolutionary War, Joe ate it up. His ardor was catching; Maureen was inspired by Joe's retold stories. Like Joe, she longed to do anything she could to bring peace back to her beloved valley.

Plenty of their friends had already left. She longed to do something besides watch them all leave.

Mother appeared at the kitchen door. She nodded at Maureen. What does Father need now? she wondered.

"I've frittered away enough of my afternoon," she told her friends. Then she looked pointedly at Patrick. "I have home fires to tend to."

"I'm sick of corn," Joe told Maureen as they walked between rows of towering green cornstalks. The silk on fat ears of corn had darkened, a signal that harvest was near.

"Patrick's been gone a month now. So has Robert. All the lads are gone, and I'm still stuck in this field." He shook the hoe he carried and thrust it out in front of them. "I could take this hoe and throw it in the creek. I don't care what happens here anymore. Not when there's a war going on. Not when I can hear cannon fire so close to home."

"I understand," Maureen said and pulled the hoe out of his hands. Then she put a hand on her brother's shoulder and smirked. "You're sounding like the men that used to shout in the pub."

Joe laughed and nodded. "I guess I do. I didn't know what the fuss was about in those days but I heard the passion in their voices."

"It wasn't passion. It was the effects of the beer you were hearing. It was all hot air and nothing more. Nothing has changed in Ireland since those days," Maureen said.

"True enough. And yet I do believe the day will come when Ireland will be free."

They had arrived at the end of the cornfield as it opened onto the hen house and the apple orchard. In the quiet of the afternoon, they could hear cannons firing in the distance.

"They've been going at it all day, Moe," he told his little sister. "I've heard the fighting since first thing this morning. And if you look, you can see smoke rising off South Mountain."

Maureen shaded her eyes from the strong September sun and

looked across the valley, a half-day's walk from their farm. "How long can it last?" she asked.

Joe looked toward the mountain and said nothing.

"Joe?"

He nodded without looking at her.

"You're thinking the fighting will come here?"

"No doubt about it," Joe told her. "The soldiers we've seen in the past few weeks? I don't know where they're planning to fight but it sure looks like it might be near here. Here or Shepherdstown. Maybe Harper's Ferry. We've seen too many soldiers for the fight to be too far off."

Maureen looked at the mountain in the distance. "Patrick isn't there, is he?"

"No, it's too soon. None of the boys we know are there. They've got training to do before the Army will put them into battle. Either Army—you know the Henderson boys headed South."

Maureen nodded.

As Joe fell silent, she wondered what he was planning. Father's objections were vehement. No matter what Joe said, Father shot him down. He spat out only disgust at Joe's patriotism, reminding him that loyalty to a nation led their family to heartbreak and their exile from Ireland. He reminded him of his duty to his family and the farm. He asserted his authority as head of the household.

All of it only strengthened Joe's resolve.

Maureen could see Joe's desire to enlist in his face. He stood there in silence, his eyes trained on the rising tower of gun smoke. His hands were shoved deep inside his pockets—the jingle of coins a sure sign he was planning to go soon. He wouldn't listen to his father's yelling ever again.

Maureen didn't know what to say. She rested her chin on the hoe handle and memorized this moment with her brother.

Maybe he already made his decision. Maybe this would be the last day they spent together. Even though she hated the thought of seeing him leave, she couldn't ask him to stay either.

She had so many things she wanted to say. She longed to tell him that she'd miss him, she loved him, and she'd pray for him every night.

Suddenly, he seemed to awaken from his trance and turned to her. "I suppose Mother is looking for you for help with supper. I'll take the hoe back and—and then I'll be in."

Joe stared at Maureen for a moment as if he was going to say something more. Instead, he grabbed the hoe and watched her head into the house.

Later, when Maureen put a bowl of potatoes on the table for the evening meal, Joe was nowhere to be found.

She called up to the loft for him to join them at the table. She started for the back door when she realized Joe wasn't coming in for supper.

He was probably on his way to Hagerstown. She looked at her mother and father who waited in silence as if they already knew Joe was gone.

Her mother shook her head. "It's no use, Maureen. I've already looked everywhere for him. He ran into the loft a while back, but I paid him no mind. I'd like to think he's headed to town or over to Patrick's house. Then I remembered Patrick's gone, too. And Robert."

"And Zack and Tom," Maureen murmured. Everyone had left except Joe, and now it looked like he was gone, too.

"The Henderson boys?" her mother asked. "But Mrs. Henderson told me…"

"They crossed the river and joined the Confederate Army."

"Enough, ladies." Her father stretched out his hand to his daughter's seat. "Maureen, sit down and let's have our supper. If Joe's gone, so be it. If he hasn't, then he's late for a very good meal."

Wordlessly, Maureen sat in her place across the table from Joe's empty seat. Before she could answer, her mother shot her a warning look. Instead, she picked up a fork.

Supper passed without a word. Maureen saw the grief in her mother's eyes. Her father sat stone-faced, staring into his empty tea cup long after she and her mother had cleared the table.

Joe didn't say goodbye.

Maureen's heart ached for her stubborn, brave brother. She knew it might be a long time before they saw him again.

DIVIDED LOYALTIES

Even though it hurt, she was proud of him. And envious.

Joe left to serve his country. Why does it matter that I'm a girl? I can't stay here and do nothing when there's a war going on.

CHAPTER 2
POCKETFUL OF COINS

The gun was heavy. Its weight surprised and frightened Maureen as she held the old pistol, cold, dark and dull, in her hands. She'd seen her father's gun many times, but this was the first time she'd ever handled it. She lifted it carefully from the cupboard drawer.

"This gun is not something you'll be needing to use, girl," her father once told her when he was cleaning it.

Now, she decided as she turned it over in her hands, I might need it. Father might have a few choice words to say when he discovers it missing. That can't be helped.

Joe had been right about the battle coming to Sharpsburg. Two days ago, the Army of the Potomac and General Robert E. Lee's Confederate Army had met on battlefields north of town. After one long, fierce day of battle, skirmishes continued sporadically for a second day. With no way to escape, Maureen and her parents huddled in the kitchen, praying and waiting for the silence that finally came at dusk.

When Maureen rushed out to tend to the terrified chickens, she found Eliza weeping in the orchard.

"I couldn't stand it another moment," Eliza told Maureen as she fell into her friend's arms. "Amy's in a state over Robert. He wrote to tell her his regiment was marching so she concluded he was in the fighting. Mother and Father have been on their knees for hours and hours."

Then she looked into Maureen's face, worry and fear clouding her blue eyes. "Do you think Joe was there, too?"

Maureen shook her head. "I don't. He's only been gone for a few days, hardly enough time to do more than sign the enlistment papers."

Maureen sent her friend home with a promise to meet in the

morning. While fighting wasn't an option for girls, no one was going to stop her from finding out what happened to Robert.

The light of a new day hadn't dimmed Maureen's resolve even though now she worried about what she was getting herself and her friends into. She had seen plenty of the rough looking characters that made up the Union and Confederate armies and they frightened her. She figured the gun might save her life.

She shoved it into the worn canvas haversack along with a few beaten biscuits, a bottle of water and her shawl and then shouldered the bag. She reached into her pocket for her mother's egg money, rubbing the smooth, cool pennies with her rough, sunburned hands.

Maureen had promised to meet Eliza before sunrise. Already a hint of pink light glowed through the window. She was late. She was also excited and scared. From the sounds she'd heard for two days, she feared what she'd see when she reached the battlefield.

She quietly pulled open the rough-hewn front door and glanced one last time around the silent cabin. As she closed the door, she thought about her mother and father and hoped they wouldn't worry about her.

As soon as Eliza saw Maureen nearing her house, she raced to her. "Did anybody see you go?"

"After all the noise and fright of the fighting, my parents are sound asleep. Our house is like a tomb," Maureen said. "How about you?"

"I was terrified Amy was going to blubber loud enough to wake Papa before I could get her out of the house." Eliza looked with pity at the younger girl. "All she did for the past two days was cry."

"Can you blame her?" Maureen said.

"Amy!" Eliza whispered, gesturing for her petite sister-in-law to leave her hiding place. "Maureen's here. We've got to go now. Come on."

Amy peered out from the low-slung branches of the apple tree, a handkerchief to her very red nose.

"Are you sure you want to go?" Maureen asked. Amy looked more like a frail and frightened child than the wife of a Union soldier

12

as she peered out from under her lacy bonnet. She was seventeen, a year younger than Maureen and Eliza. Before Robert joined the army, she was always filled with laughter.

After receiving Robert's letter, her worries only grew. The past two days were nearly unbearable. The armies brought the war closer than any of them expected. By the time the first cannon was fired, it was too late to flee. All they could do was cower in their homes and pray for the boys on the battlefield. Maureen couldn't imagine how the young wife suffered as she waited.

Amy pushed aside the branch and marched toward Maureen and Eliza.

"I have to find mah husband." Her voice was soft, her tone firm.

As they turned to walk toward town, pink streaks filled the sky as gold-edged clouds signaled dawn was arriving. Though it was September, it was already warm and humid, one of the last days of a hot summer. Drops of perspiration slid down Maureen's spine. The morning dew soaked into the hem of her skirt and the sodden fabric wrapped around her ankles as she walked.

Once they were out of sight of their homes, Eliza pushed off her straw bonnet and then linked arms with Amy and Maureen.

Eliza filled Maureen in on how they had waited out the two days of fighting. "Look at my fingernails. Another day of fighting and I would have had to chew on my fingertips."

Amy nodded though she said nothing.

On the empty country lane, the girls felt quite alone. Usually by this time of day, the narrow road was filled with farm wagons bringing produce, eggs and milk to town. Maureen struggled to steady herself, though her heart pounded against her chest. She held tightly on to her haversack to keep her hands from shaking. It was too quiet now that the battle was over. Every rustling of leaves or snap of a twig sounded loud as a thunderclap. Maureen started and turned at every sudden noise; she had never been so scared.

And what is that smell? It was acrid, reminding Maureen of a wood fire but sharper than that. This foul smell hurt her nose and sickened her stomach. It smelled metallic like iron, sour like rancid meat. And it wouldn't go away, instead growing more powerful as they walked.

They passed by woods that led to one of the area's biggest farms. Though the cooler air was welcome, the girls worried about what was in those woods. They stepped carefully, listening.

A fierce growl disrupted the peaceful twitter of birds. One man hidden by the trees snarled fiercely. Then another shot back an angry response. Although the girls couldn't understand their words, they heard the men's fury. The girls froze, reminded that the road they traveled still might not be safe. Enemy soldiers might still be nearby. Scalawags and other hangers-on had been reported preying on unsuspecting townspeople.

Maureen's mouth went dry as her arms tensed. She looked slowly at her companions and reached for her haversack. As suddenly as the voices erupted, they died down, and the women exhaled with relief and hurried on.

Bright sunlight filtered through the woods, tossing a dappled pattern at the women's feet. Something is wrong, Maureen thought as they neared the junction where the woods ended. The last time she walked here, the corn had grown tall enough to shade the road. Today, though, she saw a bright sunny path ahead. Has the corn already been cut down? she wondered.

Instead of corn so tall it obscured the view of the valley stretching to the violet Catoctin Mountains, they saw soldiers sprawled across the landscape. The corn had been flattened into the earth, trampled by combat. Wagons and cannons lay in ruins among the craters and scorched land. Hats, canteens, guns and shoes were scattered around them. The air was filled with the sounds of suffering and cries for help. They had reached the battlefield.

Maureen shuddered when she realized how close the fighting had come to their little farm, a walk of less than a half hour away. Her thin veneer of courage was quickly fading.

What are we doing here?

Fallen soldiers were too numerous to count. Wounded men cried out for help. Many gathered in small knots. They tended to each other's wounds or waited in a daze for help. For others, it was too late. Already, troops spread out on the battlefield, dressing survivors' wounds and giving them whiskey or morphine to dull the pain.

Alongside them, grief-stricken civilians stepped carefully among the men. Women pulled their shawls tightly around their shoulders. Men clutched hats to their chests. Their faces were filled with fear, worry and sadness. Some came looking for loved ones. Others stooped beside injured men, bringing water and aid.

As the three women scanned the faces of the fallen, shadowy buzzards spread their wings wide overhead and soared silently in ever-shrinking circles.

Amy stumbled, and her friends rushed to catch her. She sucked in her breath as she surveyed the terrible sight. "Look at them, so many of them."

Amy put her hand to her brow to shade her eyes from the rising sun. She surveyed the ranks of soldiers, some in gray, some in blue, some in no distinguishable color, all lying side by side. In the distance, a trim white farmhouse stood heavily damaged, a sentry of dead soldiers at its base.

Nearby a woman crouched, recognizing someone. She called his name, at first hopefully, and then in great despair as she realized her loved one was dead.

A raven perched nearby, looking over her shoulder, ominous and horrible. She yelled at it to go away before falling to her knees next to the man on the ground.

Similar scenes spread out across the flattened cornfield as the slanting morning sun lit the valley.

Maureen longed to comfort the men as they slowly passed by. A soldier resembling Joe called out to her. She knelt beside him, horrified by his blood-soaked clothes. She wiped his perspiration-drenched face with her handkerchief and offered him one of her biscuits. Even though he refused it, another man's hand rose quickly to claim it. She wished she had more. This man—any of these men—could be Joe, she realized. It was almost too much to bear.

A cool breeze caressing her cheek could not assuage the sorrow welling in her heart. It seemed disrespectful to pick their way past the dead soldiers, their heavy boots landing so close to the faces of men on the ground. Eliza and Amy held each other up, terrified that one of these lifeless faces would belong to Robert.

Amy's chin jutted out with determination. She pressed her lips into a thin line as she walked. She never looked away from the faces.

Eliza followed her determined sister-in-law. On they walked, past scores of wounded and dying men.

Maureen feared recognizing boys she knew. She knew soldiers on both sides. Any of them could be here, though she remained hopeful she wouldn't find her brother. Joe enlisted only a few days ago. It would be weeks, at least, before he would see fighting. She hoped he would never see anything like this.

What was heroic about this? What did it accomplish? Sick to her stomach, she followed her friends.

Amy, desperate to find out what happened to her husband, took the lead. She walked slowly, whispering Robert's name as if she thought he would sit up and answer her.

Eliza followed behind her, holding her embroidered handkerchief to her nose. Maureen stopped to hand out the rest of her biscuits to bleeding men, to wipe their faces and speak a kind word. She despaired that she couldn't do more. Cannon fire disturbed the quiet of the early morning. It sounded far away to Maureen, perhaps near the Potomac.

Will the fighting return here? Maureen prayed for peace. Here, in this hell.

And this was hell. She was sure of it. The moaning of the wounded men and the keening of the grieving women. The scent of gunpowder, fire, rot and blood that lingered in the humid air. She thought of their little patch of bright green, bristling with nearly-ripe corn as she looked at this once verdant field, crushed, scorched and blown away.

Tiny yellow and white butterflies danced among the wildflowers that had survived. Maureen watched them as they fluttered among flowers she might never have noticed on any other day. She didn't want to search anymore, even though she knew she must.

Maureen gathered her courage to continue walking and find the truth. Amy and Eliza needed her. They were desperate for news of Robert. She only hoped they wouldn't find their answer here on the battlefield by Antietam Creek.

CHAPTER 3
ANGELS ON THE BATTLEFIELD

The shadows were growing longer and Maureen yearned to sit down. Her feet ached as much as her head. She and her friends had passed hundreds, maybe even thousands, of soldiers. They stopped beside many of them, offering what little food and water they had until they ran out.

Still, they had not found Robert. With each passing hour, a hint of relief mixed with their anguish.

"We'll find him alive and well," Eliza promised again and again. Her voice was filled with distress. Eliza counted on the protection of her brother. Older by five years, he had always been kind to her, never teasing her the way Joe teased Maureen. Eliza was a lot like Robert. She was as kind and caring as he was. As he *is*, Maureen corrected herself. She began to wonder if what they were doing was crazy. There were bodies as far as she could see.

Are all of them dead? Where are they taking the wounded?

Amy continued, never faltering. Maureen watched as the slight young woman strode on in search of Robert. Her expression serious, her fingers constantly twisting her wedding ring, Amy looked at every face. "Please don't be Robert," she whispered time and again as she approached a man with dark curls like Robert's, with a trim mustache like his.

Though the sun began to sink behind the trees, the grim task of burying the dead was already underway. There were many like Amy, for whom the search for loved ones continued.

Maureen saw two women, dressed alike in black trimmed in white lace. They walked side by side, seeming to float among the casualties. Together they would stop by each man. If the man was conscious, they would bandage his wounds. Otherwise, they would touch each body and if it was still warm, if he was breathing, they

18

would call for help. Then while they waited, they would kneel on the hard ground, cross themselves and pray for his soul.

Maureen was still watching the pair when she heard Amy gasp and fall beside a Union soldier staring unseeing at the sky.

"Mercy's sake," Amy whispered. "I know him. I knew him. He was a friend of Robert's. They went to college together at Mount Saint Mary's. His name was Sam, Sam Winterstone. He was the funniest boy I ever met. He told terrible jokes, but he enjoyed telling them so much we all laughed. One girl laughed hardest of all; they were married the same month we were. I think they have an infant son. Oh, dear Lord." Amy wept silently.

Maureen and Eliza knelt beside Amy and put their arms around her.

"I don't think I can go on," she said at last. "I don't know where Robert is—" She looked out across the battlefield. "I don't believe he's here."

She slumped to the ground and pulled her shawl around her thin shoulders. Her bright blue eyes seemed sunken and her face wan after the long day.

"We'll find him," Eliza promised once again. She patted her sister-in-law's shoulder.

"I know we will." Amy nodded. Her eyes shone with tears as she hugged Eliza. Though they were related only by marriage, they looked like sisters, both with pale golden hair pinned away from their young faces.

Maureen looked away to wipe her cheek.

At that moment, the two women in black appeared beside them. "You poor dears," the tall one said as she placed her hand gently on Amy's shoulder. "Have you lost someone? Maybe one of these young lads here?"

"No, ma'am," she shook her head. "I knew this boy, but I am looking for mah husband. I haven't heard from him since before the battle. He wrote to tell me his regiment was coming to Sharpsburg so I know he might be here. I had to look. After the fighting, I had to come in case mah Robert needed me. Like these men needed someone…"

19

Amy bowed her head to sob.

"It's getting late. You shouldn't be out here when it gets dark. It will be dangerous—so many strangers about. Are you far from home?" The woman stooped down to look in Amy's face. She gazed at her with a kind smile, waiting for an answer. Amy looked from the woman to Eliza and Maureen without answering.

Maureen spoke up. "No, ma'am. We don't live that far away. We want to keep on looking, at least for a little while longer."

"It's so close to sunset though, my dears. I don't think you should be on the road after dark." The tall woman sounded worried.

"Our mothers will worry if we aren't back," Eliza answered.

"I suspect they're worrying already," Maureen admitted. All three had left their homes without a word to their parents. "They don't know where we are."

"Heavens," the woman exclaimed.

"We're hoping our mothers think we're at each other's houses," Maureen explained.

"If we aren't home for supper," Eliza added, "you know how they'll worry. Your father will be furious."

Maureen nodded. Before she could say a word, Amy spoke up.

"I don't know how I can leave here without Robert. What if he's sufferin' alone? Or…dyin'?"

"You won't find him in the dark. And you can't be any help to him if you get hurt out here." The woman with the smile held out her hand. "Come. Walk back to town with us. We're staying with our cousin's family. If you like, you can rest a bit before you return home. We'd be happy to share whatever we have."

Amy nodded, and her friends helped her rise from the ground. "I don't think we should impose, ma'am."

"Nonsense, it wouldn't be an imposition." The woman with the smile briefly put her arm around Amy's thin shoulders.

Her tall companion interrupted. "We understand if you don't want to stop, but you must be starving. At least take some food for your walk home."

The short, middle-aged woman smiled at the girls again. Her dark, deep-set eyes were warm as she reached out to each of them with slim, soft hands. "And it would be polite of us to introduce ourselves. My name is Patricia and this is my sister Angela."

She gestured toward the tall, lithe woman with a long oval face and kind blue eyes behind metal rimmed glasses. "We're sisters, both of us widowed last year."

"We came to see if we could be of service after the battle," Angela added. "We have a little medical training—we worked with our father and Patricia's husband, they were doctors in Annapolis—although I've spent the last two years teaching girls not much younger than you how to sew. We seem to be praying more than healing anyone here."

Angela sighed and pointed a little farther up the road at a bullet-riddled farmhouse with lights glowing in the first floor windows. "It's not too far. And it's certainly warmer than it is out here."

The three girls wrapped their shawls more tightly to ward off the growing chill. They introduced themselves as they walked with the sisters, telling them about Robert and Joe and their families.

The setting sun lit up the house where the sisters were staying. Like others on the edge of town, it had suffered the blows of shelling. The chimney had crumbled. Bullets had sheared away the top corner of the house.

"How did you endure the fighting so close to you?" Maureen asked as she surveyed the damage.

"We hid in the cellar," Patricia explained. "We arrived on Monday a week ago to visit our cousin and his wife. Sadie has been quite ill, and my cousin begged us to come. Not very good timing, now is it?"

She smiled for only a second before continuing. "When we first saw the soldiers, we assumed they were marching to Pennsylvania. We certainly didn't expect a battle here—did you? Then they stopped just over that ridge and began fighting. We prayed all day for God to keep us safe. And he did. This morning, once we were sure it was quiet, we came out on the battlefield to see how we could help. My cousin begged us to go with them. They are collecting their daughters—both married to Union boys—and going to Sadie's sister's house in Ohio."

DIVIDED LOYALTIES

"I can't blame them," Maureen said. "I'm surprised you didn't go with them."

Before Patricia could answer, Amy suddenly asked, "What will they do with all these boys?"

"It may be days before they get to them all. The army has sent out medical men to dress wounds and start moving them to hospitals. The dead, well, they've already started burying them," Angela told her. "We hear there are thousands of them."

"I'll never forget the young man we found early this morning. He was trapped under his dead friends," Patricia recalled. "That man had been struck in the head and when he came to, he couldn't get out. Angela and I tugged and pulled all those bodies off him. And he was fine, except for a giant welt on his forehead."

"He thanked us and asked where his regiment had gone," Angela added. "We called over an ambulance driver to take him to the big field hospital."

"Field hospital?" Maureen looked up, her face full of new hope after their long futile search. "Where's that?"

"They were taking him to one at the Pry House," Patricia answered. "General McClellan has troops at the house. Now the barn is filled with wounded men, poor souls."

"Do you know where the house is?" Amy's eyes were bright with curiosity.

"North of the battlefield, farther up Boonsboro Pike." Patricia pointed past the battlefield they had scoured all day. "It's not too far from here, maybe a half hour's walk."

"Perhaps you could stop there tomorrow," Angela suggested as they arrived at their house. "We've been talking about volunteering there or at one of the other hospitals."

"Now there's no sense standing out here when we have nice comfortable chairs inside." Patricia invited them in. "Come in. At least for a moment. I'm sure you could use the rest, even for five minutes."

She led them to a cozy parlor, or what was left of it. Crumbled bricks were piled on the hearth, and a ragged crack crossed the wall from the hole in the ceiling. Books that had fallen from the

22

shelves littered the rag rug. A thin layer of plaster dust covered every wooden surface as well as the divan where Patricia suggested the young women sit. The room was cold and would stay that way since the fireplace had been demolished.

The five women sat quietly for a moment. Maureen knew courtesy required she continue a friendly conversation and yet words seemed unnecessary after all they'd shared during their long day. And frankly, she was tired and her feet hurt. She knew they all must be suffering from sore feet.

She found herself thinking about the Pry House. An idea glimmered. She needed to know more.

"You were talking about the field hospitals." Maureen leaned forward. "There are others?"

"Oh, heavens, yes. There are so many injured boys. One hospital couldn't contain them all." Angela said.

"There's a powerful need for nurses," she added after a moment.

"Oh, Maureen. The way you've gone on about serving your country, that might be the way you could help." Eliza grabbed her friend's arms. Then she turned to the sisters, "My friend would be a great nurse. She has been taking care of her father all summer. He fell and broke his leg."

"And he's been miserable ever since. Nothing I do pleases him." Maureen shook her head. "Much as I like the idea of helping, I don't think I can."

"Why ever not?" Angela asked. "You probably have as much experience as some of the ladies already there."

Maureen frowned as a crease formed between her eyebrows. Then her face lit up as she considered Miss Angela's idea. After so many hours of wondering how she could serve her country, this woman had proposed an idea she'd never thought of. The ladies of Sharpsburg had been talking about some kind of a ladies' aid society, for sewing uniforms, canning vegetables and knitting socks.

Maureen was certain she could do more. What about nursing? She wasn't sure she'd be any good at it.

At home, all she did was make her father grumble. She feared she didn't have the skills a room full of suffering soldiers needed.

Patricia smiled and placed her hand on Maureen's shoulder. "Don't mind my sister. Angela gets a little too bossy sometimes."

"Maybe I do," Angela answered her sister and then turned to Maureen. "I know I saw a spark in your eyes. I do believe you could do your country a heap of good in one of those hospitals. Maybe it's something you should think about."

As much as the woman's words stirred her heart, Maureen had her doubts. She smiled as she thought about visiting the hospital the ladies had mentioned. "I will. I think maybe we'll be going there tomorrow if Amy has her way."

Amy nodded.

"Well, then," Angela said. "You look up the head nurse and see if they don't need your skills."

"Angela, don't be so bossy," Patricia chided her sister.

Maureen smiled. "It can't hurt to ask."

Maybe she wasn't very good at caring for her father, but maybe the needs of the wounded were so great the nurses would be willing to take anyone. Even me, Maureen thought. It would be one way to help.

Beside her, Amy sighed and brushed a stray blond curl from her face, tucking it into what was left of the neat bun that had been so carefully pinned early that morning. She stared silently into the dark fireplace. Her shoulders sagged and her eyes had lost their usual luster.

Patricia patted Amy's hand. "Maybe you'd like to tell me about Richard."

"Robert," Amy corrected her.

"I'm so sorry. I meant Robert."

"Not much to tell really," Amy shook her head. She spoke softly and slowly. "Mah family moved here from Richmond when I was twelve. I met Robert when he was in his last year of college."

Amy's face took on the glow of love as she spoke of her husband. "He has these beautiful brown eyes that sparkle when he laughs— which he rarely does. He's a serious young man most of the time. We fell in love, and we got married after graduation last summer.

We celebrated our first anniversary just before Robert enlisted and I moved in to stay with Papa and Mother Brennan."

"No children yet?" Patricia asked.

Amy blushed. "Not yet."

"Patricia, you shouldn't be asking such things." It was Angela's turn to scold.

"Why ever not? Plenty of young brides have children right away. I did. So did you, as I recall."

Angela laughed.

"I didn't mean to make you blush, Amy," Patricia added.

Amy laughed nervously. "I—well—you'd think I'd be used to that question by now. Everybody's waiting for a baby."

"Perhaps you would like something to eat?" Angela jumped to her feet, effectively changing the subject. "You must be starving."

"No, thank you, Miss Angela." Maureen shook her head and stood. "In fact, I think we ought to be going."

Eliza reached out to help her sister-in-law stand. "Yes, Amy looks tuckered out. We better get her home."

"Yes, poor lamb," Angela said as she walked them to the door. "Keep safe."

"We'll pray for you," Patricia added. "Tomorrow you'll find Richard."

"Robert," Angela whispered.

"Yes, Robert."

CHAPTER 4
ONLY BOYS

Maureen rushed through her morning chores. She had plenty to do before she met up with Eliza and Amy.

Reassured by her father's soft snoring that her parents were sound asleep, she rekindled the fire, drew water from the well and checked on the chickens' water and feed.

Once water was heating on the hob and she had restocked her haversack with apples and bread, she took care to keep the front door from creaking as she slipped out.

"And where might ye be going so early?"

Startled, Maureen turned to find her mother sitting on the porch chair, fingering the black beads of her rosary.

Maureen drew a deep breath. "I think ya know, Mother. And I'll not let ya stop me."

Her mother held her hand out to take Maureen's. "I'd be daft if I thought I could. I knew you'd go last night and so did your father. You know your father is opposed."

"And are you?"

"Maureen, you're eighteen now. At your age, I was married with a wee one on the way. I was a grown-up woman and so are you. You're old enough to make that decision."

Maureen didn't know what to say. Her mother's eyes searched her face, and Maureen knew she needed to tell the truth.

"Then you know I'm going back, Mother." She pulled her shoulders back and straightened her haversack.

Her mother dropped her hand and nodded. "I would prefer if you stayed home safe and sound. As I said, you're old enough to make that decision. Now go on. I'll be praying for you just as I'm praying for your brother."

Maureen exhaled as she ran down the lane. She looked back

26

once and found her mother looking away, her lips forming the words of her prayers.

Eliza and Amy rushed down the front lawn of the Brennan homestead a few minutes later and fell into step with her.

"Papa told me your father was furious," Eliza said in greeting.

"It wasn't the homecoming I'd hoped for," Maureen muttered.

"What happened?"

"Father stopped at your house to shoot the breeze with your da. Father said something about the girls and Uncle Raymond said he thought we were all at my house. They spent the afternoon looking for us. By the time I got home, he was beside himself with anger and worry."

Eliza nodded. "Papa was so glad to see the two of us, he just wrapped his arms around us and told us supper was waiting. Amy thanked him and said she'd just as soon go to bed."

"What I'd do for a father as kind as yours. When I walked into the house, Father was so angry he couldn't speak to me. As soon as Mother caught sight of me, she jumped out of her chair, asked me if I had supper and then lit into me about how irresponsible and unfeeling I was. Oh, was she disappointed."

"Papa was beside himself, too. Still, we all got out of the house again this morning," Eliza said.

"I was afraid Papa Brennan would bar the door before we could leave," Amy added.

Maureen couldn't help but notice how frail Amy was looking. Her skin was sallow, and her eyes were tired. Maureen wondered if the poor girl had been able to sleep.

I would have liked a good night's sleep, Maureen thought ruefully.

As her friends chattered on, Maureen considered how she'd explain her way out of today's disobedience. Her father had made it clear during a tense supper the previous night she wasn't to leave the house.

Maureen had pleaded with him, trying to explain what Eliza, Amy and she had seen on the battlefield and how they wanted to help Amy search for Robert. She thought—wrongly, as it turned out—that he would understand. Her father paid no attention to what she had to say and instead told her in his gruff way how wrong she was. She was sorry to see disappointment on her mother's face. Even as she pursed her lips and shook her head, she reached out to touch her daughter's hand. Maureen didn't know what to make of her mixed signals.

Finally, in frustration, she said something disrespectful and stalked out of the kitchen. Later, when her mother came into her bedroom to talk to her, she feigned sleep.

Maureen was baffled. She expected them to be proud of her. She remembered her father's speeches about love of country and duty to family. That's what sent her out to the battlefield. If searching for her cousin on the battlefield wasn't right, then she didn't know what was.

She had made up her mind by then, and early the next morning, out the front door she went. She'd expected to leave without a word. Her mother, always one step ahead of her children, was waiting for her with love and her prayers. Maureen's heart warmed as she remembered.

"Maureen?" Eliza said. "You aren't even listening."

"Oh. Sorry, you were telling me something your father said." Maureen brought her attention back to the present.

"I promised to bring Amy home for supper," Eliza explained.

"We're not children." Amy sounded bitter. "I'm a married woman, a married woman with a husband fighting in a war. It's mah duty to know where he is and if he's well."

As they neared the places of death and misery they saw the previous day, Maureen had second thoughts. She didn't know if she had enough courage to face it all again. She did regret leaving her parents to worry.

She wanted with all her heart not only to search for her beloved cousin but to find a way to express her gratitude to the country that had welcomed her. She wanted to defend it after she heard the marching of heavy boots in front of their house, sounds that recalled the English soldiers in the Ireland of her childhood. So she struggled to put aside her fears and misgivings as she resolved to find a way to make a difference beyond the boundaries of their little farm.

Without realizing it, the girls slowed down as they reached the edge of the battlefield. The shortest route to the Pry House went past the same fields where yesterday they had seen hundreds of soldiers lying dead and wounded. The memory made Maureen suggest another route.

"Let's take the road through town instead. It's not much—"

"Mercy's sakes!" Amy interrupted. "I forgot mah weddin' band. I never take it off. But mah hands began to swell in the night—Lizzie, we have to go back." Eliza looked at Amy and then Maureen.

"You don't need it, do you?"

"I can't see mah husband without my weddin' band. It isn't proper. We have to go back."

Maureen nodded. "Go on then. Get your ring. It shouldn't take too long. I'll keep walking and meet you at the Pry House."

"It's so far to walk alone," Eliza protested.

"It's broad daylight. We haven't heard even a hint of gunfire today, and now there are plenty of people on the road," Maureen assured her. "I'll be fine."

Maureen watched her friends walk away as she readjusted her haversack, comforted by the weight of the gun inside.

It is broad daylight, she told herself. The guns are quiet. There are people on the road.

She tucked a curl behind her ear, mustered her fortitude and marched into Sharpsburg. She looked for a friendly face but saw only strangers. She was glad to see the Confederates had left, ordered back to Virginia. The men in their place didn't look any better: Union soldiers, lounging near the tavern, on the front porches of businesses, loitering by Toohey's store.

At the sight of them, Maureen quickened her pace. She held tightly onto her haversack and tried not to look left or right.

At the corner of Main Street, Maureen had planned to turn right, the direction of Pry House. Then she caught sight of a man as he stumbled and fell. Maureen looked around to see if anyone went to his aid. No one did.

I can't just let him lie there, can I?

No, she decided, and turned away from her planned route to

29

help. Dressed in tattered brown pants and a dingy white shirt, he spoke with a slur. She thought he was drunk—until she saw the brown stain on his shirt. Was that blood?

"I'm looking for my buddy, ma'am." His voice was weak and hoarse. "They said I might find him here. Could you help me up? I gotta see him."

His hand shot out and he smacked her across the jaw as she leaned toward him. The blow knocked her down onto the dusty road.

"Sorry, ma'am," he apologized. "Are you hurt?"

"Just my pride." She rubbed the tender spot on her face and smiled weakly.

She readjusted the haversack strap that had fallen off her shoulder and brushed the dust and dirt from her skirt. Then she wrapped her arm around his. It took all her might as she supported his broad back and hooked a hand under his elbow to lift the big man. He was unsteady on his feet, so she leaned against him to prevent another fall.

"Where are you going?" she asked.

"Inside that church there." To her surprise, he pointed to the little white chapel Maureen attended every Sunday.

"Are you sure?" she asked. The battle-worn church looked quiet enough for a Saturday morning. Then Maureen noticed the battered oak pews that had been dumped unceremoniously by the cemetery.

"Pretty sure, ma'am." He grabbed the gate post to steady himself and pulled a cap from his pants pocket to cover his greasy honey-colored curls.

Maureen gasped when she saw the gray wool and the crossed rifles. *What am I doing? Helping the enemy?*

"Will you be all right now?" she asked, hoping to hurry away.

"If you can just help me inside, I'd be obliged." He pressed his free hand on that brown stain and exhaled heavily.

"You're hurt, aren't you?"

"Yes, ma'am." He answered her with a nod. "Shot yesterday as my unit retreated."

"I thought the battle was over by then."

30

"Mostly, but we got caught in a skirmish. Them Yankee boys didn't want to let us go without a fight."

Maureen said nothing as she rushed to get him inside so that she could get back on the road. She wanted nothing more to do with this man or his army.

"Why aren't you in the hospital?" She struggled to guide him to the church entrance.

"I was. Doc patched me up, and I left to find Charles. You know, my friend."

Maureen pulled open the heavy wooden door to a place she didn't recognize at all. Instead of pews, rows of men lay under blankets. Instead of the low sounds of a hymn, men moaned in pain. Instead of beeswax and incense, the stench of infection overwhelmed her. Maureen held back at the door as the soldier limped inside and forgot her.

Her stomach lurched as she faced a room filled with Rebel soldiers.

The Enemy.

She hung onto the heavy iron door handle to keep from falling to her knees as she watched a man and a woman lean over the beds of injured men on the far side of the sanctuary.

"Ma'am?" whispered a fair boy with blond curls wet with thick black blood. She turned to a boy to her right, lying on a rough pallet. She recoiled from the sight of his wounds. "Could you bring me some water?" he asked, his voice labored and husky.

She hesitated for a moment. She wanted to turn her back, but her conscience and her kindness forced her to go to him. Maybe, she rationalized, I'll be helping someone in his last moments.

She found a bucket of warm water and a dented tin cup under a window. She picked a dead fly from the water, dipped the cup and took it to him.

He looked at her gratefully and choked down the water. She wiped spilled water from his cheek with her handkerchief as he lay back silently on his cot.

Then she rose to face ragged rows of men, their young faces scraped and gashed, bruised and mangled. Enormous bandages, stained with blood, covered faces and scalps. Rough blankets and even cast off clothing were draped over each soldier. She couldn't tell who was dead and who was asleep.

What an unholy sight in this holy place.

As she turned to leave, she heard her name.

"Maureen," called a boy in a torn Confederate jacket. "Over here."

He was one of Joe's friends. Blood stained the front of his coat, and his feverish face was smeared with dirt.

"Tom," she said. "You've been hurt."

"I've been waiting for my mom." Tom's eyes searched hers as he talked. "I want to tell her—I want to say goodbye. And I'm sorry to be leaving her."

"Don't say that, Tom," Maureen countered. "You'll be fine."

"I want her to know I was with Zachary all through the battle. At first, we watched from up on a hill. The Union Army fought our battalions near the Miller's Cornfield early in the morning. It was bad, so bad I thought we was losing. The Yanks kept on coming. Our unit—my brother's and mine—knew it would be our turn soon enough. And when it was, we fought hard. We fought for each other. We was brave. We didn't run. No sir." He paused and spoke quietly. "I wish Zack was with me now. He didn't make it, you know."

His voice faded away as he closed his eyes.

"Tom!" Maureen cried. "Tom, please." She brushed the fringe of black hair away from his damp brow. "Please, Tom."

He didn't hear her.

Maureen backed away. She choked back a sob as she threw open the church door and ran into the hot sunshine. She stumbled and fell in the churchyard, her face wet from weeping. She reached for her handkerchief, now stained with a Rebel's blood.

The sun was too bright. The grass was too green. The breeze too soft.

She'd seen the enemy and found they were only boys. How could she not help them? She wondered—even as she feared she had betrayed her country.

I helped the enemy, Confederate soldiers who might have shot at Robert or Joe.

These boys were so much like her brother. Tom was Joe's friend. His brother Zack used to pull her hair. Like Joe, they heeded the call to serve—even though their loyalty led them to the Confederate Army.

Once friends and neighbors, now they were the enemy.

Burdened by shame for giving aid to the boys inside her church, Maureen wondered if helping Union soldiers could ease her guilt and atone for her sin.

She learned a lot in the months she'd tended to her father after his fall. She did everything from changing the bandage on the deep gash that split his thigh to bringing him his meals. He still suffered great pain from his injuries, and she learned patience even if he never did.

Father's pain wasn't anything like this. She'd never experienced death so raw and brutal. She'd only seen a dead body once before. And then, the body of their neighbor was neatly laid to rest in his Sunday best clothes in a carefully built wooden coffin.

Her head pounded. She couldn't think anymore. She sat there, numb to the squirrel gathering acorns from the oak tree that shaded her, deaf to the migrating flock of robins twittering among the first fallen leaves of autumn. On any other day, Maureen enjoyed the world around her. This, however, wasn't any other day. She had seen a nightmare brought to life.

There was more to come, she realized as she remembered Eliza and Amy.

They must be at the Pry House by now, wondering where I am. Would the Pry House be as bad as this?

Could it ever be worse?

CHAPTER 5
PRY HOUSE

Though the white trim looked faded against the deep red brick, Pry House stood proud and sturdy on the highest point of the property. Square and solid, it looked over fields that were recently decimated. Corn rows were flattened. A single harried-looking chicken cackled from its hiding place under the front porch. Cows and horses lay dead in the pasture.

Officers in blue woolen uniforms lounged on fine upholstered furniture set out on the sloping lawn. Maureen waited for her friends under a tree, out of sight of the soldiers.

At last, Eliza and Amy came marching down the farm lane. Maureen jumped up and came beside them. Together they scanned the scene before them. "I can't believe...this beautiful house...the family furniture—out there on the lawn—" Eliza stammered.

Her observations were cut short when an ambulance wagon rushed beside them, barreling toward a big white barn to the right of the house. Stretcher bearers ran to the wagon, lifting men who moaned or cried out as they were moved. A nurse in a dirty white apron stretched her hands, reaching to those who could walk on their own. Before the wagon was even empty of its human cargo, another pulled beside it. And then another.

"Come along, Lizzie." A crease formed between Amy's blue eyes.

"We shouldn't be here." Maureen's fears were making every step difficult. "This is no place for us."

"Nonsense." Amy's steely tone surprised Maureen. "If mah Robert is hurt, he might be in that barn." Amy led her friends past groups of soldiers who silently watched the women. They picked their way over the rutted dirt lane until they stood in the large dark opening of the barn.

34

Amy twisted her now-recovered wedding ring and glanced at Eliza and Maureen.

She's as scared as I am, Maureen thought, as they peered into the darkness.

The musty old barn was cavernous with a steeply pitched roof. Weathervanes topped each of the two cupolas. Oil lanterns provided the only real illumination inside the dark space. The scene was hardly serene. Doctors and nurses scurried about as men cried out for relief from their suffering. Many lay quietly on their pallets, bloody sheets a testament to the extent of their injuries. Those with less severe injuries sat up in their cots or crowded near the doors to absorb the sunshine and breathe fresh air. Odors of hay and manure mixed with the smells of men, pungent and raw.

Maureen shrank from the scene at first, even though she soon realized it was a far better sight than she'd seen in the church. It was an Eden compared to the Hell of the battlefield.

One of the soldiers, someone feeling better, whooped as the women entered the ward. A middle-aged woman looked up and with a disapproving glare hurried over to them. From the looks of her apron, she was the nurse Maureen had seen helping men from the wagon.

"May I help you girls?" she asked gruffly.

Maureen could only stare at the nurse's disheveled appearance. Her dingy, dirt and blood-streaked apron covered a stiff black dress. Most of her iron-gray curls were caught up under a battered Union cap. Beneath her faded gray eyes, dark circles told of long hours without sleep.

Amy wordlessly looked at the other two, her eyes bright with worry, her fingers working her gold band.

Maureen realized she couldn't speak and she stepped forward.

"Good morning, ma'am," she stammered. "Um, my friends and I-I mean, um… Amy Brennan here is looking for her husband. We wondered if he might be here."

"We had a Brennan here yesterday, poor soul. He's left us." The nurse reached for her patient list. Amy gasped, and the nurse looked up from her handful of handwritten notes.

"What was his first name, dear?" Her voice was softer now, the crease between her eyes fading away.

"Robert," Amy said.

"No, wasn't a Robert who passed."

The three young women exhaled.

"Now I don't have the names of all the patients yet. Some are difficult to identify until they wake up. And some we just plain get wrong,"

She looked over the list and muttered names: Charles Henry, Leonard Howard, Keith Murray, Joseph O'Neal…."

"Joe?" Maureen said. "How—"

Eliza tore the list from the woman's hands. "It couldn't be our Joe." Her eyes scoured the pages.

"Miss…" The nurse eased the list back into her own possession. "If you don't mind."

"Is that my dearest Amy?"

Amy gasped at her name and turned to search the beds before her. In the second row, a young man feebly raised his hand.

She flew to Robert's bedside, knelt beside him and caressed the hand he stretched to her. He was sitting up, his legs covered by a brown blanket. His face was bruised and swollen.

Amy seemed to notice nothing amiss as she fell into his arms. "Oh! Robert! Robert!" She laughed merrily.

Eliza turned to walk to them until the nurse stopped her. "Give them a moment."

"But he's my bro—"

"And she is his wife, is she not?" the nurse replied.

Eliza clutched her friend's arm. "I can't believe we found him," she whispered. "I need to know about Joe…"

Maureen turned to the nurse. She had to know more. "Miss—"

"Larkin," the nurse answered. "Yes, dear?"

"What about Joe?" Every muscle in Maureen's body tensed as she braced for bad news.

Nurse Larkin leafed through her dog-eared pages.

"Yes, I know we had a patient by that name here," she said. "He was one of the first patients. An older man, he—"

"Older man?" Maureen exhaled as her arms relaxed. "It couldn't be my brother then."

"Oh, no, this was a man old enough to be your father. At least. Too old for battle in my opinion. Here he is." She handed the list to Maureen so she and Eliza could study it.

"I don't see——" Maureen looked up for an answer. Eliza took the pages, finally focusing on the name she sought.

"Maureen, it's a different spelling." Eliza grabbed Maureen's hand and squeezed it hard. "It's spelled O-N-E-A-L. And he's from Conshohocken, Pennsylvania." She stumbled over the town's name. "It's not our Joe."

Eliza's face glowed with the news, her eyes shining, her smile wide. She almost seemed happier than she had when she saw Robert. Maureen was surprised by Eliza's elation, but not too surprised.

"Our Joe, is it?" She waited for an answer.

Eliza blushed and looked down at the list. "Of course, I'm glad for you and your family," she stammered as she hugged the papers to her chest. She turned her attention to her brother and sister-in-law. "They look so happy," she said quietly. Maureen followed her friend's gaze as she wondered why Eliza wouldn't admit her growing affection for Joe. Maureen already suspected it.

They looked on at the sweet reunion they had hoped for.

Robert pulled Amy away to look at her and wipe tears from her cheeks with his crumpled handkerchief. Maureen wondered at the love she saw in the newlywed's faces. They spoke quietly to one another, nodding their answers. Hints of a smile began to light up their faces. Wasn't that the same light in Eliza's eyes only a few minutes ago?

Robert's face was cut up, and his left eye was blackened as if he lost a boxing match. Amy looked him over, running her hands down his arms to the blanket that covered his legs.

He shook his head to a question from Amy and wrapped her arms around his neck.

"He must be breaking the news to her," the nurse said.

"News?" Eliza asked.

"He can't walk," she said. "Doc don't know if he ever will again."

"Oh no." As Eliza started to go to him, Maureen held her back. "Not yet; let the news sink in with Amy first."

"He'll be fine. He's healthy. He tells me he's a teacher. He can certainly go back to the classroom. What does he teach?" the nurse asked.

"Music. Up at the college in Emmitsburg," Eliza said.

"A college professor." The nurse looked impressed. "He'll be able to handle that. I'd have worried if he taught children. He won't have to worry about those college boys."

"What happened? Do you know?" Eliza asked.

"Took a bullet in his back. I know that sounds bad, but in the craziness of the battle, guns were going off every which way. He seems like the valiant type. I don't think he's the kind who'd run. Who's to say how it happened?"

As she spoke, Robert leaned toward his wife and whispered in her ear. She blushed deeply and turned to smile at him.

Then she leaned to whisper in Robert's ear. He laughed aloud, put his hand on his wife's belly and kissed her. There in front of rows of wounded men.

"Now they're sharing secrets." A knowing smile creased the nurse's face and crinkled her eyes. "I'm sure he'll be fine now."

"Why?" Maureen pulled her gaze away from the couple.

"That's something between a man and his wife," the nurse answered.

After a moment of silence, Eliza blushed, too. "Oh," was all she said.

Eliza started to hand the patient list back to Miss Larkin and then stopped when she noticed a familiar name at the top of the page.

"Patrick Toohey!" She showed the name to the nurse. "Is Patrick here?"

"Came in yesterday," Miss Larkin said. "Poor boy."

"Oh Maureen, could it be?" Eliza turned to the nurse. "He's an old friend of ours. You should go see him, Maureen."

"Me? Why me especially?" Maureen said.

Eliza rolled her eyes at Maureen and sighed dramatically. "Maureen. Haven't you been paying attention? Patrick's been sweet

38

on you since the church social earlier this summer."

Maureen couldn't imagine why Eliza would say such a thing. Patrick was friends with her brother, so she knew him well enough. She didn't even remember much about the church social except how hot it was…and how Patrick kept bringing her glasses of punch as she sat with her mother.

"Go see him," Eliza urged. "I know he'll be glad to see you."

Maureen hesitated, and Eliza asked the nurse, "Would it be all right?"

"Should be fine," Miss Larkin said. "I'll take you over."

"Go, Maureen," Eliza urged. "I'll visit with my brother. Go on."

As they passed by the young couple, Maureen couldn't help but overhear their conversation.

"Can you stay?" he asked. Robert touched the curve of his wife's cheek with his fingertips.

"How could I ever leave?" Amy replied.

Eliza stopped and cleared her throat as Maureen and the nurse moved on.

"Your friend is pretty beat up. A bullet grazed his belly, and his eye's pretty bad," Miss Larkin told Maureen. "I can see he's awake. A minute or two can't hurt. Only a minute now."

Maureen's heart beat fiercely in her chest as they walked through row after row of narrow cots. Many of their occupants were sleeping so she stepped carefully. Each man bore the marks of battle: burns and bruises, heavy bandages covering grievous wounds. She didn't want to look as she neared Patrick's cot.

What will I say? She had never given him a moment's thought. The son of the town's shopkeeper, Patrick was well known around Sharpsburg. He was a nice enough boy, usually a bit of a flirt.

The nurse left her as they reached his cot. The bandage that covered one eye couldn't obscure his fair looks. Though he was 18, he still had a boyish face. It was round and sprinkled with freckles. His eyes were the color of the sky and fringed with long dark lashes. Those eyes were fixed on something over his head. He didn't even look at her.

DIVIDED LOYALTIES

"Morning, Patrick." Maureen forced a smile. A thick bandage caked with blood covered his right cheek and eye. She wondered about the bullet wound as she noticed his fair skin was moist and flushed.

She looked up to see what he was looking at, but saw only the rough wooden rafters of the barn high above them.

"Ma'am," he whispered. She looked at him and realized he didn't recognize her. "Could you move over a bit? That angel up there is talking to me, and you're in the way."

She sat on a stool beside his bed and studied his face, still transfixed on the ceiling.

"An angel?" she asked.

"Yes, don't you see her? She's beautiful with long curly dark hair and a shining face. She's smiling at me. Do you see?" he asked, never looking at Maureen. "She says I'll be in heaven soon. Isn't that wonderful?"

"No, it isn't," Maureen said flatly as she realized he was delirious. She moved into Patrick's line of sight and continued. "You're not ready for heaven yet. We need you here. Your mama needs you. Joe needs you. I need you."

"You do?" He turned to focus on her face. "Where's Mama?"

"She'll be here soon," Maureen lied. She had no idea if Mrs. Toohey even knew her son was here. She decided to stop by the store on the way home to make sure she did know.

"Oh, good." He turned his gaze back to the ceiling. "Oh, the angel's gone now. I expect she'll be back again soon."

He closed his eyes and sighed.

"Patrick," she called to him softly. His only answer was a second sigh. She sat there for a moment, desperately trying to shut out the cacophony around her. Visitors looking for their loved ones trickled into the makeshift hospital. Those who found a relative who had survived the battle shouted with joy. At the same time, Maureen heard cries of grief, too.

"I'm sorry," she heard a nurse say to a young mother with a toddler in tow. "He died in the night."

The woman pulled her child to her and crumpled under the

news. Maureen's throat tightened at the sight of such pain. When she had left the house yesterday to see what had happened after the long hours of battle, she hadn't bargained for this.

She started as someone lightly touched her on the shoulder. Maureen looked up to see Patrick's mother.

"I'm glad to see my son is in good hands." Mrs. Toohey's pink face lit up with a broad smile. Patrick's mother was about the same age as Maureen's. With her red hair tucked under a girlish straw bonnet, though, the short, round woman looked younger.

"He's been waiting for you." Maureen jumped up from the low stool. She didn't know whether to stay or go as Mrs. Toohey turned her attention to her son.

Patrick woke at his mother's touch. "Maureen came to visit me, Mama. Wasn't that grand?"

Mrs. Toohey took Maureen's hand and smiled at her son.

"Maureen is still here, Patrick," she explained.

He turned, startled to see her. "I thought you were here yesterday."

Maureen blushed.

"No, today. I just got here. You're a little confused."

"How long have I been here?" Patrick asked. "It feels like weeks and weeks."

"Only since yesterday," Mrs. Toohey said. "Don't you remember?"

Patrick looked confused as his eyes darted from Mrs. Toohey to Maureen.

"Yes…It was only yesterday?"

He drew his arm from under the blankets to wipe his damp brow. Maureen was worried about his fever and went to get him water and a cool cloth while he and his mother talked.

When she returned, Patrick was recounting the hand-to-hand combat that might have cost him the sight in his right eye.

"They're moving lots of men to hospitals in Baltimore and Frederick. Other places, too," Patrick said. "The doctor said my injuries aren't bad enough. I'll stay here for a while before getting back to my regiment."

"That's good news," Mrs. Toohey said. "I'll be able to come and visit."

Maureen wiped the dampness off Patrick's flushed face and offered him the cup of water. "I wonder if they'll move Robert."

"Could be." Patrick's flush deepened as his hand touched hers on the cup. "Could be."

He held her gaze for a moment before taking the cup. A blush rose in Maureen's cheeks.

Mrs. Toohey smiled at her shyness. "I'm sure your papa needs me at the store," she said to Patrick. She leaned over to kiss her son and then rose. "And you need your rest."

"Yes, Mama. Will you be back tomorrow?"

"Of course, son."

"And you, Maureen? Will you come and visit me, too?"

"I'd be happy to," she answered him.

"Good." Maureen sensed Patrick's gaze on her as she walked away. When she turned for a final glance before she looked for Eliza, he was still watching her. How had she never noticed before? She was flattered. And happy. Amid all this pain, she found a little spot of joy.

Mrs. Toohey stopped Maureen after leaving her son. "He looks much better than he did yesterday," she said hopefully. "He was out of his head. Today he seems better. But his face is so beat up. I don't know about his eye. Doctor said he may never see out of it again." Mrs. Toohey paused for a moment. Then she straightened up. "At least he's still got his arms and legs. And they're not sending him to a big hospital. So I guess his wounds aren't considered grievous."

"That's all good news," Maureen replied.

"I hope you'll be able to visit him again," Mrs. Toohey said. "He talks about you all the time. He asks about you in all his letters."

"I didn't know," Maureen began to say.

"I thought as much. He's been too shy to talk to you or even write you a letter, hasn't he? Maybe some good will come out of this."

She smiled at Maureen. Then to the girl's surprise, Mrs. Toohey kissed her cheek. "Thank you, my dear."

She was gone before Maureen could reply.

"How's Patrick?" asked Eliza as she came up to Maureen.

"He looks terrible. He's feverish and a little delirious. He's got a huge bandage on his face, and he could only look at me with one big puppy dog eye," Maureen said.

"Didn't I tell you?" Eliza asked.

"It may be because he's delirious," Maureen replied.

"You wait and see. I know Patrick Toohey." Eliza's smile spoke volumes.

"What are you not telling me?"

Eliza looked down at her hands though she said nothing.

"Eliza…"

"I fell in love with Patrick when I was 12 years old." A blush turned her cheeks pink. "I kept waiting for him to notice me. He never did."

"Oh, Lizzie," Maureen sighed.

"It's fine. My heart found someone else, and Patrick noticed my best friend. So maybe one day he'll be a relative." Eliza smiled. And it was Maureen's turn to blush.

"I want you two to fall in love and have a wonderful life filled with children," Eliza continued.

"I don't think I should—"

"Yes, you should. Patrick is already in love with you."

"I don't want to be the cause of your unhappiness."

"You won't be. It wasn't meant to be, don't you see? I'm glad for you. Glad for both of you."

Eliza stopped and looked in the direction of Patrick's cot. "So you'll be back to visit?"

"I promised Patrick and Mrs. Toohey I'd come tomorrow."

"Mrs. Toohey asked you back?" Eliza was surprised. "She knows a good match when she sees one."

Maureen blushed again and changed the subject. "Are you ready to go home?"

"Yes, we should leave. Amy's staying with Robert. I want to hurry home and tell Mama and Father we found him. They've been worried sick."

Maureen nodded, and they set out under the warm summer sun.

They ignored the catcalls of the soldiers leaning against a spreading oak.

After the anguish of yesterday, Maureen was a little light-headed today. Their search for Robert had been successful. The newlyweds were reunited. Their joy could not be dimmed by his injuries. At least not today.

And was there more news? A baby on the way would explain why Amy had looked tired and a little green.

"Did you know about Amy?" she asked Eliza.

"I don't think anybody except Amy knew," Eliza said. "She must have been waiting to tell Robert first. Isn't it wonderful? It will be good to have happy news to go with the sad."

Eliza was silent, her eyes focused on something far away as they walked back on Boonsboro Pike. "I don't know how I'm going to tell them," she said finally.

"Patrick said they're moving some of the men to other hospitals," Maureen said.

"Robert is being transferred to Baltimore. They have to rebuild the railroad bridge first. Confederates blew it up. Robert told us it might be another week or so," Eliza said.

"And Amy? Will she go to Baltimore?" Maureen asked.

"She plans to. She has family there she can stay with. I expect Mama will want to go with them."

The two girls found the walk home went quickly now that their mission had been accomplished. Their step was light, their chatter lively. Amy had giggled again, Eliza told Maureen.

Maureen had to admit to herself she was excited. She couldn't believe Amy's good fortune in being reunited with her husband. Even seeing Patrick had been good. Though his wounds were not serious, she worried about his fever and his eye. She'd return tomorrow to check on him, as she'd promised Mrs. Toohey.

She hadn't thought about love before, though it was clear Eliza had. And now her heart seemed to be set on Joe. "Our Joe," she had called him.

This was no time for Maureen to think about love. She had a mission. Even though she hadn't spoken to the nurse, she knew she would when she returned. The two sisters were right. The hospital was short-handed.

Maureen was sure she could help all those suffering young men. She wanted to serve as a battlefield hospital nurse, like Miss Larkin.

The question was, would they have her?

CHAPTER 6
A GIRL'S DUTY

Maureen burst into the house filled with news, but before she could say a word, she saw the rage that darkened her father's eyes. He sat at the kitchen table, his elbows resting on the table. Then, as the door slammed shut, he turned and glared. Her announcements died in the tense air.

"Thank you, dear Lord!" her mother exclaimed. She jumped out of her chair, clapped her hands together and rushed to Maureen.

"Kate, contain yourself," Daniel ordered. He turned in his chair with difficulty to look directly at Maureen. "I need to have a word with your daughter."

Maureen saw her mother's face turn to stone as she reached out for her daughter. Though she said nothing more, she touched her daughter's cheek, looked deeply into her eyes and then went to pick up the tea kettle. Maureen glanced after her, glad for her support, before turning to face her father's wrath.

Maureen had dreaded this encounter even though she hoped her news would help her avoid it. She was wrong.

"You have a lot of nerve, Maureen Regina O'Neill." His voice was carefully modulated, even and unwavering.

Maureen knew better than to trust the tone. Her father's eyes burned dark, the darkest she'd ever seen them. She never feared her father. Today she wondered if she should.

"Father," she began. "I have the most wonderful news. You'll be so happy—"

"Happy?" The growl in his voice turned her joy into sadness.

Slowly, she sat down on a kitchen chair. He wouldn't strike her, she was sure of it.

Even so, she was staying out of his reach just in case.

"Girl, I don't know if I'll ever be happy with you again. Your defiance is beyond my comprehension. I thought your mother and I taught you to respect your elders, to honor your mother and your father. To obey us.

"Your disregard for our wishes goes beyond anything we could imagine. Your mother has been sick with worry. The men on the roads out there are dangerous. They might have killed you. They might have—"

"Father, how could I turn my back on Eliza and Amy?" she retorted. "Of course, I knew it was dangerous."

"And yet you defied me," he growled.

"There's no good answer to this, Father." Her voice was gravelly. Her head pounded. Her fingernails cut into her hands as she clenched her fists tighter and tighter.

Then she did something she never did: she raised her voice. "I did what I thought I must do. I didn't plan to defy ya. I had to go."

"Enough theatrics, girl," he shouted. "I'm so sick of hearing what my children think they must do. Don't we have enough to worry about with Joe running off to fight in a war that makes no sense at all? 'I have to go,' he told me. He sounded just like you, full of himself. He talked of patriotism, duty to his new country. Then he walked out of here and never came back—after I forbid his going. He should have stayed home to help with the farm. That is where his patriotism—his loyalty—should have been."

"I'm proud of Joe," Maureen spit back. She bounded out of her chair and strode over to him, her fists clenched, her face level with his. "I'm proud he joined the Union Army. Our country is at war. Our new country and home. One we gave up our Ireland for."

"I told you that is enough. You don't remember how it was in Ireland, the losses we suffered in those last days. The deaths we—" Daniel stopped himself for a moment.

Then he lowered his voice. "You don't know anything about the costs of war."

"Don't I now?" Maureen was incredulous. "I know the costs. In the past two days, I've seen it all. I've seen the death and the injuries—and the sadness of wives and mothers. Joe could have been there, Father. We could have lost him. Just as Eliza and Amy were

47

afraid for Robert. Even so, I know Joe is doing a brave and noble thing. I wish I could go too."

Maureen's father tried to jump from his chair, but his weak leg forced him down again. He scowled at her and Maureen felt so much anger that she never expected to see from her father. He was always a man filled with laughter. Since his accident he had changed. His conversation once dripped with honey. Now, her mother said, he got his way with vinegar. Today she could taste its acid bitterness.

"No more of your guff, Maureen Regina O'Neill," he said. "You'll go nowhere. You are my daughter, and you'll stay home and tend to your chores and help your mother and me. The world beyond our door is no place for a girl. Not that you're of much use to either army. Judging from the past few days, I'm not sure you're of much help here." He looked away, a frown etched across his whisker-covered cheeks. He folded his hands into tight fists and stared into the flames of the low fire burning in the hearth.

Maureen stared at her father while she weighed her response. Angry as she was, she decided not to echo his tirade. "I'm sorry you feel that way," she said in the calmest voice she could muster. "I'm sorry I have been such a disappointment."

Afraid she would spit out something angry, Maureen ran from the house. She willed herself not to cry until she could get far from her father. She heard the back door slam as she ran across the yard and then skipped over hens who scurried toward her for food. She raced past the squash plants heavy with fruit. She dove between the feathery stalks of corn, seeking a hiding place where she could think.

When she could no longer see the house, she collapsed onto the ground. And there, wedged between the woody stalks and a fringe of leggy weeds, she wrapped her arms around her legs, leaned her head against her knees and sobbed. Hot tears burned her eyes and she wiped them on her skirt.

Her father's cruel words rang in her ears. She wiped salty tears on her sleeve and muttered. Not of much help, he says, after I've done for him. Her head pounded and her heart raced.

I hate him, she thought and almost immediately regretted the thought. She knew she didn't hate her father. She remembered the sadness that enveloped him when they first arrived in America. Though he said nothing, Maureen remembered her mother saying Father couldn't be consoled for the loss of his homeland. After a few bitter months, he grew resigned to his new situation and began referring to Sharpsburg as home. This summer, with his leg so painful, he had been just as bitter. He didn't talk much except to grumble.

Maureen quieted down and listened to the corn stalks swaying in the light breeze. The shadows between the corn rows were growing. The slanting sunlight was golden, lighting up the wings of flies and the dust that floated on the warm air.

She sat in silence, ruminating on the growing division between her father and herself. Memories stirred in her. She thought of the Irish men who longed for freedom from British rule and of the stories of valiant Irish soldiers who gave their lives for American liberty. Duty to country was deeply ingrained in her heart. She felt it as strongly as Joe did when he spoke with such passion about his willingness to sacrifice everything to keep their adopted homeland free.

She might be just a lass, but she felt that same ardor. Her gratitude to the land under her feet was limitless. And the need was so great. She thought of Miss Larkin and the few women who worked with her. They worked tirelessly to help an endless stream of soldiers. Boys, unattended, cried out in anguish, waiting for the care they needed so desperately.

Have I been such a disappointment to ya, Father? Have I now, when I tended to your wounds, ran your errands, brought you your meals? I'll show you.

She was tired of feeling such bitterness and disappointment from the father who once used only tender words to speak to his children. She had always trusted her father's opinion. No more. She knew she'd be in trouble again. Even so, she was going back to Pry House tomorrow.

Her country needed her. Those soldiers needed her. Then, to her surprise, she thought of Patrick. Something new and exciting happened as she sat beside him today. It might not be love—she didn't have time for that anyway.

She knew, nevertheless, she was anxious to visit him again.

She rose stiffly from the ground once the daylight started to slip away.

She straightened her faded dress, smoothing the bodice she had so carefully sewn with old lace trim and neat pin tucks. She was proud of her work on this, her first grown-up dress.

As she emerged from the corn rows, she caught sight of her mother. Her back was to Maureen as she cooed to the hens that had gathered around her feet. Maureen wasn't sure her mother knew she was approaching.

She steeled herself for another confrontation. Then when her mother turned, instead of disappointment Maureen saw something unexpected. Her mother's expression was soft and sympathetic as opposed to angry as her father had been. She walked to Maureen and wrapped her arm around her waist as they walked toward the house. The simple gesture surprised and warmed her. Her mother and father were always a team when it came to disciplining their children. Her mother's reaction was something unusual.

At the back porch, she stopped and turned to her daughter with a look Maureen could only read as strong. Her mother was petite, but her will was giant-sized. Maureen knew that well enough.

"I just spoke to your father. I hadn't told him I saw you go this morning." Mother's tightened her firm but gentle embrace. Such signs of affection were unusual for her mother. Though she lavished hugs and kisses on them when they were little children, she had far less use for them now that she and Joe were grown.

"Your father doesn't understand," she began.

"No, he doesn't," Maureen replied.

"He wants to keep you safe. He's worried sick about Joe. We haven't heard a word from him since he left. We didn't even get a proper goodbye." Maureen thought she heard a touch of bitterness in her mother's voice. Perhaps it was regret.

"Father would have started in on Joe just like he did with me." Maureen could taste the acid in her words as she pulled herself free from her mother. "Joe couldn't get Father's blessing. And he was tired of all the arguments. So he just left."

50

"That he did and your father won't be consoled. What have you decided to do? I know you've already made your mind up."

Maureen nodded.

Her mother looked into her eyes, causing Maureen turned away, afraid it might hurt to look at her mother.

"I don't know," she started to say. Then she sighed. "I'm hoping the nurses at the Pry House hospital will let me help out there. I learned a lot taking care of Father's injuries this summer."

"Right ye be. That you did." Her mother laid her trembling hand on the porch rail. "Your father kept you running. He relied on you as much as he did me. I know I couldn't have done it without you."

"Mother, I," Maureen began. "I know I'm asking a lot of you—"

"I know," her mother said. "Your father is going to be angry. Just as he has been angry since his fall. I'm sad to see it's the way he is now. He can't farm. He can't keep you or Joe under lock and key. And he's angry about it. If you think you can help those soldiers, go."

Maureen saw tears in her mother's eyes and a lump formed in her own throat, touched by her mother's show of emotion. She never cried in front of her children. Maureen wondered if she ever cried for her home in Ireland. Or if she cried for Joe. Even when they were little, she didn't take much stock in crying. She usually scoffed at them when they tried to get their way with tears.

Maureen waited as her mother swiped at her damp cheek. "I'm not running away. The hospital is only a few miles away."

"Yes, I know. And I know the day will come when you will be needed farther away," her mother predicted. She patted her daughter on the shoulder. Maureen had never loved her mother more. She knew it had taken a lot for her to cross Father to support her.

"Thank you, Mother." Maureen wondered if she had ever said that before.

"Now I best be getting back to your father." Her mother smiled at her before disappearing into the house.

Unwilling to face her father anew, Maureen strolled across the lane to Antietam Creek. She walked under trees whose leaves were now tinged with yellow and red. Summer was at an end. Cooler weather had finally replaced the humid summer heat. In a few days, the whole valley would be ablaze in autumn color. Nights would soon be chilly.

It wasn't long before she was lost in her thoughts. What would she say to Miss Larkin? How would she explain how she could be of help to the makeshift hospital? Options were few for a girl to serve her country. As her thoughts wandered, doubt crept back in because she didn't know which would be harder: spending her days working among those injured soldiers or telling her father she was going to do it.

It was dark when Maureen returned home. She could feel the electricity in the air, still charged with her father's anger. He struggled to his feet when she entered. Instead of talking to her, her father limped to the little, stuffy bedroom he shared with her mother. He glanced at her with anger etched all over his face. Then he closed the door. His rebuff hurt.

"He doesn't understand, Maureen." Her mother wiped her hands on a tea towel and placed a bowl of stew on the table. "Now sit down. I waited supper for ya."

"I'm going to see Miss Larkin tomorrow. I know Father said I should stay here." Maureen picked up her spoon. "I know you understand, don't you, Mother? If you'd seen all those poor boys, you'd know why I want to go. I can't help but think of Joe when I see all those soldiers."

Her mother nodded as she sat beside her. "God forbid he gets hurt, though if he does, I know I'd want a nurse like you to help him get well."

Maureen heard the catch in her mother's voice. She knew she'd practically worn out a rosary praying for her son. She ran the black beads through her fingers every morning and every evening. By now, Holy Mary must be tired of hearing about Joe in Mother's prayers, Maureen thought.

They talked late into the night. Maureen told her first about Robert and Amy and then described the scenes she had witnessed.

She left out her experience at the Sharpsburg church, unable to admit to her mother she had helped Rebel soldiers. She didn't mean to help the enemy. It just happened. She didn't know if her mother would understand her kindnesses to boys who had chosen to fight for the other side, boys who might have aimed their guns at Robert, Patrick and Joe.

"I hear Father Murphy won't be holding church services in the morning," her mother said as she finally rose to clear away the dishes. "It's been turned into a hospital like the Pry House."

Maureen held her breath for a moment and then said, "I heard something about that. I heard the Confederates took it over."

"Confederates!" her mother exclaimed. "They are still here? I thought the Union Army sent them all packing across the Potomac." She shook her head as she went back to her dishes.

"I don't think those men are anything to worry about, Mother." Maureen put her bowl in the dishwater. "They're pretty bad off. At least, that's what I heard."

Maureen picked up a towel to dry the dishes her mother washed. Feelings of sadness overwhelmed her as she worked beside her mother. She'd never again be a little girl without a care in the world. She wasn't sure if this was what adulthood felt like. There was one thing she knew for sure: Her childhood had slipped away.

CHAPTER 7
PATRICK

"Finally." Miss Larkin was smiling.

Maureen took a deep breath and snipped the ends of the bandage. Her hands shook as she had wrapped layer after layer of clean cloth and tied it just the way Miss Larkin wanted. Finally, she'd gotten it right. After three humiliating tries. Miss Larkin had laughed it off each time and told her to do it again. Maureen was relieved to see the nurse's approving smile.

"Now cut this bandage off my arm and let's see if you can dress a real wound." Miss Larkin held up the practice bandage to be snipped off before she led Maureen to the bedside of a soldier whose arm had been amputated. With her mentor watching, Maureen gingerly held what remained of the soldier's arm. She swallowed hard and willed her hands to stop trembling as she wrapped the bandage the way she had been taught. Relieved, she covered the gruesome wound, the worst she had ever seen.

"Good girl." Miss Larkin turned to the pale boy-faced soldier. "Feel better, Private?"

"Yes, ma'am," he nodded.

Maureen looked at his weary face and wondered if he meant that. She swore she'd keep an eye on him. He was trying to be brave—and she knew what that was like.

She picked up her supplies and willed her nerves to settle down.

"That's all for today, Maureen. I'm pleased with your progress," Miss Larkin said. "You can see your sweetheart now."

Maureen wanted to object, even though she couldn't stop the heat from rising to her cheeks. Though she'd only been working at the hospital for a week, the gossip had started. The soldiers were worse than women. They caught onto Patrick's obvious affection very quickly.

Every time she handed a man his breakfast or the afternoon letters, she knew she'd get teased. The first day had been humiliating. Maureen couldn't remember ever being the subject of such talk. She didn't like it. Then, she realized, the men meant well. Their little jests were said with affection. They were sweet, she decided, so she held her tongue and smiled at each comment as she went about her day.

She didn't have time to fret over things so trivial anyway. Her schedule was busy. In the mornings, she delivered breakfast and then helped those who couldn't feed themselves before she ran errands and assisted the nurses and doctors.

She hoped her skills were improving. She'd learned how to administer medicine, and she could spot a fever. She'd watched the doctors set broken bones and stitch gashes together. It wasn't easy, but she was learning. She figured out how to steel herself before she looked at soldiers' horrible injuries. And it didn't take long to set aside her shyness when a man needed clean linens or a clean face. Even though her tasks were exhausting, Maureen threw herself into her work. She wanted to prove she was capable of what was expected.

While she worried about how her colleagues might judge her work, Maureen was pleased to be the object of someone else's attentions. She could feel Patrick's eyes follow her as she hurried across the crowded space.

Still, she was careful not to let his attentions distract her. Beyond an early morning greeting, she avoided speaking to him until mid-afternoon when her work was done. By then, everyone had eaten their breakfast and dinner. The sun had warmed the air and yellow jackets buzzed in the dusty beams of light that slipped in between the barn's wooden siding. Most of the men dozed.

Patrick always waited for her arrival. In the beginning, he sat up ramrod straight in his cot. In the last two days, though, she found him out of bed waiting for her in a chair near the barn's entrance.

Maureen was glad for his new waiting place. She appreciated the opportunity to breathe in fresh air as much as she enjoyed their meetings. She tried not to gulp it after a morning spent in the sour, still air of the makeshift hospital. Though some patients had been sent to other hospitals, the place was still crowded. The smell of old barn mixed with sickness was as strong as ever.

After her bandaging lesson, Maureen was more than ready for some fresh air and sunshine. She tucked a loose curl back into place and looked for Patrick. She smoothed her white apron, dirty as usual after a day's work. As she passed by Miss Larkin's little desk, the nurse called her.

"Miss O'Neill? There was one more thing." Miss Larkin motioned to the stool beside her desk. "I want to tell you how good your progress has been these past few days. For an untrained nurse, you are quite capable. I've seen your patience and kindness with the boys. Those aren't qualities I see in every nurse."

Miss Larkin praised Maureen's work, recounting all the things she had done just a few weeks at the hospital.

"My dear, you have the gift of healing. You know in your heart what needs to be done, and you do it. I know you feel a little shy and maybe even a little queasy sometimes. Even so, you go ahead and do what these boys need."

Maureen felt her spirits rise. She was astounded that her work had been noticed. Gift of healing? Me?

"I don't do anything special," Maureen argued. "I—"

"You saved that young Toohey boy's life, you know."

Maureen was stunned to hear the nurse's words and sat back on the stool. "No—"

"The boy was dying; his fever was sky high, and we couldn't get it to come down. And there were so many crying out in pain, so many bloodied and broken…well, we didn't hold out any hope for him."

"Dying," Maureen repeated, her voice only a whisper as she thought about his confession to her. "I didn't know."

Miss Larkin put her hand on Maureen's shaking arm and nodded. She praised Maureen's strict attention to the boy even as he suffered through hallucinations and burning fever. "Your persistence made the difference. Even his mother told me how comforted she was by your diligence."

Maureen thought about the subject of their conversation waiting for her near the hospital entrance. Patrick looked so healthy now. It shook her to think he could have died.

"Thank you, Miss Larkin," Maureen said.

"One of my colleagues is setting up an enormous hospital camp up in Smoketown. It's about a mile north on Boonsboro Pike. Do you know the area?"

Maureen shook her head.

"Not much to know, really. Not much of a town. A couple of sheds and cottages. In any event, Maria Hall, a very capable nurse—she nursed Mr. Lincoln's poor little boy Tad after his brother Willie died of typhus—" She paused to look for any flicker of recognition in Maureen's face, but there was none.

"She's setting up the camp, and she's sorely in need of nurses. I've recommended you. Now it's a different sort of place than this. It's close enough to go there and give it a good looking over. I think you should because I believe it would be too far for you to walk to every day from your house as you do now. You'd have to live at the camp. I want you to consider very carefully. It's almost ready, so you can see the living arrangements. It's rough. And you'd receive a small salary for your work."

A million thoughts, a million questions raced through Maureen's head. She was flattered, of course. It had never occurred to Maureen that her work had been noticed. No one had ever praised her for her accomplishments before. It gave her a new sense of pride.

Then she thought about the soldiers. She might not know all their names but she did know who would tease her, refuse to eat breakfast, or talk her ears off. She'd miss them.

Most of all, she realized, she'd miss Patrick. The thought of leaving him made her consider turning down Miss Larkin's offer.

But she wouldn't. She had come here to help her country, hadn't she? Living away from her parents, that would be challenging.

What would her mother and father say to that? She couldn't even imagine what she'd say to get their permission. Or did she even need it?

She had to admit, she'd be glad to escape her father's stifling silence every evening. He'd greeted her news that Miss Larkin had agreed to allow her to work at the Pry House with nothing except a grimace. And he hadn't talked to her since.

Miss Larkin waited for an answer.

"I am so grateful for your kind offer."

"You're saying no, aren't you?" Miss Larkin said.

"Oh, I'm not saying no. But I do want to think about it. I want to say yes. I do." Maureen leaned toward her. "May I think about it? I'll tell you for certain tomorrow."

"Yes, of course." The nurse's smile was kind, as usual. "I expect you'll need to talk it over with your parents. In fact, I've written a note to them, asking for their blessing. Miss Hall is quite young herself, though not nearly as young as you. I think you would get along splendidly."

She handed the note to Maureen who slipped it into her pocket. "Thank you, Miss Larkin." She jumped up from the stool and returned to her search for Patrick.

"You'll do an excellent job at Smoketown if you decide to go," she heard Miss Larkin say.

Maureen couldn't wait to tell him her news. What would he say? Would he be proud she had been singled out? Would he miss her?

Then she couldn't find him. Where is he? She thought impatiently as she looked toward the usual places. He wasn't by the entrance. Nor in his bed. He has to be here somewhere. She went outside and, putting her hand up to shield her eyes from the afternoon sun, scanned the hills. He came around the side of the big white building, a bouquet of flowers already wilting in his clenched hand.

Patrick blushed as he presented them to her. "For you," he said with a shy smile. "You've done so much for me. I thought these might please you."

Her hands brushed against his as Maureen took the gift. Patrick's eyes softened, though his gaze never wavered. She was touched.

"Thank you," She clutched the spindly Queen Anne's Lace and purple clover to her chest.

She didn't know what else to say as she stared at the limp blossoms. Her heart thumped so loudly she wondered if Patrick heard it. She looked up from the flowers, and her eyes shyly met Patrick's.

Patrick led her to a vacant space on a low wall that stretched out beyond the barn. It was hardly private with so many other soldiers warming themselves on the sunny lawn.

"You look different today," she said.

"I feel different. I feel well again," he said. "And the doctor told me today I'll be discharged soon."

"Already?"

"Soon as my eye is a little better healed. The bandages are off—as you can plainly see. It doesn't look too bad, does it?" Patrick asked.

Maureen had made a point of sitting on Patrick's left side to avoid seeing his wounds. She was reluctant to look at his right eye, now covered by a black patch, and his cheek where a thick red scar served as a reminder of his day in battle. It was still hideous.

"No," she lied. "You do look much better. And what about your gunshot wound?"

"Bullet just grazed me. Hurt a lot at first, but it's pretty near healed now." Patrick lowered his voice. "I could show you."

He moved as if to unbutton his shirt.

"I'm sure it's fine." Maureen shook her head.

Then he began to laugh. So did Maureen.

Patrick took her hand. "Feels so good to laugh again."

"I'm glad you're feeling well." She looked at the flowers in her lap for a moment and then again at Patrick. "But you'll be leaving…"

"No, I'm not. They need more help here so I have orders to work here, at the hospital. I'll be here. Where you are."

Patrick looked at her a little more bravely than she had seen before. How was she going to tell him her news? She couldn't. Today was not the day for her news. Let him have his happy moment.

"Oh, Patrick," she began.

"You're always on my mind, Maureen." Patrick turned to look at her, fire beginning to kindle in his eyes. He reached for her hands with his own, trembling and clammy. "I haven't told you this. Well, I have to."

Maureen trembled nervously. She steeled herself for—what she didn't know. "Yes, Patrick?"

He looked at her hand resting in his own and, swallowing, looked at her. "I haven't even told my mother this. I don't think I ever will."

He paused for what seemed the whole afternoon.

"What is it, Patrick?"

Finally, he looked at her again, with a blush rising to his cheeks and an awkward smile.

"I know I should have thought of my mother as I lay dying on the battlefield."

"You weren't dying."

"Yes, of course. I didn't know it then. I lay there thinking those were my final moments on earth. I could barely see with my eye swollen shut. I had a headache so fierce I couldn't lift my head. I couldn't move without pain ripping through my guts. I heard moaning and crying all around me. Men calling for their mothers, for God, for an end to the pain. I could see one of my buddies beside me, his eyes wide open even though he wasn't looking at me. A Reb was slumped on top of him. I think maybe it was the man who I was fighting with. I didn't think I'd ever forget his face, but perhaps it's best I have."

He had turned away from her, his eyes fixed on the rolling field that spread out before them. He seemed to be looking at the battlefield where he had lain. Maureen wondered if he remembered she was beside him.

Then he looked at her again. "You were my only regret. I mean, not knowing you. I promised myself if I survived, well... I thought of you in those terrible moments. I should have thought of my mother, I suppose."

He smiled at her, this time with a little more confidence. "Still, it was you I thought of. I kept thinking how sorry I was that I would never see you again. And then suddenly there you were. Not you, not really. I saw an angel with eyes dark as yours, and hair brown and curly like yours."

"I was there," Maureen said.

"No, you hadn't arrived when the angel appeared. She looked just like you. It must have been a dream. She was asking me to come

60

with her, and I thought, well maybe I should. But before I could go to heaven, you came. You told me not to go. You did, didn't you? Or was that part of the dream?" Confusion passed across Patrick's face.

Maureen smiled at him. "I did tell you it wasn't your time. I told you we needed you here."

"You did, didn't you? Then, well, then I knew I loved you." His blush deepened.

"Then kiss her, you dope," a soldier lounging behind the wall shouted out.

"Yeah, what are you waiting for?" said another man next to him. They laughed. Patrick blushed. So did Maureen.

"Shut up and mind your own business," Patrick replied.

Then he looked at Maureen. "Maybe they're right," he whispered to Maureen.

He leaned in as he spoke and pressed his lips against hers. Maureen could feel the warmth of that kiss spread through her face to her heart to the hands that rested in Patrick's. She never wanted it to end.

"About time," the soldier said.

Patrick and Maureen separated and looked at one another. And they laughed.

CHAPTER 8
DECISIONS

The sun shone brightly in the afternoon sky, thought Maureen hardly noticed. The autumn breeze lifted the dark tendrils off her neck and she wrapped her shawl more tightly. She turned north on Boonsboro Pike instead of turning south toward home.

Maureen didn't feel like the nervous girl who had arrived at the Pry House less than two weeks before. She stepped along the road with a new confidence. Confidence that came from encouraging words. It also came from a sense that she was loved by someone that wasn't related to her.

She was excited, sure she was doing the right thing, Maureen strode down the road with purpose. She laughed to herself as she recalled that awkward moment before Patrick kissed her. And suddenly, she saw the sunshine and the long country road that stretched out beside cornfields undisturbed by bloody fighting.

"Gift of healing," Miss Larkin had said. As she walked down a road filled with wagons and pedestrians like herself, Maureen looked forward to seeing Smoketown, the place she might call home for the next few weeks. Or maybe even months.

Lost in her thoughts, she pulled an apple from her haversack.

"That looks delicious," said a female voice behind her.

Maureen turned, surprised.

"I don't believe she remembers us, sister," the woman said to her companion.

"Of course I do, Miss Patricia." Maureen was happy to see the familiar faces of Angela and Patricia. Both were dressed alike in lace-trimmed black just as they were when Maureen first met them on the battlefield.

"I was beginning to think we'd never catch up to you. Where are you off to in such a hurry?" Angela asked with a smile.

"I'm walking over to Smoketown, a new hospital—"

"Why yes, we've just volunteered to work there when it opens tomorrow. Will you be there?" asked Patricia as she eyed Maureen's apple.

"Would you like an apple?" Maureen pulled two from her sack. The winding road toward Smoketown narrowed as they turned off Boonsboro Pike, but with the field hospital and battlefield so close it was clogged with traffic. Ambulance after ambulance raced past the three women as they trudged along the hilly road lined with a dense, dark copse of trees.

"It's been such a terrible time." Patricia rubbed the apple on her skirt. "We spent a few days on the battlefield helping find men who were still alive."

"And then we started counting the dead," Angela added. "Ten became twenty. And then a hundred. And then thousands."

"We couldn't go on," Patricia said. "It got so bad. Flies and vultures everywhere. We had to wrap our faces to continue. After a while, we couldn't do it anymore."

"We've been helping out in one of the hospitals," Angela added. "We decided we'd be more help at Smoketown."

"That's where I'm going. Have you seen it?" Maureen asked. "What's it like?"

"Not much to look at." Patricia shrugged. "Rows of tents set up in the dirt. Most of them are in the sun, but there are woods there so some of the tents are shaded."

"You'll like Maria," Angela added. "She's young and energetic and very good at ordering those soldiers about."

Maureen thought about the head nurse's unusual name: Ma-RI-ah. She tucked the pronunciation in the back of her mind and then asked, "Are you going there now?"

"No, we're staying with a friend, Suzanne Keating, along the Smoketown Road. We couldn't stay at my cousin's house anymore. The damage from the battle, you know," Angela said. "Suzanne opened her house to us until the hospital is ready."

"Too bad she couldn't lend us her carriage, too," Patricia added.

"The Confederate Army took her carriage." Angela shot a look at her sister.

"Really! I didn't realize that." Patricia chuckled softly. "My apologies to her. Here I've been wondering why she was so stingy with her carriage and, well…"

"So, Mrs. Keating lives near here?" Maureen asked.

"Yes. She and her husband have a farm a little farther down the road a piece. Her husband and mine met at college." Angela explained. "I wonder if you know her?"

"I may have seen her in church, but she and I don't travel in the same circles," Maureen answered.

"I thought everybody knew everybody around here. Why, there can't be more than a thousand people in Sharpsburg."

"Yes, that's true, I guess," Maureen told Miss Angela. "But no one pays attention to the children, and I'm still one of the children and will be until I'm married."

"I'd have thought you would have a husband by now. It seems all the girls are marrying before their men go off to war." Patricia's eyes were wide with curiosity.

"Patsy!" Angela exclaimed.

Maureen blushed and chuckled. "Afraid not. I've been too busy helping with the farm and my father this past summer to be looking for a husband."

"I'm surprised a husband isn't looking for you," Patricia smiled.

Maureen blushed again.

"Maybe he is, sister dear." Angela nodded at the young woman.

Maureen's blush grew hotter as her thoughts returned to Patrick. She became silent as a twinge of guilt rose in her heart. If she went to Smoketown, she knew she would be separated from Patrick. She held out little hope that the Army might reassign him to work with her. She worried she might lose something wonderful before she even got a chance to experience it. He might not like her going away. He might get angry. Maureen's emotions were a conflicting jumble.

She knew going to Smoketown was right. Miss Larkin had asked her specifically. She chose her for her "gift of healing."

Maybe it was a way to get rid of me. Maybe, maybe I'm not really any good at all. I kept making mistakes. And as Father always says, I'm just a girl. Maybe that means I'm not—

"Did you hear me, Maureen?" Angela asked. "Is something wrong? You have such a frown on your face."

"Oh, I do? Um, no, nothing is wrong. I was just thinking."

The sisters' eyes twinkled as they smiled at Maureen. She blushed.

They arrived at the stone pillars marking the long narrow lane to the Keating farm. It was here that the two sisters stopped to bid her goodbye. Angela bent to kiss Maureen.

"God keep you until we meet again," she whispered. "I expect it will be very soon. Maybe even tonight. If it's late when you've finished meeting with Maria, I want you to promise you will stop here for the night."

Maureen heard it as an invitation, and yet she knew it was a directive. "I was hoping to get home before supper tonight. My father and mother worry about me," she began. "If it's too dark to go home then yes, of course, I will. If you don't think Mrs. Keating will mind."

"Suzanne Keating will be happy to have such a lovely girl as yourself." Then Patricia surprised Maureen by winking at her.

Maureen smiled. "Then perhaps I will be back," she answered, though she had no intention of spending the night anywhere except home.

They waved farewell, and she turned back down the road.

It wasn't much farther, Angela had told Maureen. Past the cornfield, she pointed to the edge of a stand of trees. Beyond that was the field hospital.

Although it had already been a long day, Maureen pushed aside her weariness and her doubts to keep walking.

I am being silly. I should be thrilled to have this chance.

CHAPTER 9
ONE MORE DAY

The corn beside Maureen was high and golden, untouched by the recent fighting. A breeze ruffled the tassels that topped the tall stalks as a rooster crowed.

Not too much farther to go, she thought as loneliness set in.

She adjusted her haversack, squared her shoulders and looked ahead to the wisps of woodsmoke that signaled the camp was near. Then something rustled at the edge of the field and Maureen's loneliness turned into apprehension.

An angry voice made her jump and she stooped down, hidden by the cornstalks.

"I know you're in there, girl," a man called in between the tall rows. Some fifty feet away, a wiry man in faded and worn clothing clutched a long rifle. His clothes might have been gray once, or blue once. He might have been a soldier. She couldn't tell whether he was young or old. His curly hair stuck out in all directions with a color somewhere between light brown and gray.

She trembled as she crouched under the cover of the corn, praying she wouldn't be seen.

"Come on out and I won't hurt you," he ordered as he peered between the golden rows of corn.

Maureen stayed as silent as she could, fearful he would turn on her if he saw or heard her. Slowly, she reached into the haversack, now empty except for her father's gun. She curled her fingers around the handle, threading her finger into the trigger.

Suddenly, a petite woman with skin as dark as Maureen's hair bolted from the corn stalks near her. She stumbled and fell at Maureen's feet, her eyes bright with fear and anger. Her black skirt was torn; buttons had been ripped from her lace-edged blouse. The pale blue scarf wrapped around her head was askew. She gasped for

66

air as the man advanced, his shining, pale eyes darting from Maureen to the other woman. Maureen realized she wasn't much more than a girl, probably younger than herself.

"Well, lookee here." The gunman shouldered his rifle as a grin spread across his grizzled face.

As he came closer, Maureen thought perhaps he was a soldier. His clothes had a trim military cut, and the brass buttons on his coat looked like those of a uniform. His shirt was untucked. His feet were bare. His face was heavily scarred from a knife or bayonet.

The way his watery blue eyes glittered made Maureen fear he was dangerous. He might be mean, or he might be mean and crazy. She kept her hand on her gun.

He pointed his rifle at the woman at Maureen's feet. "Don't you even think of moving, little Miss Sally." He turned his gaze and his gun on Maureen. "It looks like we have company."

Sally picked herself up while the man was still talking and raced away. He took aim and fired.

Her pace was no match for the speed of a bullet. Maureen heard a blood-curdling scream as the woman's body slammed into the road. Her ears rang from the report so close by, though she didn't dare move. She strained to see if Sally was still alive.

Then the man turned his attention and his gun on her. He paused to reload, keeping his eye trained on her.

She gripped the pistol as sweat slid between her fingers and the trigger. She prayed feverishly that she wouldn't have to use it, prayed that he would just go away. "Please. Please don't hurt me."

"Now what makes you think I'd hurt a pretty little thing like you? I wouldn't've hurt Sally if she hadn't of run."

His voice was edged with a sweetness that made Maureen's blood curdle. She fingered the trigger and calculated how she would make her only shot count. She knew she could only get one shot. And she knew she wasn't good with a gun.

Her heart pounded painfully in her chest until the moment she waited for came. He looked down at his gun.

She whipped out her pistol, aimed with both hands, shut her eyes and fired.

The gunshot threw him down on his back, his rifle flying through the air. She raced for his gun, watching as blood spurted from his neck.

"You little devil," he rasped, an ungodly gurgle in his voice as he struggled to get up. "I wasn't never gonna hurt you."

He collapsed and blood pooled under his head, but Maureen didn't wait to watch him die. After she scooped up his gun, she backed away, her heart pounding. She turned and ran from him, from the girl he had shot, away from her sin. She struggled to breathe as fear and anger bubbled up.

Then guilt made her stop and turn around. Maureen couldn't go on until she knew if that girl was dead.

Filled with panic and dread, she ran back to her, keeping her eyes from looking at the man bleeding in the field. The girl looked like a small child lying there face down on the road, her white blouse stained with drops of blood. He had shot her all right, but it was only her left hand that oozed blood.

Maureen couldn't tell how badly she had been hurt. She gently turned the girl over to see if she was still alive. At Maureen's touch, the girl trembled in pain. Then she opened her eyes and cried out.

"You're alive!" Maureen exclaimed.

"Of course, I'm alive. I fell to the ground so he wouldn't shoot twice. Then I realized he got me." She raised her bloodied hand.

Maureen tore off a strip of her underskirt, ripping it into a bandage. She willed her hands to stop shaking as she wound the fabric around the girl's thin wrist and tied a knot. Then Maureen wrapped her hand around the girl's narrow waist before asking, "Can you walk?"

"Can you carry me?" Though the girl spoke in a deep monotone, her widening brown eyes made Maureen wonder if Sally was kidding her.

"The cheek of ya," Maureen retorted and helped her onto her feet.

"We've got to get your hand looked at." Maureen hesitated for a moment, wondering where she could take this girl. The new field hospital was close, but it wasn't open. Then she thought of

68

the sisters. They would surely help her. And they were closer than anywhere else she could go. "I have friends at that farm over there. They're nurses."

The girl looked skeptically at Maureen. "No proper white lady is letting me in her house."

"You're not a runaway, are you?"

"Certainly not," she shot back, her eyes shining with indignation. "My mama bought our freedom when I was a little girl."

She held up her hands, a crease forming between her big bright eyes as she examined the bandage wrapped around her left hand. "These have always kept food on our table. I'm a seamstress. And I'm good. Well, I was." She turned over her hand to examine the bandage.

"Who was that man?"

"Can't say as I know." The girl shrugged her delicate shoulders. "He came after me while I was walking home. I made bandages for the soldiers, and after I delivered them, I headed up this road and there he was. It was as if he was waiting for me. He muttered something about a reward and then he grabbed me and tore at my clothes. I've never seen anything like it. I think he was crazy. He didn't hurt me none. I was so scared I ran into the corn rows and thought I lost him. I was wrong, wasn't I?"

"So he thought you were a runaway slave."

"Suppose so."

Maureen was shocked by the lack of emotion in the girl's voice. She shuddered to think what might have happened to the girl if she hadn't gotten away.

Maureen tightened her grip around the girl's slender waist her as they walked down the road to the Keating farm. "Well, looks like you're safe now, Sally."

"My name ain't Sally," she countered. "My name is Ernestine."

"That man called you Sally."

"Well, I am not no Sally. My mama named me Ernestine."

"And I'm Maureen."

"Proud to know you, Maureen," Ernestine said. "You really think the white lady will let me in?"

"I don't know the white lady, but I know the sisters visiting her. They'll help you, I'm sure of it."

Maureen threw the offending rifle deep into the cornfield before they walked silently back to the farm. She looked at the setting sun and knew she wouldn't make it to the Smoketown hospital today— and she wasn't going to make it home tonight. She worried about the young woman beside her. Ernestine cradled her injured hand and said she hoped her mama wouldn't worry about her.

Maureen nodded. She hoped her parents wouldn't worry, either. Yet she knew they would. And she knew there would be hell to pay when she didn't come home until the next day.

It couldn't be helped, she thought as she led the girl up the lane. She took a deep breath as they walked toward the house.

It was a grand place, with its sweeping porch held up by pillars two stories high, old oak trees that hinted at the estate's age, and shadows of fine thick draperies at the window. The stately Keating mansion intimidated Maureen. She'd never been in a place like this. Ernestine put her hand in Maureen's as they neared the front door.

"Go 'round back," Ernestine advised, pulling on Maureen. "No use making a scene on the front porch."

Maureen looked at her, confused.

"They ain't going to let a girl like me in the front parlor, Maureen," she said. "I've been to houses finer than this. I delivered baby clothes at the Johnsons a while back, and their house is about the finest in the county, and I knew to go to the back door."

Ernestine didn't wait for Maureen to answer. She turned down a path that led to the kitchen door. Maureen followed.

"How can I help you?" growled the portly, gray-haired housekeeper who answered the door. She looked from girl to girl with a frown. She let her frown rest on Ernestine a second longer than was necessary.

Maureen's voice squeaked as she answered. "I'm looking for two ladies who are staying here. My friend Ernestine has had, um, an accident and needs their help." She waited expectantly while the woman paused and looked at them with a squint that made Maureen wonder if she could see them clearly.

70

"She ain't coming in here," the woman said.

"Please, ma'am," Maureen replied. "Just look at the poor girl's hand."

"That ain't my problem. Good day." She started to close the battered door, but Maureen stopped it with her heavy boot.

"We're not leaving." Her tone was insistent. "My friend needs help. I know Miss Angela and Miss Patricia are here. Please get them."

"Mrs. Keating won't abide none of you people in her house," the housekeeper growled again.

"I ain't coming in your house, lady." Anger flashed from Ernestine's eyes. She started to say something more, and then suddenly she swayed, tried to grab the railing to steady herself and fainted dead away.

"Please, ma'am." Maureen pleaded with the woman as she stooped to help Ernestine.

"I'll get Patricia," the woman finally said.

Ernestine came to as Maureen cradled her head. She struggled to sit up, moaned softly and reached for her injured hand. The two girls waited quietly for the sisters to come, looking out on the wide expanse of pasture.

They waited only a few more moments before Patricia burst out the back door.

"What's this?" she asked, looking from the girl she knew to the smaller girl tenderly holding her hand.

"Had a bit of an accident, have you?" She knelt in the dusty yard beside Ernestine. "May I?" she asked before peeling away the bloodied remnant of Maureen's underskirt from Ernestine's hand.

"Quite an accident," she murmured as she uncovered the wound. "What happened?"

"A man with a gun was chasing Ernestine though a cornfield down the road," Maureen explained.

"He shot at me. I almost got away, but he got my hand." Ernestine bent her head to get a closer look at the dark red wound.

"Yes, I would say he did. Let's get you in the house. It looks like your nurse here did a good job," she added, nodding to Maureen.

The housekeeper blocked the door. "The Missus wouldn't want no strangers in the house." She glared at Ernestine.

"Alma," Angela appeared, her voice steely. "Mrs. Keating is more generous than you give her credit for. Let the girls in."

Alma hesitated, looking with hatred at the injured girl. Angela looked at the housekeeper pointedly. The housekeeper scowled and backed away from the door while keeping her eye on the newcomers. Maureen scurried past her, uncomfortable under Alma's unwelcoming glare.

The sisters sat Ernestine down on a stool beside the fireplace and ordered Maureen to pour water from the kettle into a basin on a nearby table. Once Patricia and Angela cleaned up the blood, they wrapped it in clean white cloth strips.

"It's not as bad as I feared." Angela looked at Ernestine with a smile. "The bullet only grazed the side of your hand. I think you'll be able to use it again soon if you're real careful with it now."

"I hope so, ma'am," Ernestine answered. "I need my hand to sew. My mama counts on me to help her."

"You probably need some good food in your bellies, both of you," Patricia looked from Ernestine to Maureen with a sympathetic smile.

"And you must be exhausted." Angela wiped the girl's face and turned to the housekeeper. "Alma, this girl needs a bed."

"I have to draw the line at that." She shook her head.

"Alma, this little girl—how old are you Ernestine?"

"Old enough to know better, my mama always says," she answered.

"You couldn't be over 14," Patricia said.

"If you say so." Ernestine sounded tired.

"Alma, have a little pity on this child. She needs some rest and some supper before we send her back to her mother," Angela said.

"Ain't no way she's sleeping in this house," Alma retorted, and then sighed. "I guess it would be all right if she slept in the barn."

Patricia opened her mouth to object, as her sister nodded. "Thank you, Alma. That will do."

"It won't do at all," Patricia muttered as they escorted Ernestine to the barn and made up a place for the girl to sleep with fresh straw and a thin quilt.

"This isn't much." Angela looked at the results. "It's warm and fairly clean."

"I'll bring you something to eat at supper time," Maureen said.

"I'd best be going home, ma'am." The girl frowned as she looked over the makeshift bed. "My mama will be waiting for me."

"Not till tomorrow," Patricia patted her hand and bade her to get undressed and climb under the quilt. "It's too late to be out on the roads. Rest now. Food later. We'll get you home in the morning."

"Maybe some tea would do you good?" Angela asked. "I know I'd like a cup."

"No, thank you, ma'am." Ernestine's shoulders drooped as she smiled weakly. "I'm not much in the mood for anything right now."

"Well, then, we'll leave you to your rest." Angela pushed the other two out of the barn ahead of her.

"Poor child," Angela said.

"Poor child, indeed," Patricia said. "We better thank our God in heaven that Mrs. Keating's housekeeper let her stay in the barn. Mrs. Keating wasn't about to welcome Ernestine, free or slave, into her house. She may not be a slaveholder, but she's no abolitionist either."

"Mrs. Keating?" Maureen asked. "I thought you said—"

"It's a complicated subject around these parts," Patricia tried to explain. "Mrs. Keating is a good and generous woman, except when it comes to this. I can't understand it at all and you, being a newcomer to this country, must find it puzzling. But these people have been divided on the issue of slavery for two hundred years. White and colored people just don't mix too well here is all."

"Ernestine will be safe with a roof over her head for tonight. Tomorrow morning, we'll take you to the hospital, and we'll take Ernestine home—unless she needs more tending to," Patricia told Maureen and Angela as the sisters rose to leave.

Maureen decided to return to Ernestine until supper time. After the girl had nibbled at a little food and gone to sleep, Maureen tiptoed to the room made up for her. She burrowed down into the

73

downy linens in a maid's room at the far end of the house, ready for sleep. The night was cool, but the quilt was soft and warm. She wondered that she should be given a bed for the night and another girl no different from her would be hidden away in the barn.

It doesn't seem fair, and it doesn't seem right.

It had been a long day—frightening and troubling. As tired as she was her eyes simply would not close as her mind raced through the events that took her from the Pry House hospital to her terrifying encounter on Smoketown Road.

She'd left the hospital full of excitement. Patrick. Her new assignment. And then in a blink of an eye, she faced danger like nothing she had experienced before. That man was going after Ernestine and then Maureen. And then she'd killed him. Dead. He had to be dead.

Was it murder? Did I murder a man?

Before today, Maureen couldn't kill anything except a chicken. She'd wrung plenty of necks. But when her brother tried to teach her to shoot, she followed along only grudgingly. She didn't want to hunt. She wasn't going to kill a squirrel or a deer. Ever. She couldn't even bring herself to shoot at a fox harassing her hens. She'd shot plenty of tin cans, pine cones and other inanimate objects and Joe was pleased with her aim. He never could, however, convince her to aim her gun at a potential meal.

When Maureen packed her father's gun in her bag, she didn't really believe she'd use it. She brought it for protection, thinking she might wave it around if someone frightened her. She had heard about marauders and ne'er-do-wells who followed the troops and had been terrifying families in these parts.

She touched that cold metal again and again as she reached into her bag for another roll or an apple. That gun kept reminding her she wasn't safe. It reminded her she was on her own. It never occurred to her she might murder someone.

But on this very day, she aimed that pistol and fired a bullet into the body of a man. He might still be lying in that field, growing colder in the evening dampness. She didn't want to think beyond that. Maureen forced herself to defend her own actions.

Maybe she did save Ernestine's life. She probably saved her own. Even if that horrible man wasn't going to kill her, he was going to hurt her. She was sure of that. And that was something she didn't want to dwell on at all.

It made her shiver to remember the terrifying look in his eye. He was no better than that fox sticking his snout into the henhouse.

And yet she didn't kill the fox.

But she did kill that man.

I had to. Otherwise, he might have come after me and then attacked poor Ernestine, lying in pain on the road. Maybe he'd have killed both of us.

This was danger as Maureen had never experienced it. She cried from fright when her family's pub burned in Galway. She was frightened of all the strange people she saw when she arrived in America. She looked on the soldiers marching past her farm with suspicion. She heard the echo of cannon fire and seen the carnage of war so close to home.

And yet, until today, no one ever threatened her life directly. Never before did she feel compelled to protect herself. Maybe her father was right. Maybe if she stayed home, she would have been safe. If Ernestine stayed home, she'd have stayed safe, too. But Ernestine had to work. She had to travel those roads.

And so did I. I wanted to help find Robert. I wanted to work in the hospital. I wanted to visit Patrick. That has meant going out on those roads.

Maureen thought about Ernestine as her body grew heavier with sleep. What about her? Maureen didn't remember the last time she spoke to a person with skin dark as Ernestine's. She never noticed them in town and never at church. She spent most of her waking hours on their farm where she only saw her relatives.

She knew about slavery, of course. She knew it was one of the reasons for this terrible war that was tearing apart her new country. She'd seen enslaved men, women and even children walking past their house. She never really gave them much thought until today.

It wasn't right for that wounded child to be alone in that big, dirty barn, Maureen thought again, and her conscience got the better of her. She crawled out of her warm bed and crept down the narrow hall, down the servant's stairs and through the now-empty kitchen. She eased open the back door and hurried over the cold, hard-packed ground to the barn.

"Maureen? Is that you?"

The girl was startled to see Patricia wrapped tightly in a thick black shawl, sitting in the straw beside Ernestine. "Yes, ma'am. I was worried about Ernestine."

"Me too," Patricia said. "I didn't think the poor child should be alone in here all night."

"You ladies don't have to worry about me," Ernestine mumbled. "It's not so bad. But if you all keep up with your chattering I won't get any sleep at all."

"It's too cold out here for you," Maureen said. "I've got this big warm bed with a nice downy comforter." She looked at the older woman to see if she would object. Instead, Patricia wore a hint of a smile. "It's too cold for you too, Miss Patricia."

"Maureen's right." Patricia rose from her bed of straw. "Let's get you in a proper bed."

"If you don't think I'll get in trouble..." Ernestine's voice was husky from weariness.

She wrapped herself in the thin quilt before gathering up her shoes and dress. "The straw isn't so bad. Still, I don't think I was sleeping alone."

She shook as if to rid herself from whatever vermin might have been sharing her warm place in the straw.

"Good night, girls," Patricia whispered. She turned to walk toward her bedroom as Ernestine and Maureen collapsed into bed.

"Isn't this better?" Maureen asked.

"Sure is," Ernestine said. "Warm and toasty."

Maureen heard the girl's breathing grow heavy and even as the darkness of night closed in. The sun had risen when a gentle tapping at the door woke her.

"There's a wagon ready," Angela said after Maureen opened the door. "We'll take you to the field hospital and then take Ernestine home to her mother. If I can find her."

"She's here," Maureen said. "Still asleep."

Angela peered around the door to see the girl nestled under the comforter. She gently woke Ernestine and asked to see her hand. "How does it feel?" she asked.

"It's sore," Ernestine said. "I think it looks better though."

"I think it looks much better. Now dress quickly and come downstairs." Angela got a gleam in her eye. "Don't let Alma see you. She'll have a fit if she finds out you've slept in her bed. Hurry along now. We don't want to make the driver wait."

Maureen was excited to ride in a wagon. Used to relying on her two feet to get her where she wanted to go, she hadn't been carried anywhere in years. The last time she had a chance to take such a ride as this was when the family moved to Sharpsburg. They spent their first winter in America in Philadelphia, staying with her Aunt Priscilla's family. Father arranged for a wagon to carry them from the train station to the little log cabin.

"It's fast!" Ernestine exclaimed as the horse pulled the wagon through the gate and onto Smoketown Road. She hid her head under her hand-crocheted shawl, coming out only as the horse began to move in a steady rhythm down the road.

Maureen held her breath as they passed the cornfield where she had shot that man the day before. She glanced at Ernestine whose expression remained impassive, as if she hadn't remembered the ordeal they had encountered there.

The man is gone. Either he lived, or someone moved his dead body since yesterday.

She shivered as she thought of his menacing face and the way he pointed that rifle.

They directed the driver, a gray-haired man who looked as if he could be related to Alma, to drive to the Smoketown field hospital before going on to complete an errand in nearby Boonsboro.

"And we'll drop this young lady at her house, too," Patricia told the driver.

They said very little on the short drive from the Keating farm to the field hospital. Maureen was still dazed by the events of the previous day. Ernestine assured her she was feeling much better and that her hand was healing nicely. Yet her young face was drawn, and Maureen wondered if she really felt as well as she said.

DIVIDED LOYALTIES

The sisters looked out as the scenery unfolded before them.

"Here, driver," Patricia said a few minutes later.

They stopped beside a cluster of canvas tents hugging the edge of the forest with curls of smoke rising above them. Men scurried to and fro, setting up line after line of clay-colored tents stretching as far as they could see.

Ambulance wagons and men on horseback hurried past them on the busy road, kicking up a thick cloud of choking dust.

With bloody and battered men leaning against trees or lying on the rough ground, it wasn't a sight for the weak of heart. Maureen closed her eyes and willed her stomach to settle.

"Will you be all right, Maureen?" Angela asked.

"I'm sure I'll be fine," Maureen said as she climbed from the wagon.

I'm not sure I'll be fine at all. I'd rather stay with you nice ladies, but I promised I'd be here.

She turned and smiled her brightest smile. "Thank you for everything."

"Maureen," Ernestine called and jumped out of the wagon to run after her.

"Yes?" she said, turning.

"Thank you. Good luck."

Maureen hugged the girl. "I'll miss you."

"Oh, go on," Ernestine said though she smiled at Maureen.

CHAPTER 10
MISS HALL

The wagon drove away and turned out of sight before Maureen entered the hospital camp. This place made the Pry House look like a castle. Dust swirling through the hot air and smoke from the campfires made it hard to see how far the rows of tents stretched.

A grove of tall trees provided the only respite from the unseasonable heat. Smoketown wasn't much of a town before the war. A couple of houses and the blacksmith shop that gave the place its name was all.

Now Maureen saw it would soon be a bustling metropolis. Even in this state of confusion, doctors were rushing to see to men carried here from the battlefield. By the mess tents, stoves sent up clouds of steam and the smell of grease. Near them, people were filing in and out of other tents that looked like offices of some sort. Maybe a chapel or post office. Everywhere ambulance wagons were still bringing wounded men in.

Though the pink of dawn was only beginning to fade as the sun rose in a brilliant blue sky, wounded Union soldiers had found seats in the shade of the trees.

A sergeant whose head was wrapped in a thick white bandage leaned against a post, smoking a cigar.

"You looking for someone, Miss?" he asked Maureen as she hesitated beside him.

"Miss Hall," she said.

"Miss Maria should be in that tent there." The sergeant pointed at an open tent. "Don't worry. She don't bite." He threw down the cigar butt and bowed politely.

Maureen peeked into the tent where the sergeant had directed her and saw two women, one older and one younger, with their heads bent over a notebook.

DIVIDED LOYALTIES

Not wanting to disturb their conference, she stood outside, uncomfortable amid all the pandemonium surrounding her.

Maureen's eyes wandered to the tent next door where she could see through the open flaps two rows of cots neatly lined up. Each cot held a man covered with a white blanket. Most patients were still sleeping, except for the man near the door. He was sitting up, looking worried.

"Nurse?" asked the young man. "Do you think you could help my buddy here?"

"But I'm not a nur——" Maureen began to object and then thought better of it when she saw the man in the next bed over.

He was lying on his back, bandages around the crown of his head and both arms. Breakfast rested untouched beside his cot. He looked to be about Joe's age with auburn hair and ruddy complexion.

"How can I help?" She put down her haversack and leaned over the man.

He looked only at the ceiling.

"He ain't talking." The young man looked at his silent neighbor, a look of pity on his face. "I'm not sure he can even hear. I do know he can't eat by himself."

"Do you know his name?" Maureen asked.

"Rusty something. Everybody calls him Rusty. I think it's on account of his hair."

Maureen knelt beside Rusty's cot. She picked up the bowl of tepid oatmeal and asked, "Rusty, are you hungry? Would you like some of this?" She turned and whispered to the man beside Rusty, "It looks awful. What's your name?"

"Bill. And yeah, it's bad. They say it's porridge. I, for one, think they used it to make the casts on Rusty's arms before serving it for our breakfast."

Bill's eyes twinkled even as he grimaced. A heavyset boy with thick golden curls, he sat up in bed, his left shoulder enshrouded in bandages and his right eye blackened.

"He'll eat it," Bill added. "Try."

Maureen offered a spoonful of the grayish gruel. Rusty glanced at her for only a second, looked at the spoon and opened his mouth.

80

He continued to eat what she offered until the bowl was empty.

She looked around for a napkin to wipe a bit of lumpy cereal off his face. "Here, ma'am." Bill offered his crumpled handkerchief.

She wiped his face, and he closed his eyes.

Poor fellow.

"Thank you, ma'am." Bill accepted his handkerchief and shoved it a pocket. "We saw some serious action the other day. When they put Rusty beside me yesterday after his operation, I recognized him from our unit. Can't say I know him exactly."

"Can I get you anything, Rusty?" Maureen leaned over the man to look at his face.

"He hasn't said a word to anyone," Bill offered.

Rusty opened his eyes and looked at her, though he said nothing. Maureen patted his arm lightly, and he flinched, a look of terror passing over his face.

Then she heard the sound of the two women she was waiting for as they entered the tent. Their conversation stopped when they spied the young woman between the cots of the two young soldiers.

"And who have we got here?" The younger woman studied her with a patient air.

She didn't look much older than Maureen, but she spoke with an easy confidence. Her dark eyes, set between a sloping forehead and high cheekbones, peered kindly at Maureen. Her pale blue dress was clean and plain, decorated only by two pearl buttons at her neck.

Maureen suddenly grew shy before this lovely woman. She radiated authority as she clutched a big black notebook. "Yes, child, what is it?" she asked again.

"Answer Miss Hall, girl," the older woman chided her.

"I was sent to see you, Miss Hall. Miss Larkin at the Pry House sent me," Maureen stammered.

"Miss Larkin? Ah, yes. She sent word that she was sending someone. We sure do need the help." Miss Hall tapped her book. "I'll take care of this, Miss White," she said to the other woman and then turned back to Maureen. "Come with me."

Maureen glanced at Bill for a second before she hurried after Miss Hall to the hot nursing office tent. Miss Hall took a seat on

81

a funny chair beside the desk as she set her things down. Its back appeared to have been roughly sawn off.

The woman saw her look at it and smiled. "I asked to have the back cut off—like Miss Barton's. Have you heard about Miss Barton? I met Clara in Frederick and was struck by the looks of her chair. She had cut the back off like this. Too much to do to be dawdling in a comfortable chair, she said. And you can't dawdle in this chair, let me tell you."

Maureen nodded though she said nothing.

"Maria," called a man entering the office, his nose buried in records he was holding. Maureen recognized him as Sharpsburg's town doctor. In his somber black frock coat, Doctor Lee looked like he was making a simple house call.

His appearance was far different from the doctors she had seen at Pry House. They were coatless, with sleeves rolled above their elbows and dried blood on their clothes and faces.

"Forgive me," he said as he looked up. "I didn't realize you had company."

"Doctor Lee," Maureen addressed him before Miss Hall could answer. "Um," she stammered, not sure what to say.

"Why, it's Maureen O'Neill. How's your father?"

"You know this girl? I found her tending to one of my boys. She seemed to have a kindly bedside manner." A hint of a smile crept into her authoritative expression.

"I'm not surprised. She did a fine job nursing her father after his fall."

"She's coming to work here. She comes highly recommended."

"She'll be a good addition to the staff here." Doctor Lee handed some paperwork to the nurse. "These are instructions for the men I just treated. They're pretty bad off."

"Yes, Doctor," she answered as he hurried out of the office.

Miss Hall turned her attention back to Maureen, studying her face. "You're a bit young. Miss Dix won't like it a bit."

"Who's Miss Dix?"

"Dorothea is in charge of nursing. She's put me in charge of this camp. And she's left strict directions for the nurses' appearance.

I think we can make an exception in your case. Miss Larkin likes you. The doctor likes you. And from the looks of it, you were doing a good job helping my patient. Let me see where I can use you. I need you. Maybe Miss Dix won't like it: she wants her nurses old and plain."

"But you're—"

Before Maureen could say "beautiful," Miss Hall was gone.

Maureen felt out of place as she waited to see if she would return.

The office was spartan enough. Dust floated through the air and fell on a pile of blankets stored on the ground behind the tiny desk and chair. Piles of papers rested on a notebook smeared with ink. She had expected an orderly place, but it looked as if everything had been left unfinished.

Maureen already liked Miss Hall. She seemed like she was working hard to get the hospital under control. Just as Maureen began worrying that she wasn't coming back, the nurse burst back into the tent.

"I had to talk to the doctor before he got away. Then we got a new patient; man with a gunshot to the neck. Can't figure out how that happened. It wasn't a battle wound as far as I can tell. Too new," Miss Hall explained as she rifled through a stack of pages.

Maureen froze at her words, glad the nurse couldn't see her expression. She wondered if it could be possible the man she shot was here—not lying dead out on Smoketown Road.

"Then your new friend called for me," Miss Hall continued. "Bill tells me you were right kind to Rusty—and that's something he needs right now."

Maureen pushed away thoughts of the man with the gunshot wound and listened.

"Would you spend the rest of the morning with Rusty? You're the first one to get him to eat. Everyone has been so busy, and your sitting with him might do him a world of good."

"Bill asked me to help. I didn't do anything special," Maureen demurred.

"It's a good thing he stopped you. That boy is going to need a

lot of attention, and you see we aren't set up yet for proper nursing."
Maureen could tell Miss Hall used her gentle ways to get things
done.

"I guess I could." Maureen hesitated for only a second. Although
she needed to get home, she wasn't eager to face her father's anger.

"Good girl." Miss Hall smiled. "All you have to do is sit with
Rusty. Talk to him, read, tell him about your family. See if you can
get his real name, too. No one seems to know it. He didn't have a
single item in his pockets to say who he is."

Miss Hall stopped for a moment as if to emphasize the need
for his name. "Stay with him for dinner and then afterward I'll call
a carriage to take you home. Come back tomorrow, and we'll get
to work. Make sure to bring some warm clothes. It could be winter
before we get all these boys well again."

With that, Miss Hall was gone. Maureen realized the nurse
hadn't asked her if she would be returning tomorrow. She had no
doubts that Maureen would be back.

Only, Maureen wasn't sure. Her doubts returned.

*Do I want to work here? I'd be practically living in the woods, far from
family, far from Patrick.*

Then again, maybe she needed to be here. Maybe this was what
she was destined to do.

The image of the man she shot interrupted her thoughts. She
shivered and wondered if he had survived. If indeed he was here,
how was she going to stay out of his sights? She dreaded the thought
of seeing him again. She shook her head and pushed her fears and
doubts away.

For now, she'd check on Rusty. Then she'd find out if that man
was here before he found her.

CHAPTER 11
CHANGES

When the carriage finally stopped in front of their little house, it felt like the trip had taken hours. Maureen was tired; more importantly, she was frightened. She knew her father was going to be angry with her again. And angrier than he'd been before. She knew her mother would have worried. Maureen never stayed away overnight ever before in her life. She braced for another tirade as she walked in the door.

Her father was sitting in his usual place by the fire when she entered the house. She greeted him and waited for him to look at her. He just sat there unmoving, a frown on his face as he ignored her. She looked around for her mother but didn't see her.

Desperate to do something, she poured herself a cup of tea and then poured one for her father and set it beside his chair. As she bent toward him, she noticed her father's black curls were considerably grayer these days. His worry for his son (and Maureen, too, she realized) coupled with his pain was taking a toll. He was looking older than his forty-six years.

Finally, he turned his face toward her. The look in his eyes, deep-set and dark like her own, broke her heart.

"I feared you were dead," he said simply. "When ya didn't come home last night, I was certain of it. And now we've waited all day for you. Where have ya been?"

A pang of guilt shot through her. "I'm so sorry, Father." She knelt beside him, meaning every word she said.

His look, one of worry mixed with anger, was hard to face. "If I could have come home earlier, I would have."

She told him about Ernestine's run-in with the man who assaulted her and how she helped the girl after she was wounded. She told him about getting help from Angela and Patricia. "They told me it would

85

be safer to spend the night with them. I couldn't walk home in the dark."

"You shouldn't have had to think about walking home in the dark. I still say a girl's place is in her family's home. Especially now. What proper girl goes out on the road at a time like this? It's not right. I'll be expecting you to stay home and help your mother now."

"But Father——"

"There will be no arguments." He spoke harshly and turned away from her.

"Ah, but there will be!" Maureen summoned all the strength she could as she stood beside his chair. Today she needed to stand her ground.

"I will not be staying at home. I have been hired to work at a new hospital. I've got a job to do, Father. A real job. Here's a letter from Miss Larkin asking for your blessing." Maureen held out the missive and waited for a response. Her father didn't even look at it. "The nurses need help, and they've asked me to come. That's where I've been all day today. What's more, the hospital is far away, too far to come home every night. I'll have my own tent there."

"Tent? Your own tent?"

Good. He's listening.

"The hospital is made up of canvas tents—must be a hundred of them north of Sharpsburg. The nurses stay there, too. I plan to go there tomorrow."

Her father shook his head and rose stiffly. Once he rose to his full height, Maureen felt small. Though not a big man—not as tall as Patrick—her barrel-chested father wielded his power like a sword. His eyes darkened as he lifted his chin and squared his shoulders. He lowered his voice and spoke each word crisply.

"Maureen Regina O'Neill."

She trembled to see his wrath aimed at her. She shrank back as he stared down at her, a deep frown creasing his face. Back in his pub days, he frowned in the same way when an argument veered toward violence. Never before, though, had he looked at her this way.

She wasn't backing down. She stood toe to toe with him, defiance flashing in her own dark eyes.

His Irish brogue was clipped. "It seems you no longer wish to be a part of the O'Neill family. So be it. If you leave this house tomorrow, don't come back. I mean what I say. You will no longer be welcome here."

The air between father and daughter froze.

"Father, you don't mean that." Maureen hoped she misunderstood. Her legs threatened to crumple under her, and she grabbed hold of the back of her father's chair.

"Ah, but I do, Maureen."

Maureen couldn't look at his dark, hostile eyes. Unable to speak, she fled into the yard where her mother was picking squash in the chilly autumn evening. She glanced at Maureen and returned her gaze to the leggy plants beside the back porch rail.

"It's awfully late to be working in your garden, Mother." Maureen looked up at the sky, growing dark with only traces of dusk in the western sky.

"I was gathering the eggs when I heard you come. Then I saw the squash and thought I should get them in before the frost kills them."

Her mother silently picked the rest until her basket was full. Maureen knew there was more behind her mother's simple words. Though she never confronted her husband, she always had a way of making sure her children knew where she stood.

Maureen welcomed the silence as she looked up into the darkening sky. With no moon or clouds to block them out, the first stars twinkled brightly overhead. Stunned by her father's ultimatum, Maureen's thoughts were in turmoil. She was angry and hurt, disappointed in her father, worried he might never let her back in the house again.

Would he really turn me out forever?

Maureen couldn't imagine not having this home to come to. She had grown to be a woman here. Since their move from Galway, this farm had been the center of her universe. The place where she and her brother dreamed of the future. The future they imagined included this home, this farm, this yard.

She remembered nights like this when she and her brother would lie out in the field and look for their favorite constellations: Orion, the Big Dipper and the Pleiades.

Sometimes they would see a star streak across the sky. Joe told her to wish on it, for good luck.

I'd like to see one of those stars now, so I could wish for Father to see my point of view and change his mind.

"Your father was very worried," her mother finally said.

"I'm sorry I made you worry." Maureen leaned down beside her mother to pluck squash. "Even the small ones?"

"Might as well. They won't be a bit of good if we get frost tonight. I do worry, you know. I pray every night that you'll be safe. Your father worries he'll lose his only girl." She wiped her hands on the gingham apron she always wore, and she put her bowl on the step. She stepped onto the porch to lean against the rail.

Maureen stood beside her. She dug the note from Miss Larkin out of her pocket and handed it to her mother.

"I've been asked to work at the new hospital in Smoketown. I want to go. But I'll have to stay there; it's too far away to come home every night."

Maureen paused. Her mother nodded as she read the note without comment.

"When I told Father, he said I couldn't come back home. Did you know he would say that?"

"Your father said what he thinks will keep you home. And safe. He's afraid for you." Her mother carefully folded the little white sheet and tucked it in her apron pocket.

"He can trust me to be careful. Why doesn't he see that?" Maureen asked.

"Of course he trusts you. It's the rest of the world he doesn't trust. You know the stories. We've heard about people stealing possessions off dead men on the battlefield and even soldiers who went crazy after the battle and turned their guns on civilians."

Maureen shuddered.

"I assume that's why you took your father's gun," Maureen's mother said quietly.

"I didn't know you knew," Maureen answered.

"I open that drawer every day. Your father's gun might be stored under that old cloth, but I still know when it's not there. The drawer is much lighter to open. I noticed it the first day you left."

Maureen said nothing.

"I hope you haven't had to use it," her mother said.

Maureen still said nothing.

After a patient pause, her mother looked at her hands. "Then I'm glad you had it. It's kept you safe."

"Mother, I—"

"It's best kept between you and God. These are terrible times. As much as I don't think it's safe for a young woman to be out alone, I respect your need to help. Mrs. Toohey tells me you've made a difference in her boy's life." She paused a moment and then added quietly, "And so did Mrs. Henderson, Tom's mother."

Maureen looked at her mother. She knew then that Maureen had helped those Confederate boys.

"Mrs. Henderson? How did she know?"

"Father Murphy told her," her mother answered. "He said he came in after you left and stopped to talk and pray with young Tom. It was just before he died, you see, and Father said Tom seemed at peace. Father Murphy said he thinks that was because of you. Hard to believe poor Tom's gone now."

Maureen nodded as the color drained from her face. She had been found out.

"Mrs. Henderson told me it meant a lot to her to hear that. She's grateful to you for helping her boy," her mother said. "Now you know and I know he was a Confederate. He was also Joe's friend. I can't blame you for helping him."

"Mother, I knew it was wrong to be helping those Rebel soldiers. I mean they were boys that may have shot at Robert and Joe. But I knew Tom. I knew he was Joe's friend. I'm not sorry I helped him."

"I know, my dear. You wouldn't be you if you didn't help someone who needed you. I'm proud of what you've been doing. I'm still waiting to hear from Joe."

Then she fell silent for a moment before turning to say, "You go to that hospital and help those boys. Send them home to their mothers and sweethearts. And then you come back to me and your father. Do you hear?"

"But he said—"

"Don't mind what your father says in the heat of anger and worry. Some things are worth fighting for. Some things aren't. You must learn which battle you need to fight. Remember that. Maureen, I've been in your shoes. I've learned how to stand stood my ground with Daniel O'Neill."

Her mother was silent as she gazed up into the clear night sky. "I see how you love this country. I understand—more than you know—how much you want to help. Go tomorrow. And when you can, come back home. I'll be waiting for you. And I know your father. He'll be counting all the days that you are away."

She smiled, and yet Maureen saw the worry, too. She wondered how many rosaries her mother had prayed for her son. And she suddenly thought, How many rosaries had she offered for me?

"Yes, Mother," she said and, looking up, saw a star streak across the nighttime sky.

CHAPTER 12
NO PLACE FOR A GIRL

Maureen rose early the next morning, determined to go to the Pry House to visit Patrick for a few minutes before starting on her way to Smoketown. For the entire four miles, she rehearsed how she would tell Patrick about her new assignment. Not a single one of her speeches sounded right. As the big white barn came into view, she grew more worried about what she would say.

She was still walking on the path when she saw Patrick jump up from the chair by the entrance. She knew by the way he limped that the pain from his wounds still bothered him.

She smiled as they met and a deep blush rose to his pale cheeks.

"I've missed you." Patrick took her hand and looked around. After he was sure they wouldn't be seen, he kissed her cheek. "Where have you been?"

"I got caught out after dark last night. I was running an errand for Nurse Larkin up to the new hospital in Smoketown. Sunset is coming quicker now, and it was too dark to keep on walking. I figured it was safer to stay with my friends than walk home in the dark," she said. She prayed for forgiveness for omitting parts of her story. "My father is furious with me. He told me not to come home again."

"That doesn't sound like your father." Patrick took her hand as they strolled to the hill behind the hospital. The countryside spread before them in waves of green and gold. From this place, it was impossible to tell there had been a battle close by.

With Patrick by her side, Maureen experienced a comforting peace she'd never known before and one she needed so much. She knew his injuries still hurt him even though he did his best to be strong when she was near. In little gestures, he showed his affection: by the way he held her hand, warned her of a rock on the path, found her a comfortable seat.

91

"I can understand how much he wants to protect you. These are terrible times. I'm sure your father will come around," he said.

"I hope so," she said.

They walked in silence to the hospital entrance. She hoped he couldn't see how troubled she was. She tried so hard not to think of Ernestine and that man, her move to Smoketown, her inevitable parting from Patrick, her father's harsh words.

Ah, but he must have sensed something. Always so shy, he squeezed her hand.

She responded with a smile and then asked, "When do you start your new duties at the hospital?"

"Doc says another day or two officially, but I'm already running errands and doing some other things around the hospital." Patrick frowned. "He still don't know about my eye. My vision is still very blurry, and he can't say for certain if it will improve. At least it doesn't look nearly as awful as it did." He touched the raging red slash beneath his eye patch.

"Looks like it still hurts."

"Nah. If I was home with Ma, yeah, it would hurt like hel— the dickens. But here, I ain't gonna complain."

Maureen was confused.

"My problems don't seem too bad after you look at these other men. I still have all the limbs I was born with," he told her. "And besides, I've had you visiting me. There are lots of lonely people here, missing their mothers and their girls."

Maureen blushed and looked around the hospital. He knew she could see what he saw. Pry House seemed to be getting busier. Plenty of mothers, daughters and sweethearts sat by their men, reading letters and sharing confidences. More men were smiling, sitting up and beginning to get well. But for every man with a visitor, there were at least two who were alone.

Patrick's usual chair waited for them at the entrance, along with another. Maureen smiled as he waited for her to sit before taking his chair.

"They've been moving everybody they can to big hospitals in Baltimore and Philadelphia and other places. Some poor suckers had to walk all the way to Frederick, even though they were injured. That's twenty miles! You know about the new field hospitals at Smoketown and Locust Spring. Lots of men are being sent there." Maureen hoped he didn't see her start. "Eliza came to visit yesterday after you left. She said Robert was about to be transferred."

"Did she say when they'll be sending him away?" she asked.

"You make it sound like he's going to prison! No, a railroad bridge was blown up during the battle. It's been rebuilt, and they've started transferring men. He should go any day now."

Maureen usually enjoyed the easy affection growing between them but on this morning, she was unsettled. Guilt nagged at her for keeping Patrick in the dark about her future. She fumbled with a long piece of grass, smoothing it and tying it into knots as an awkward silence grew between them.

Then, suddenly, she jumped up to leave, too afraid to tell him about Smoketown. "I really should be going."

"But you just got here." Patrick stood to protest. "Aren't you spending the day with us? You're not leaving now, are you?"

"Not yet. I, um, I have another errand I have to attend to. I have to talk to Miss Larkin." She took a step and turned to him again. "I expect I'll see you before I head back."

Maureen hated herself for losing her nerve. She knew she should have told him before now and she knew she should tell him now. The trouble was, she didn't know how. She was afraid he would be angry that she was leaving just as he was starting a new assignment here.

"Maureen." Patrick pulled her close, his eyes darting quickly left and right before settling on her big brown eyes. "Thank you, you know. I should have said it before. Your visits have meant the world to me."

When he reached for her and enfolded her in his arms, her breath caught. She loved the feel of his warm strength.

How can I ever tell him I won't be back for a while?

She tried not to tremble, tried not to cry. But her feelings were so intense. She pulled away from him and turned to go.

I have to tell him.

Maureen turned to confess everything. His eyes were so bright and full of love. She couldn't say it. Instead, she touched his hand softly.

"I'll be back, Patrick. I promise." She ignored the bewildered look on his face.

I hope it's soon.

Eliza stormed up the lane toward Pry House. With tendrils of blond hair and the blue ribbons of her bonnet trailing behind her, Eliza looked like she was angry and on a mission. She strode up to Maureen at the hospital entrance, breathless.

"I've just had a fight with Mama." Her usual cool demeanor had been replaced by frustration. "She's going to Baltimore with Amy and Robert—Did you know Robert is on his way to a hospital there? Mama's going because she doesn't think Amy should go alone. She won't let me go with them. I begged her. I told her I could help, and then she said it was better for me to stay home. There's nothing to keep me here."

She ran a hand behind her neck in an unconscious effort to tame her flying hair and ribbons.

"So what are you doing here?" Maureen asked.

"I came looking for you. I want to volunteer like you are. I was figuring I could do something for Miss Larkin. She's been so kind to Robert." Eliza paused for a second and frowned. "I'm no use at home. Papa just snapped at me, something he never does. I know he's worried. He doesn't need me around. Mrs. Burns is there to cook his dinner. I'm just in the way."

Maureen watched as her friend's face and demeanor softened. "I only want to help. Can I do something here?"

"I'm sure Miss Larkin would be happy to have you. But I won't be here. I've been asked to work at a new hospital about a mile from here." She patted her haversack.

"You are? A different place? Is Patrick going there, too? Do you think I can work at the new hospital? We could work together."

"It's different from here, Eliza. You can come with me and see Miss Hall and take a look around. I'm going now. It's more like a camp than this is. The nurses sleep in tents, just like the patients. And it's much bigger. I'd say there are more'n a hundred soldiers, a lot of them very sick. And there are bound to be bugs and cold nights and lots of mud and dirt."

She could see Eliza thinking about that for a moment. "What does that matter? I can be brave," Eliza replied and then asked, "What about Patrick?"

"I just went to see Miss Larkin about that. I asked her if there was a chance he might be re-assigned there. She said no, so I haven't told him I'm going yet."

"You haven't told him you won't be here?" Eliza's eyes grew wide with astonishment.

Maureen could hardly look at her friend as she shook her head. "I have not. I don't know how to tell him."

"Maureen O'Neill, Patrick's going to be furious."

"He's so excited about his new assignment. But his orders are for this hospital. Soldiers have already been assigned for nursing duties at Smoketown. What do I say?"

Eliza put her hand on Maureen's arm and looked her square in the eye. "You have to tell him and if you don't, I will. Just tell him you and I are going to work there. It's where we're needed."

She paused for a moment. "I know my mother wouldn't like me going, but she'll be busy in Baltimore. I can't do a thing to help Robert. Anything will be better than doing nothing at home. And I can't sit around waiting for a letter from Joe..." Eliza blushed.

"From Joe?" Maureen asked.

Eliza silently shook her head. Then she nodded. "You know about Joe and me. I have fallen in love with my dearest friend's brother. You know that, don't you?"

Maureen took her friend's hand. "I thought so. Joe never said a word, though I did wonder why you, my best friend, never told me."

"It's just so new. This summer we—well, these things happen. Then one afternoon he came by, kissed me and said he'd see me soon. He'd joined up that day."

Maureen waited for her to say more.

All Eliza said was, "Take me with you."

"If you're sure…" Maureen paused for a second. "I would certainly be happy to have a friend there."

As Maureen picked up her haversack, Patrick rushed out of the hospital with his eyes on an envelope in his hands and practically ran into the two young women.

"I thought you'd gone. I looked everywhere for you," he said to Maureen, a hurt look on his face. Then he brightened and turned to Maureen's friend. "Hello, Eliza. Your brother's with the doctor now. He just sent me with a letter for the General."

"Maureen and I were just talking about—"

"We have to go, Patrick," Maureen interrupted.

Patrick looked from girl to girl.

"You're going now?" He frowned. "Looks like you two are cooking something up."

"As a matter of fact, we are," Eliza said. She looked pointedly at Maureen and went on before Maureen could stop her. "We're going to work at Smoketown. Maureen and me. The nurse there asked Maureen to help out. They're desperate for help, and she agreed to go. I'm going to go, too."

"To Smoketown? That is hardly a place for a young lady." His frown deepened. "It isn't proper. For one thing, you know nursing isn't a job for well-bred ladies. It was one thing to help out while you were visiting me but this…You have to know that."

Maureen could feel her temper rising, first with Eliza and then with Patrick. But before she could speak, he continued. "And then do you really know how awful it will be? It's supposed to be so much worse than this? They've been having a rash of those catching diseases, lots of dysentery and you know … One of the doctors was saying those fellows are pretty bad off. What do you know about nursing them boys?"

Maureen looked at him as he spat out those last hurtful words. "How dare you speak of the nurses that way. How dare you talk to me at all about this. You were perfectly happy to have me work at Pry House when you would be working with me. You certainly didn't think I was doing something disreputable while I hurried around nursing all those boys here or when I sat by your sick bed. And, as a matter of fact, I don't recall asking for your opinion," she said. "And how dare you raise your voice to me."

Eliza stood by for a second transfixed by the spat erupting in front of her. Then, seeing soldiers gathering at the sight, she found a seat out of the line of fire, yet close enough to hear.

Maureen stormed away from Patrick, her cheeks aflame. Patrick followed.

"It's dangerous, Maureen. You're asking for trouble. I don't want you to go."

"I don't think you have a say in what I do, where I go or who I talk to," Maureen replied. "And I won't be alone. Eliza's going too. You've volunteered to help your country. So has Robert and so has Joe. Now it's our turn. We can't fight the war, but we can help the men who do."

Maureen stopped long enough to regain her composure. Then she looked Patrick squarely in the eye.

"I don't have to answer to you." Then still glaring, she turned on her heel and walked away from Patrick.

Patrick followed, his face red with anger.

"You have to answer to somebody," he retorted. "Smoketown is no place for a girl. Certainly, no place for you and Eliza."

She winced at his words and stretched her hand out as if to show him the hospital before him. "You have no idea what you're talking about. These hospitals are filled with girls, girls like me who care about boys like you, soldiers who are suffering and need care and comfort." She paused and pointed at his face. "You needed a girl when you were suffering here. When you saw angels. When you were thirsty, bloody and in pain. You needed me then, and now you turn on me. As if I'm a little girl who needs guidance."

She turned, defiantly, and jutted out her chin and waited while he clenched his fists so tightly the knuckles turned white.

And then his face softened so dramatically that Maureen sensed a change of direction in his argument. He looked down, cocked his head to the left and reached for her hand. She noticed how he still grimaced in pain, but she hardened her heart.

"I love you, Maureen," he told her in almost a whisper. "I care about you and want you to be safe. I need you. You're all I think about, all I thought about on that battlefield. I need you."

Maureen's heart began to soften at his sweet words. Yet, she heard echoes of her father's harsh words in Patrick's.

No, you can't manipulate me, Patrick Toohey.

She bit her lip, pulled her hand away and wiped it on her skirt. "Do you now?" Her tone was icy.

"Yes…Maureen." His eyes pleaded with her.

Maureen was unmoved. She crossed her arms. "Love?" Derision dripped from her lips. In the angry, silent moment that followed, Maureen realized Eliza—and a small crowd of soldiers—were looking on in amazement. Their argument had become the center attraction at the hospital entrance. She was mortified, both by Patrick's scolding and the witness of the crowd. She lowered her voice. "You insult me like this, shout in front of all these people. Is that love? I don't think so, Patrick."

Patrick waved his hand at her as if he was dismissing her. "Maybe I don't need you. Not like this." He eyed her scornfully.

It was too much for Maureen. She didn't need him or his contempt. She wanted to go to Smoketown. She had promised. Nothing, and she meant nothing, he said could make her change her mind. "I'm going to Smoketown. I'm leaving now. And you can go to the devil."

Miss Larkin rushed over, shoving her stethoscope in her pocket and wiping perspiration from her face.

"Maureen, may I see you a moment?" The nurse took Maureen's elbow to lead her away.

CHAPTER 13
ON THEIR WAY

"What happened?" Eliza raced after her friend.

Maureen dashed down the hospital lane full of rage after the double dressing-down she had received.

"It was awful, Lizzie." Maureen slowed down to allow her friend to catch up. She closed her eyes and shook her head. "First Patrick. Then Miss Larkin. As if I had done something wrong."

"What happened?" Eliza asked again. "You two were becoming the talk of the hospital. The men near me were taking bets on who would win. Odds were on you, but I think their fellow soldier was the sentimental favorite." Eliza shook her head. "You can't just talk to them like that."

Maureen sped up as she turned north on Boonsboro Pike. Her face was white with anger. "Like what? Standing up for myself? Telling Patrick to mind his own business? As if he can order me about. I want with all my heart to help. It's my country, too."

If she stopped to admit it, she was horribly embarrassed. But she knew she was right, and she wasn't backing down.

"Maureen." Eliza struggled to keep up with her and when she finally did, put her hand on her friend's shoulder to stop her. "He's in love with you. He's been in love with you for ages. Even I know that. I could never go into his father's store without him asking how you were or what you were doing."

Maureen wasn't sure if it was the blood pounding in her ears or the anger that made her tremble. Now Eliza was telling her Patrick loved her—as if that made everything all right.

No, it didn't.

Maureen wiped her damp eyes and pressed her cool fingers against her hot temples.

"He had no right to tell me what to do. No right. He's not my father. I didn't even let my father tell me what to do." Her blood was boiling. "And neither did you. Did you?"

Eliza blushed. Maureen knew she had made her point.

"And then Miss Larkin scolded me for arguing in front of the men," she said quietly and began to walk again. "How embarrassing."

"She still wants you to go to Smoketown, right?"

"Yes, she does," Maureen nodded. "She praised me for being brave enough to go there."

"Brave enough? What does that mean?"

Maureen related how Miss Larkin had told her how enormous the place was, almost too big for the staff that was there. "She spoke so highly of Miss Hall, saying she was doing the best she could. You'll love Miss Hall. Even if she's young, she's so dedicated that she was assigned to run the hospital by Dorothea Dix."

"Dorothea who?"

"Miss Hall says she's in charge of all the nurses all over the country."

They continued down the road in silence. Maureen kept up a furious pace as she struggled to contain her anger. Eliza lagged behind and finally stopped.

"Can we slow down, Maureen?" she pleaded. "We have a long way to go."

"It's not far, just a little farther down Keedysville Road before we turn."

"I can't go as fast as you. And besides, I'm getting hungry."

"We'll be there for dinner. In the meantime…" Maureen stooped by the side of the road to reach into her haversack and rummaged around. "I know I brought some rolls and apples." She pulled out her extra socks and chemise, and lay her father's gun on top of the clothing.

"Maureen!" Eliza exclaimed, worry twisting her face. "What's that for?"

Maureen shrugged her shoulders. "Patrick said the world could be a dangerous place. I want to be prepared."

"So you think you need a gun?"

Maureen forced herself to remain impassive. "You never know," was all she said. "Here they are." She unwrapped two rolls and two apples from a blue gingham towel and handed one of each to Eliza.

Eliza took them, her attention transfixed on the gun before her.

"Don't tell anybody I got this," Maureen added. "Not a soul. Promise."

"I promise." Eliza shook her head. "But I don't like it."

Maureen wrapped the gun in the towel and placed it at the bottom of her haversack.

Eliza bit into an apple as a look of worry spread across her face. "And I'm not going to forget you got it."

Maureen calmed down as she walked toward Keedysville. Traffic had picked up since the battle ended. Ambulance wagons mixed in with the carriages and farm wagons. None of them gave right of way to people on foot. And there were a lot of them.

Maureen looked at the faces of those who passed. She saw sadness and worry. She saw men and women lost in thought or chattering away. She didn't see anyone she knew. At least not until they passed the first houses in Keedysville.

"Ernestine!" Maureen cried as the slim girl hurried toward her with a package under her arm.

Ernestine looked puzzled—as if she had a lot on her mind.

"Ernestine," Maureen greeted her again.

"Well, if it ain't Maureen." The girl smiled in recognition.

"How nice to see you again," Maureen said. "How's your hand?"

"It hurts," Ernestine said matter-of-factly. She held up her hand, still bandaged in thin white strips of cloth. "It ain't kept me from working though. My mama wasn't about to let me lie about while she had baby clothes and bandages and who knows what else to sew."

Eliza looked at her friend and then at the stranger, a quizzical expression on her face. "Well, Maureen, aren't you going to introduce your friend?"

Maureen blushed and made the proper introductions.

"I don't have time to dawdle, so I best be going. Nice meeting you, ma'am," Ernestine said to Eliza as she turned and hurried down the road.

Maureen ran after her, eager to talk to her away from Eliza.

"Are you feeling better?" she asked Ernestine.

"I really am."

"I have to ask: Do you know anything about the man who, well, who attacked you?"

"No'm," Ernestine shook her head. "I think he was plumb crazy so he went after us. Me first and then you. I'm glad you killed him."

"I don't think I did," Maureen admitted. "I just heard there's a man with a gunshot wound to the neck at the hospital at Smoketown— you know where the sisters dropped me off the other day?"

"Lord have mercy," Ernestine exclaimed. "I thought the roads were safe from the likes of him."

"I thought I should warn you. Keep a look out when you're on the road."

"And you're going to work at that hospital there? Aren't you scared?" Ernestine asked.

"I am. But I said I'd go, so I am. My friend Eliza's coming with me."

The girls said their goodbyes again, and Maureen ran back to Eliza.

"Who was that girl?"

"Ernestine?" Maureen answered. "Just a girl I met along the road. We got to talking while we were walking. She's a seamstress. Lives near us."

"Since when have you been friends with a colored girl?" Eliza asked.

Maureen looked at her with a frown. "I told you we just met on the road."

"What happened to her hand?"

Maureen stammered. "She, well, um, she told me what happened. Got bit by a mean dog, I think she said."

She couldn't miss the odd look Eliza gave her but now was not the time to remember the day she shot that man.

The rest of their walk into Keedysville was quiet. Though the town was hardly more than a mail stop, its Main Street was lined with trim two-story houses and a couple of shops. The hatter in the tiny millinery was famous for his craftsmanship, and his shop drew people from all over the county. A general store lay in the center of town.

As the two girls passed the store, a woman flanked by two Union soldiers flew out the door. She was dressed plainly, except for the flower-bedecked bonnet on her head and the lacy shawl wrapped around her pale gray dress. She held a small notebook in her gloved hands, and she appeared to be reading off a list of orders to the young men.

She paused as she led them down the street. "Can you read?" she asked them.

The men nodded.

"Then I don't need to read all of this to you. Make sure you find everything on this list. Tomorrow, look over the list and be sure to get everything you couldn't get today. Do you understand?" the woman asked with impatience.

"Yes, ma'am, Miss Barton," said one of the men while the other nodded again.

"What's your name again?" she asked the silent one.

"Sergeant Brady, ma'am," he told her.

"Sergeants are getting younger every day," she said. "You understand what I'm asking you, do you not?"

"Yes, ma'am."

"See that you get it all."

"Good afternoon, ladies," the lady greeted Maureen and Eliza as she passed. "You look as if you are looking for someone."

"No, ma'am," Eliza told her. "We're on our way to Smoketown."

"To visit or to work?"

"We're going there to work," Maureen explained.

The woman shook her head. "Desolate place that. Dirt and disease. Those poor men, so sick, everybody's afraid to move them." Then seeing the concern registering on both girls' faces, she smiled.

"Of course, Miss Hall is doing the best she can. I'm sure with you girls working there it will be all the better. I must be going. All the best to you, girls," she said as she hurried down the lane.

As the two young women turned onto Smoketown Road, Maureen found her argument with Patrick replaying in her thoughts. She knew by the look on his face and his harsh words their budding romance had died before it started.

She was the type of person who liked to please people and now she'd displeased everybody, from her father to Patrick, and even Miss Larkin had had a few stern words. She closed her eyes and trembled. She knew she was doing the right thing, even though she had her doubts. Patrick's angry words only fueled her insecurity.

Then she remembered that the man she shot might be here too.

What am I thinking coming here? Why don't I turn around and go home?

When she saw Miss Hall at her desk, her resolve returned. She wanted to help just as this great lady was.

Miss Hall closed her book as the two girls approached and greeted them.

"So glad to see you, Miss O'Neill. You'll be happy to know Rusty said his first words after you sat with him. In fact, he asked for you. You just may have the healing touch," she said to Maureen and then turned to Eliza. "And you brought a friend?"

Maureen, encouraged by Miss Hall's words, smiled as she introduced Eliza and said they were ready to work.

"I've got a growing number of very sick men here," Miss Hall explained. "For the most part, they're good men. Boys really. These soldiers need you, and I am so grateful you are here."

She turned to Eliza. "And you, Eliza, have you also worked at the Pry hospital?"

Eliza blushed to the roots of her golden curls. "No, ma'am. I was just... My brother's a patient there, and I visited him almost every day. He's going to Baltimore and well," she explained, glancing at her friend. "When I found out Maureen was coming here, I decided to come along. I'm not doing much good sitting at home, worrying."

"And what have your parents said about you coming here?" Miss Hall asked Maureen.

Maureen shook her head. "My da calls me a bad daughter. He forbade my going, but I left anyway. My mother has given her blessing."

"It's only my father at home. My mother is going to Baltimore to be with my brother Robert," Eliza said. "I told my father I wanted to be a nurse. He's so busy with his work, I'm not sure he even heard me. I figure it's safer than when we were wandering the battlefield looking for Robert."

Miss Hall looked at her with interest as Eliza told the story of searching with her sister-in-law until they found Robert.

"We found him after searching for a day and a half," she said. "My mother was sick with worry so she was relieved when she heard the news about my brother. She and Amy—Robert's wife who is expecting—have gone to be with him in Baltimore where he'll receive more treatment. We're all praying he might walk again. We still don't know."

She paused for a moment, and Maureen wondered what she was about to say when Miss Hall stood up.

"If you don't mind getting your hands dirty, changing linen and serving meals, I'm happy to have you." A hint of a smile teased at Miss Hall's lips. "Lord knows I need every extra hand I can get."

Miss Hall took them on a quick tour of the camp. "The other nurses said they'd show you around more thoroughly later," she told them.

The number of badly injured men crowded into all those tents staggered Maureen. As they passed by, curious eyes peered from behind the tent flaps. Knots of men, some bandaged, some missing limbs, lounged near the trees that provided the only shade from the sun.

The fetid air, smelling of smoke, blood, rotten food and unwashed bodies, surrounded them. Miss Hall warned them to watch where they stepped.

"This is much worse than the Pry House hospital," Eliza whispered to Maureen.

"And it's so much bigger," Maureen said.

As if she heard them, Miss Hall explained, "Every day is an uphill battle here. There aren't enough people to keep everything neat and tidy the way it should be. We barely have enough people to look on the men here. We have upwards of 500 very sick men. It's not only their battle wounds. They've come in here with typhus, dysentery and now all sorts of lung ailments and rashes. These farm boys come in here and catch everything townsfolk get when they're children—so they're really sick."

She stopped in front of one last tent.

"This, my dear girls, is where the nurses stay," she explained. "Go on in and make yourselves at home. At least as well as you can. You'll meet other nurses inside. They'll get you settled. I'll put you to work later."

A familiar face greeted them as they entered the dim, musty tent.

"Miss Angela!" Maureen exclaimed.

Angela's face brightened with a smile as she recognized the two girls. "Miss Hall told us to expect a new nurse today, and there are two of you! I'm so glad to see you. Patsy, look who's here."

Patricia came inside the tent behind the two young women and wrapped her arms around their shoulders.

"Welcome. We have two beds left, and we just put another blanket on them. It's getting cooler in the evenings, isn't it?" Angela asked, her kindly eyes crinkling as she smiled.

Miss Angela led them to two cots with rough white blankets like those on the soldiers' beds and handed them the white pinafores the nurses wore.

"Now get yourselves settled and we'll be back shortly," Angela ordered, and the two women scurried away.

Eliza and Maureen dropped onto the thin mattresses of their cots. "Not much of a bed," Eliza sighed as she lay down.

Maureen laughed nervously and then Eliza laughed with her. Though neither knew why it set them at ease.

It had been a long day, a long walk and for both of them an overwhelming experience.

After a long silence, Maureen turned to Eliza to suggest they see what Miss Hall wanted them to do. She heard Eliza sigh as she caught sight of a tear rolling down her face before she could quickly swipe it away.

"Is there something troubling you?" Maureen asked.

Eliza pulled herself up to lean on one elbow and look at her friend. She shook her head until Maureen cocked an eyebrow at her.

"So much has happened so quickly. I hardly know how to think about everything." Eliza sat up and clutched the edge of her cot with both hands. "Doesn't it seem impossible that only a few weeks ago we were children?"

"Speak for yourself. I've been working like a dog all summer long."

"Yes, but we didn't think about things the way we are now. With the war, I mean." Eliza frowned. "I kept hoping it would end before boys we knew had to go."

"You're worried about Joe?"

"Yes, of course. Aren't you?"

"We haven't heard a word from him since he left."

"Neither have I," Eliza said. "I don't even know where to send a letter. I wrote one right after he left. I hope he got it."

"I can't believe I didn't know about you and Joe," Maureen said.

"It's all so new." A dreamy look replaced the sadness in Eliza's eyes. "And wonderful. And scary—Maureen, it's so scary when he is so far away and when I don't even know where he is."

"But Joe?" Maureen asked. "You've known each other for so long."

"I don't honestly know what happened. It was only this summer that he suddenly seemed so handsome and so kind to me. We met by accident at the creek. One hot summer afternoon, I had a row with Amy and went there to sulk. When I got there, Joe was fishing."

Maureen listened in amazement as her friend recalled Joe as someone she never knew.

Sweet and gentle, kind and considerate—he was all those things, of course, but Eliza described him as a wondrous new love.

"He never mentioned seeing me that day?" Before Maureen could answer, she went on. "I guess he never mentioned it to your parents either. I was so sure he planned to tell them. And then he left."

"Tell them what?" Maureen asked. "Do you have an understanding with my brother?"

Eliza nodded, a look of love shining in her bright blue eyes.

"He didn't ask me exactly," she said. "Only that he loved me and didn't think he'd ever meet another girl so wonderful. He said that to me, Maureen. Joe!"

"And you love him?"

"Of course I do, silly," Eliza giggled. "Enough to kiss him!"

"Why Eliza, I never." And Maureen giggled, too.

Suddenly, Eliza grew serious. "He will come back, won't he? I'll die if he doesn't."

Maureen hugged her best friend and hoped her mother was still praying her rosary.

CHAPTER 14
SMOKETOWN

Strong women surrounded Maureen all her life. Certainly, her mother was the first strong woman Maureen knew. She handled the household, children, and, of late, her injured and gruff husband, with efficiency and a no-nonsense manner. She could order her children about with a stern look.

Maureen knew better than to cross her mother. She knew her mother's family had suffered greatly during the famine in Ireland. She knew her mother and father had welcomed anti-British neighbors into their pub for a pint and another in an endless discussion about independence.

Maureen was very young at the time. She didn't remember if her family had faced any dangers because of it. What she did know was that her mother was often in the thick of the talk, a moderating force when tempers flared. Was she more involved than Maureen knew? She sometimes found herself wondering.

"Though she be but little, she is fierce." Her father used to quote Shakespeare, with a look of love and respect at his petite wife.

If her mother was fierce, so were other women in Sharpsburg. Like her mother, they handled their lives and their men with confidence.

Maureen's first week at Smoketown was nearly over, and she tried not to be intimidated by the strong women she had met. Her movements seemed awkward around proficient nurses who strode from bed to bed checking wounds, administering medicine and issuing orders. She envied the women who knew every patient's name—as well as the names of wives, children and sweethearts. They were so brave in the face of suffering. They were so smart.

Maureen wondered if she was strong enough. The work went well—even if camp life didn't. First smells of vomit, excrement and

109

rotten food assaulted her to the point of passing out. She learned when and where to hold a well-worn hankie to her nose. Then she discovered she was afraid of bugs. Who ever heard of a farm girl afraid of bugs?

"Jesus, Mary and Joseph!" she exclaimed as she pulled back the blanket on her cot after a grueling day.

She found a big brown insect burrowing in the bedding. She pulled the blanket off the cot and threw it to the ground. Then with her boot, she swept away the bug and squashed it on the cold dirt. Her face screwed up in disgust, she shook herself and then shook out the discarded blanket.

Eliza laughed at her.

"Are you sure it's dead now?" Eliza asked from the warmth and apparent safety of her cot.

"It better be—and all its brothers and sisters, too," Maureen muttered.

"Rough day, wasn't it?" Eliza asked as Maureen settled under the covers.

"I'm getting used to it." Maureen tried to smile.

"I'm not sure what I expected," Eliza said. "This surely wasn't it."

"The Pry House was a church picnic compared to this," Maureen agreed.

Maureen wanted to complain about the pain between her shoulders from all the heavy lifting and then thought better of it. She knew Eliza had suffered the same hardships, including the added grief of worrying about her sweetheart.

"I miss my bed," she said instead. "I miss my chickens…and I miss Mother."

"I miss my Mama, too," Eliza said. "So many people around us and they're all strangers."

"Strangers? You already know so many of their names," Maureen argued.

"Remembering their names is the easy part," Eliza answered. "There's so much more I've got to learn."

Conversations didn't last long at Smoketown. Something always interrupted. At bedtime, much needed sleep often left their chats unfinished.

As she drifted off to sleep, Maureen realized her friend had become one of those strong women she so admired. Once a flighty girl overly concerned about hair ribbons, Eliza adapted to life in a hospital. Besides learning all the patients' names, she handled correspondence with ease. Maureen was a little envious. She still struggled to sound out words. She screamed at bugs and was overwhelmed by the camp smells—while Eliza never seemed to notice either. The way her dear friend adapted to the dirty work of the hospital surprised her. Maureen once thought she'd never last— especially after Maureen learned about Eliza's romance with Joe.

Tomorrow, I will be stronger, she promised herself.

Maureen slept fitfully. Every tickle made her wonder if another bug was crawling on her while she slept. She shivered as the cool autumn night air seeped under her blanket. She doubted her reasons for being at Smoketown. And she worried about her family—once so close, now as divided as the nation. She wondered if her father would welcome her home and when—not if—they would see Joe again.

As she watched the darkness of night give way to the first light of dawn, she sighed and threw off her inadequate covers. She twisted her dark brown curls into a tight bun, smoothing loose tendrils that curled around her eyes. She wriggled into her worn blue dress and tied on her apron before stepping into her heavy shoes.

Morning came early for the nurses, though she was the first one to rise today. She tiptoed carefully between the cots to the basin, broke the thin layer of ice on its surface so she could splash water on her face. Shivering, she slipped out of the tent looking for coffee to fortify her spirit.

Maureen was surprised to find a bright dusting of snow covered the camp overnight. Some of the men were kicking at it, picking it up and tapping it off the low branches of trees. Maureen was surprised to see delight in the faces of soldiers so often contorted in pain.

"Morning, ma'am." A man stamping his feet against the cold. He stood up straight when she greeted him.

"Morning," she answered. She recognized him immediately. Rusty's auburn curls were now free from the heavy bandages that had encased them the last time she saw him, even though his arms were still in casts. A smile creased his face from ear to ear.

"Ma'am, I don't know if you remember me, but I sure as sh—I sure remember you." Rusty's voice was soft with a New England flavor.

"Yes, I do," she smiled. "You're Rusty. You were my first patient here."

"And not a very nice one I'd say." He hung his head and looked up at her through a fringe of red hair.

"You were quite sick then," she assured him. "You're looking well now."

"Pretty good," he agreed. "I'm getting pretty tired of these ole casts, and I'm still having trouble seeing—the doc says that I might never see right again. Well, I must be doing better 'cause I see you fine."

"Well, Rusty, it's a cold morning. Have you had your coffee?" Maureen began, until Rusty interrupted.

"Miss Maureen, I gotta ask someone. Why's everybody calling me Rusty? My name's Allan."

Maureen laughed. "Allan! I guess no one knows your real name. Everyone calls you Rusty because of your ... umm," Maureen smiled and pointed at Rusty's hair. "Seems it stuck."

Rusty grinned. "Yeah, it stuck all right."

"I'll call you by your proper name from now on."

"No need. I've been called Rusty so long I feel like a Rusty now."

"One thing's got to change," Maureen said. "We have to correct your medical record and notify your regiment. I imagine someone at home is worried about you."

Rusty shook his head. "No one, ma'am." He told her he came from Vermont, the only child of a baker. His mother died in childbirth, so it had only been his father and him. A year ago, their little shop had burned down, taking the life of his father.

"I'm so sorry. I know how awful fires are. My father's pub in

112

Ireland burned down when I was little. That's why we came to America." Then Maureen added, "But nobody died in our fire. Not even Sadie, our dog. Father got her out before it was too late."

"Really? How's your dog now?" he asked with interest.

"Poor Sadie. I miss her. Father said she wouldn't like the ship, so we left her with Jimmy Mulligan, the little boy next door."

He shook his head. "It's hard to recover from a fire, ain't it? I didn't know what to do. I didn't have anyone else. So I joined the army." Then he raised his bandaged arms. "Looks like that idea may have been half-baked."

Maureen smiled at him. Then, as she began to speak, the face of another patient caught her eye. It couldn't be, she thought. A wiry man with a bandage on his neck stood near the wooded edge of the camp, smoking a cigar and talking to another patient.

The last time I saw that man, I was sure I shot him dead.

Even as she dismissed what her eyes saw, her heart pounded, and her breathing grew ragged. He turned toward her only slightly— enough to make her start. Her breath caught in her throat and she nervously raised her hand to her heart.

It is him. Now I'm sure of it. Don't look my way.

He had the same scar across his face. He had that same hard-to-describe curly hair. And even with his face turned away from her, she recognized that mirthless grin. He'd smiled the same way when he looked away from Ernestine at her. Before she shot him.

I didn't kill him after all.

Maureen's her blood ran cold enough to stop her heart. And she wished he was dead.

"Miss Maureen, are you feeling all right?" Rusty frowned at her.

She forced a smile. "Why, yes, of course," she answered.

"You're looking a little peaked. Maybe you'd like to sit down." He moved away from the tree to lead her to a fallen log the soldiers sat on while they smoked.

Much as she appreciated his kindness, Maureen desperately wanted to get out of that other man's sight. She started to make her excuses until she realized he had moved on without seeing her. She sighed in relief and took the seat Rusty offered.

"See? Isn't that better?" he asked, offering another of his brilliant smiles.

"Yes," she nodded. "Much better."

Her heartbeat returned to normal. She breathed easily.

"Now how about that coffee?" she asked once she was recovered. Although Rusty turned her down, after that shock, Maureen needed some. From now on, she'd have to keep an eye out for that man.

She knew one thing for sure: She never wanted to face him again.

She never wanted to know his name, either. Then Eliza told her. Harvey.

The two young women were crossing the camp on their way to supper one evening when Maureen spotted him out of the corner of her eye. He was standing in his usual place, a cigar in his hand.

Maureen moved to the other side of her friend and asked, "Do you know who that is?"

"Who?" Eliza turned to see where her eyes were focused.

She discreetly pointed toward the woods where he stood alone.

"Oh, yes. His name is Harvey. I was talking to him this afternoon. Not very nice, I might add. Why?"

"He looks familiar. I don't know why but he does." Maureen looked away.

Eliza shot her friend a quizzical look. "I don't know why you might know him. He's not from around here, but he wouldn't tell me where he came from. All he said was he was ambushed on the road after the battle. Got separated from his unit or something. He said he thought he was going to die until some farmer came along. He took him in, and his wife nursed him until the Army ambulance came. They brought him here." Then Eliza lowered her voice to a whisper and leaned toward Maureen. "To tell you the truth, I think he might be a Reb."

"A Confederate? Here?"

A chill swept through Maureen and she sped up, hoping she wouldn't raise any suspicions in her friend. Once she moved between two tents where she could no longer see him, she slowed down.

"Miss Angela told me the field hospital at Locust Spring has plenty of them. So, a few Confederates might be here, too. We have to treat them all the same, I guess—Are you all right?" Eliza asked.

Maureen wished she could tell her friend. Instead, she only nodded. Now was no time to relive that awful afternoon. She was shocked with herself for wishing he was dead. She thought about Ernestine for a moment and then pushed that awful day out of her mind. It was bad enough she had to creep around every corner keeping an eye out for him. She'd learned quickly that he had a routine and she kept it in mind wherever she went. She changed the subject.

"Think we'll get something worth eating tonight?"

"I hope so." Eliza held open the mess tent flap. "The soup at lunch was so watery. And the bread was stale."

"They don't have a lot to work with, do they?" Maureen hurried inside. It was crowded with nurses, a handful of doctors and recuperating soldiers who had been assigned nursing duties.

Miss Hall, who was sitting alone, motioned to the girls to join her at her table. From the looks of her plate, supper wouldn't be much better than the noon meal. "Get yourselves something to eat. I'd like to talk to you."

Eliza and Maureen went through the mess line, grabbed their pitiful meals and then sat with Miss Hall.

Miss Hall told them about the epidemic of measles that had broken out in their hospital. She still hoped for at least one more nurse to care for the ailing patients. She needed nurses who had already had measles. And she needed nurses willing to work exclusively with these sick men for at least a week, probably two.

"Is it very catching?" Eliza asked.

"Unfortunately, it is," Miss Hall answered her. "Outbreaks of measles earlier in the war were devastating. Some men even died. I mean to contain this disease before it spreads too far."

Eliza pushed away her plate and shook her head.

"I don't think I can do. I've never had the measles, and I wouldn't like being away from the other nurses all that time.

"I understand," Miss Hall said. "I've heard that a lot."

"Do you have any volunteers?" Maureen asked.

"Just one. Miss Patricia," she said. "A friend of yours, I believe."

"And she has had the measles?" Maureen asked.

Miss Hall nodded. "Have you had the measles?"

"I did when I was little. Back in Ireland. All the children in the village got sick at the same time." Maureen remembered how the disease spread through town. So many were already weak from the famine spreading through the country. She and Joe were among the last to catch it. Joe's turned into pneumonia, and her mother had been so worried about him. Maureen hadn't thought about those days in a long time.

Although she didn't like the idea of being quarantined, she also knew it would keep her out of sight for a few weeks. Maybe it would be long enough for that man to get well and go back to his unit.

"I think I'd like to help." Maureen knew her voice didn't sound too convincing.

Eliza turned and looked at her friend in horror. "No, Maureen. You can't."

"I don't think I'll have to worry. I've had the measles. I'll be all right."

"It will be difficult," Miss Hall warned. "These men are very sick."

"It would only be for a couple of weeks." Maureen looked at Miss Hall for affirmation. "Then they'll get well. Isn't that right?"

"We figure they'll be better in two more weeks."

Eliza stared at her friend. "Please don't."

As much as Maureen didn't want to abandon Eliza, she decided it was best to volunteer for the measles tent.

"It's only two weeks. Fourteen days, Eliza. Yes, I'll be happy to go." Maureen hoped no one could tell that her heart was beating hard and her palms were sweating.

Miss Hall smiled. "I think you should sleep on it. And tell me your decision in the morning. We moved the men this afternoon. There are eight of them. Miss Patricia is already with them, and I know she'll be glad of the help."

Maureen was sure she'd made the right decision. "All right

then," she said, forcing herself to smile. "I'll think about it tonight and report to you in the morning."

Miss Hall excused herself, and Eliza turned to her with a scowl on her face. "What are you doing?"

"I want to be helpful anyway I can. If Miss Hall needs me, I'm going to to go." Much as she wanted to, Maureen couldn't tell her friend about how frightened she was of Harvey. She was grateful for a place to hide for the next few weeks. Besides, it was only measles.

Maureen tucked into her supper suddenly feeling hungry.

Eliza just looked at her friend. "Is this just about being 'helpful'? Nothing else?

Maureen continued to chew her food.

"I think you're hiding something or maybe you've gone crazy, Maureen," her friend watched her scoop another forkful into her mouth. "Not only have you agreed to work in the measles tent, now you're eating that goop."

"It's ugly, but it tastes pretty good," Maureen swallowed and laughed. "And it's a long time until breakfast."

"Yes, it is." Eliza sighed as she pulled her plate back in front of her. "Well, it's not too awful."

Maureen didn't say another word as she finished her meal. She was beginning to like her plan to work in the measles tent. How bad could it be? She remembered the itch, the headaches and the stuffy nose. It wasn't fun, but she was a child. The itching was the worst part. Then all of a sudden she was better and out of bed. She didn't think it could be any worse for a group of grown men.

Yes, she decided, volunteering will give me something interesting to do. And it will keep me out of the way of Harvey. And I'll be working with Miss Patricia.

Maureen was relieved, knowing she would be out of sight of Harvey. Maybe out of sight until that man was gone. She slept well that night, with not a single thought about the bugs.

CHAPTER 15
COMFORT AND PAIN

Eight men had been assigned to the measles tent. The tent was set off from the rest of the patients, away from the places Maureen was most accustomed to: the patients she tended, the dispensary, the mess tent. She was glad it was far from surgery and even farther from the cemetery where she had seen graves being dug nearly every day. She and Patricia had their quarters nearby.

It would be home for only a week or two, Miss Hall had promised. Then suddenly, the place seemed so small and so forlorn. Maureen wondered what she had been thinking as she looked around at the inhabitants of the eight narrow cots.

Miss Patricia greeted her with a cheery "Good morning."

"I'm so glad you're going to be helping here," she added. "The work isn't too hard. We really can't do too much for these boys. They are mostly in need of a little conversation and fellowship. They'll be glad to have a young person to talk to. They miss their friends."

"Miss Patricia," Maureen started to say until Patricia interrupted.

"Just Patricia. I appreciate the manners your mother taught you, but in here Patricia is fine. Now, let me introduce you."

Patricia leaned over a boy covered in a red rash, his face drenched in sweat. "How are you feeling, Jimmy?" she asked as she took his only hand, bumpy from measles. Maureen's stomach turned over when she looked at the mass of angry crimson spots.

"I was fine until this morning," he said. Maureen looked at him in disbelief. A bloody bandage wrapped the stump of what remained of his left arm. Another covered the foot torn up by shrapnel. And now he had measles. She wondered what the misery of a childhood disease would do to a man who had survived the Confederates' best efforts to kill him.

"My head hurts something fierce," he continued. "You were right. The fever is miserable. Can I get some more of that lotion? These spots won't quit itching."

"Of course, Jimmy." Patricia turned to Maureen. "Sit with him and introduce yourself. Then we'll meet the other boys."

Jimmy Finch was quick to talk about himself. His eyes shone as he told Maureen about his farm near the Pennsylvania line. They had apple trees and cows. He was engaged to a pretty girl who lived on the farm next to theirs. She had come with her mother and his to see him only a week ago.

"Her visit made me decide I had to get well again," he said. "Even with this stupid arm. I hope I didn't have the measles then. I don't know if Sarah has had 'em and I'd hate to find out she got the measles while visiting me."

Patricia came back with calamine lotion and showed Maureen how to apply it. "It don't look too good, but it helps," Jimmy assured her.

Maureen dabbed the pink lotion on his face and neck, along his infected arm and down his back. "If you don't mind, miss, I'll think I can take care of the rest." A blush came to his spotted cheeks.

Patricia laughed. "We'll be back to check on you in a few minutes, Jimmy."

It took most of the morning to meet all the patients. The other seven were in similar misery. Many were feverish and weak. A few were going crazy with their itchy skin. Others complained of achy muscles.

Most of the soldiers were about Maureen's age. All except Theodore. To Maureen, he seemed older than Miss Patricia—and Miss Patricia had to be older than Mother. Theodore called out as Maureen and Patricia approached his cot.

"Miss Patricia," he croaked. "Can't you make the itching stop?"

"Didn't the calamine lotion help?"

"Not too good." The man's voice was raspy, and his tone was gruff. "I feel awful. I'm still itchy, and now my throat hurts. I'm having a hard time swallowing, and I can't hardly pick my head up off the pillow."

"Have you eaten anything?" the nurse asked.

"Naw," Theodore shook his head. "I ain't got no appetite at all."

"You just rest then. Maybe an oatmeal bath would help?"

"I'd sure like the itching to stop," Theodore answered.

"My new nurse here will take care of you. This is Maureen, Miss O'Neill."

Maureen cast an alarmed glance at Miss Patricia before she sat beside Theodore. His scowl frightened her—it reminded her of her father's. Then she found out he was Irish. Like her, he was from County Galway, though he had been in the States for far longer than her family. When he spoke of his fierce loyalty to his adopted country and his pride in his farm near Philadelphia, she thought of Joe.

Theodore peppered her with questions as she bathed his itchy skin in the thin oatmeal mixture. She told him about the family farm, her parents, Joe, even her chickens, just to keep his mind off the rash.

Then Maureen turned the tables and asked her own questions. His mother called him Ted, he said, and he had never married. Instead, he took over the farm when his parents became too old for the back-breaking work. He loved his cows as Maureen loved her hens. He was proud of his fields of corn and oats. His sister Alice and her six children moved into the farmhouse after her husband's death. Theodore spoke warmly about the children and his sister. Despite his age and against his sister's wishes, he had signed up after Fort Sumter, telling Alice he had to protect the Union for her children. There would be no argument, he said.

"And now," he said with a frown, "here I am, laid up with itchy spots. I thank you for your conversation and your care. I feel a little better."

His frown transformed into a toothy grin for just a moment as Maureen took her leave. She promised she'd return as soon as she could.

With two nurses and eight patients, Maureen assumed her days would be more leisurely than in the other wards. As it turned out she was just as busy, especially at meal times. The men were talkative and invigorated by the smells of hot food. What smelled inviting looked awful. Maureen passed out plates that reminded her of the unappetizing brown stew she had often turned her nose at up. It certainly wasn't going to entice these men. Hungry as they were, most suffered from sore throats and took only a few bites.

One afternoon a few days later, when the tent was quiet, Patricia stopped by as Maureen chatted with Kevin, a soldier who was showing her a miniature of his little girl. Afraid she was doing something wrong, Maureen jumped up and stammered, "I guess I, that is, I should be…"

"Relax, Maureen." The nurse bade her to sit down again. "You're just what the doctor ordered."

"I was afraid you might think I was wasting time."

"On the contrary, your presence serves as very good medicine for these young men. They all need some good old fashioned attention—especially since they're all alone." Patricia patted the young woman on the shoulder and ordered her to continue her friendly visits. "It's so much better than a dab of lotion."

Maureen spent a few more minutes listening to Kevin as he spoke about his wife and daughter and their farm in Connecticut. "I'm hoping to get home soon," he told her. "I won't be able to fight no more, so I'm sure they'll be sending me home." He tapped on his legs, and she nodded. There was nothing below his knees, nothing except an occasional mysterious pain that made him howl.

He held a small white square of paper, almost caressing it with his feverish fingers. Maureen didn't dare ask what it was. Her reading was so bad, she had avoided requests to write letters or read from a favorite book or the bible.

He hesitated before holding out the letter to her. "Could you read it to me, please, Miss Maureen? My head is hurting so, and I'd like to hear it."

Maureen looked at the ornate handwriting and knew she couldn't make out the words. She shook her head in shame.

"I can't read very well, and my handwriting is atrocious," she admitted. "I'm sorry."

121

"I know how it is." He unfolded the paper and studied it. "I'm not much of a reader either."

Maureen wished she could read and write better. Embarrassed by her admission to the young soldier she resolved to improve her reading and practice her letters.

If only there were time. The men in Maureen's care needed constant attention. Though they were quarantined for measles, they still needed to recover from gunshot wounds, broken bones, infections and amputations.

Patricia and Maureen wiped feverish faces, brought meals and cups of tea and honey for scratchy throats, assisted the doctor and chatted with those who felt up to it. The days were long and demanding. By the time night fell, Maureen dropped on her narrow cot from exhaustion.

She rose early each morning to join the doctor as he made his rounds. Day by day, there were fewer spots and fewer fevers. With each exam, relief spilled over each man's face. The men's moods began improving as they neared the end of their time in the hot and smelly measles tent.

"Thanks, doc," Kevin smiled upon hearing he would soon be on his way to Connecticut.

"I'm going home, Miss Maureen. Home to Jennifer and little Amanda." His face shone with joy. It was a rare sight.

As he did every day, the doctor met with the two nurses and thanked them for taking care of the injured and sick.

"Is there anything else I can do?" Maureen croaked, her throat feeling scratchy. She put her hand to her throat as she swallowed.

"Same as always. Calamine lotion, oatmeal, water and a friendly face are the best medicine for our boys now." Then he added, "There's one man I'm particularly concerned about, though. Theodore doesn't seem to be improving as the others are. Can you keep an eye on him? If he looks like he's getting worse, make sure you tell me or Patricia here."

Maureen nodded. She went to see him right away and found the grizzled farmer sleeping soundly. She worried when she heard a bit of a rasp to his breathing. Checking back throughout the day,

Theodore continued to sleep. When she heard a rattling noise in his chest, she mentioned it to Patricia.

"The doctor told me to call him if he seemed to be getting worse."

Patricia nodded and sent for the doctor. Maureen was sitting beside the sleeping man when the doctor arrived. "You were right to call," he told her. "I'm very concerned about his condition."

He asked her to stay by his bed, all night if necessary. Maureen fetched her shawl and settled in her straight-backed chair to watch over the ailing man. She had grown to like the old Irishman and was worried about him. As the night grew darkest and coldest, Theodore awoke.

"How are you feeling, Mr. Theodore?" she asked when he turned his eyes her way.

"Call me Ted," he insisted. "You don't need to stay up with me. I never sleep much. Night time is my thinking time."

"I can't sleep either," she said, although her weary body disagreed with her.

He smiled weakly and held out a hand. She held it tightly and quietly they waited out the hours until dawn.

November nights are cold and silent, and that was true about this night. Not even crickets chirped anymore. Ted called it his thinking time and true to his word, he said very little. Maureen could see he was wide awake. His eyes darted about as if he were searching for something. Even though Maureen's back ached and her throat was parched, she stayed with Ted until he finally closed his eyes as the first pale light of morning appeared. Finally, his grip on her hand loosened, and she tucked his arm under his rough wool blanket. She stayed put until Patricia's hand on her shoulder roused her.

"I'll sit by him for a while. You get some sleep," Patricia told her.

Maureen rose and stretched her aching, stiff limbs and trudged back to her tent. She thought of Theodore—Ted—as she marked off on the tent pole the day that had finally ended.

She kept a tally of her days here by cutting a small sliver from the pole; this was the eighth. She hoped she wouldn't have to carve too many more. She was lonely. She missed Eliza. She thought about Patrick and Joe, her parents. At least she had grown accustomed to the foul smells and learned to look where she was going if someone was sick in the night.

As she pulled her blanket up to her chin with a shiver, she longed to sleep. And then another fear invaded her thoughts.

That man.

Even as she hid here among the patients with measles, she continued to worry about him. She didn't know if he was still in the camp. Maybe he had been released. And maybe he knew she was here. She couldn't be sure. Maureen tried to push thoughts of what she had done from her mind but as she drifted off to some well-deserved sleep, that awful day continued to haunt her thoughts.

Maureen woke to the smell of food. She jumped from her cot, smoothed her hair and tied on her pinafore. She put her hand to her throat and swallowed. That scratchy feeling in her throat wasn't going away.

Maureen hurried to help Patricia hand out plates of food, stopping first at Theodore's cot. He was still sleeping. His breathing seemed more labored, too shallow and too quick. "Mr. Theodore?" She gently prodded his arm. "Are you hungry?"

Slowly, the man opened his eyes and then rolled over, hacking and coughing. Maureen placed his breakfast onto the nearby chair and stooped down to offer help. She grabbed her handkerchief, and he hacked some more. Maureen looked away, afraid of what she might see on the cloth. She was relieved when he handed it back clean.

"I'm sorry you had to see that, miss." He forced a weak smile. "I don't think I can eat right now."

"Perhaps a sip of water?"

He nodded silently, and she handed him the cup. He drank and then fell back on his bed to sleep some more.

Maureen took his plate away and went to see Patricia.

"Mr. Theodore isn't doing very well," she reported.

"Doctor thinks it's pneumonia."

Maureen gasped. She remembered Joe's measles had turned

124

into pneumonia. What had her mother done? Whatever she did it worked.

Patricia must have seen the worry on the young nurse's face. "I'll take care of breakfast. Sit by him. I'll send the doctor over when he comes by. It should be soon."

Maureen stayed by the suffering man all day. When he finally awoke, it was late in the afternoon. Theodore seemed better. His eyes brightened as he talked about Alice and the children.

"Cassie's birthday is next month. Alice is hoping I'll be home for it. That's what I'm hoping too." He had a faraway look that worried Maureen. She leaned forward to ask him a question.

"Cassie is your sister's daughter?"

Theodore nodded. "Her youngest girl. She's ten. Gonna be eleven. I might of spoiled her a little. She's a pretty little thing with hair like yours. I kind of imagine her growing up to look like you." Theodore chuckled, and Maureen wondered if that was a bit of a blush on his whiskered cheeks.

Then a violent raspy cough wiped the happy look from his face. He grew silent and slept again.

When the doctor finally arrived, it was nearly suppertime.

"Not much we can do," he mumbled as he wrote out instructions for medicines. "His condition is much worse. No use bleeding him. Wouldn't do any good."

His tone was ominous, Maureen thought.

Soon Theodore was fighting for his breath. Maureen stayed by his side as much as she could, offering water, kind words and the medicines the doctor had ordered. She spent another sleepless night by his side.

She dozed briefly only to awake as the man suffered through more violent coughing. Night turned into day, and still she stayed nearby.

He woke about mid-morning and reached out a feverish hand. His pale glassy eyes searched her face as she squeezed his hand. By late afternoon, he was quieter than usual.

The sun beat down on the roof of the tent, making it stuffy. Maureen wiped his brow with cool water, worried the air was making it even harder for Theodore to breathe. Even then, he didn't complain.

Finally, he closed his eyes and slept again. The lines of his face smoothed out as he slept, as if the burden of worry was lifted off his shoulders. He breathed shallowly, but regularly, never moving as the afternoon light began to fade.

Patricia stopped by to check on them. "Something's wrong, Patricia," Maureen said. "I can feel it."

"I'll send for the doctor." Once her message was dispatched, Patricia pulled over a stool and sat by her young nurse. Though Maureen was comforted by her presence, she grew anxious as she waited for the doctor. He didn't arrive in time. Theodore's breath grew shallower until it stopped completely.

"I'm afraid he's gone, Maureen." Patricia checked unsuccessfully for a pulse.

Maureen started from her chair. "He can't be. He can't." Sadness filled her. "We were just talking about his family. He was hoping to be home for his niece's birthday."

She pulled off her apron and unrolled her sleeves. "How could he be dead?" she exclaimed.

"You did everything you could." Patricia patiently picked up Maureen's discarded pinafore. "Death is part of this job. You knew that."

Maureen stumbled blindly from the tent. How could Theodore be dead? When he spoke about his family hope had sprung anew in her heart. He had never complained.

Anger flooded her thoughts as she raced into the sunshine. Then she tripped over a log and tumbled onto the hard, dusty ground. She pressed her forehead into the dirt as she sobbed, filled with despair.

Maybe I have no business being here. None at all.

Then picking herself up, she sat down on the log and covered her hot, wet face with her hands. Memories of her conversations with Theodore renewed her sobs. She couldn't believe he was dead. There had been no goodbyes, no last words.

What a stupid girl I am, she reproached herself. She blew her nose and shook her head, filled with grief at the soldier's death.

She wasn't sure if she was crying for Theodore or herself. As horrible as the soldier's passing was, she felt humiliated at her lack of skill.

What was I thinking while I sat with Theodore? Why was I so blind? So stupid?

She dropped her head in her hands to cry again. Then she looked up as her hands ran over the hot, bumpy patches on her forehead and around her ears. Her throat, scratchy and swollen, hurt so.

She hoped it wasn't what she thought it was. But she knew. She had the measles.

CHAPTER 16
SICKBED

Maureen blinked open her eyes and put her hand on the cool, wet cloth on her forehead. It wasn't until she heard a familiar voice that she knew her surroundings.

"Oh, thank the good Lord," Miss Hall whispered. She was sitting beside Maureen, holding her hand.

Maureen started. She realized she was in a new place at Smoketown, in a sick bed. She turned to Miss Hall, whose soft brown eyes looked tired if relieved. "What—?" Maureen started to say though her mouth was dry, her tongue uncooperative.

"There, there, dear." Miss Hall's voice was soothing. "Don't strain yourself. You've been quite sick. We were worried we were going to lose you."

Maureen tried to focus on the space around her. It looked like the same tent where she had been sleeping, even though Miss Patricia's cot was gone. Where is Miss Patricia? Things grew blurry and then black.

The next time she awoke, it was dark. The night was cold, and the air cooled her feverish skin. Her blankets felt too heavy as if they would strangle her. Visions of the man she shot loomed in her frantic mind.

I've got to get out of here, she thought. He'll find me, and this time he'll kill me.

Maureen pushed off the blanket and struggled from her low cot. The measles had left her weak and unsteady. Her head pounded so hard her eyes ached. Her feet found the cold, hard dirt as she raised herself up. She gathered her strength, took a deep breath and stood. And sat back down. She couldn't do it. She didn't have the energy. Exhausted and faint, she sensed panic clawing its way up her throat.

I've got to do it, she urged herself.

Filled with fear, she forced herself to get up and run from the tent. Outside, she clutched her chest and breathed in the chilled, fresh air. She looked left, toward the sea of tents that stretched to the woods. She looked right and saw a silvery glint shining off a makeshift marker in the cemetery.

I guess Theodore is buried there now. Which way is home? Maureen was angry with herself for not knowing.

She started to run.

I'll figure it out, she thought. I have to get far away from here.

She ran blindly, skirting the measles tent and hopping over rough vegetation. Then she started at the sound of someone crying out in his sleep.

As she turned toward the sound, she tripped over a sharp rock and crashed to the ground. Pain seared through her ankle and she reached for it. The smell of a cigar reached her before she saw the man who offered her his hand.

"Where you off to, little lady?" he asked. Even in the darkness, she knew who it was. She might not be able to see his face—and she prayed he couldn't see hers—but she knew the aroma of his tobacco and the sound of his voice.

She shook her head and pulled away. "Suit yourself. Awful cold weather to be running around in your nightshirt, though." He limped away, and she stared at him.

He nearly caught me, she thought as she put her hand on her face. He didn't recognize me. I guess not with my face still so marked with bumps.

"Maureen!" Maureen thought she recognized that stern voice.

"Mother!" she cried out.

"No, dear. Patricia." The nurse stooped down beside her.

"I was afraid, so I ran," Maureen stammered. Trembling, she wrapped her arms around Patricia. "He's going to find me."

"Now, now, Maureen. You're safe here," Patricia said as she held Maureen close. Maureen gasped and shook her head.

"No, I'm not safe. He's here, and he's going to find me and then what? Everyone will know what I did," she said, not even brave

129

enough to look at her friend. Maureen wondered why Patricia didn't seem to understand, as the nurse coaxed her back to her own bed. "I thought Mother was here," Maureen murmured. "I guess I was confused."

"Sleep now. You'll be better in the morning." Patricia's voice calmed the girl. Maureen did feel safe when Patricia was near. Her breathing quieted down. She sighed and fell back into a deep sleep.

What an awful nightmare, she thought when she woke as the first rays of the morning sun slipped between the flaps of her tent. She looked at her hands which still bore traces of the red rash. They had itched terribly, and her skin was scored by dozens of thin scabs from mindless scratching. Her face no longer held the heat of fever, and the chill in the air made her shiver. She rose quickly to dress. Then, pain shot through her ankle and she looked down to see it swollen and purple. Stepping gingerly, she threw on her dress and shoved her feet into her shoes. Oh, that hurts, she thought with a wince.

What happened to my ankle? I can't remember a thing except the itching.

She limped her way into the measles tent, ever mindful of her swollen ankle. Patricia will tell me.

Patricia excused herself from her patient when she saw Maureen. The tent was nearly empty, except for one last soldier. "He caught the measles the same time as you." Patricia hurried over to Maureen. "Everyone else has recovered—at least from the measles."

"And now, so have you, from the looks of it," she added with a smile. "I'm so relieved. We have been so worried, we sent for your mother."

Maureen shook her head. "Mother was here?"

"She's still here. She's been by your side for the last few days," Patricia said.

"My mother is here?" Involuntarily, she touched the shadows of the rash on her face and put her hand to her hair. As if it matters. "Where?"

"Right here, Maureen." Maureen's mother had teardrops glistening on her face. It was only the second time she ever saw her mother cry.

130

"Mother. I've missed you," Maureen said as her mother folded her in her embrace. It reminded her of what it was like to be little, to be soothed as she had been when she fell and scraped her knee.

"You've been having quite an adventure, I hear." Mother brushed loose brown tendrils of hair from Maureen's face.

"Is that what Miss Patricia's calling it now?" Maureen asked.

"I'd say, heroic efforts of a nurse, followed by a severe case of measles with high fever, lung infection and a serious case of delirium," Patricia answered. "Quite an adventure for anybody."

"How long have I been sick?" Maureen suddenly felt woozy again.

"About a fortnight," Patricia told her. "After I caught you running around in the dark——"

"What! In the dark?" Maureen interrupted.

"You were quite out of your head and burning up with fever. I found you in the camp in the middle of the night. One of the patients stopped you—or I don't know where you might have gone."

Maureen tried to remember although the only thing she could recall was the man with the cigar glowing in the dark. He wasn't a nightmare, Maureen realized. She really did see him; and, worse, he saw her.

Maureen faltered. She wasn't sure if it was because of her recollection or her illness.

"Sit!" her mother ordered her. And she sat.

"You told Ernestine to be careful," Patricia said. "And you said something about being glad you shot him."

If Maureen weren't sitting, she'd have fallen down. She saw the confusion in her friend's and her mother's eyes.

"I don't remember any of that," she said, hoping no one noticed her evasion.

"You brought us a young colored girl named Ernestine who had been shot," Patricia said. "Were you dreaming about her?"

"I suppose I was," Maureen answered. "I haven't thought of her in a long time."

"Maureen, whatever made you volunteer for the measles tent?" her mother asked.

131

"I remembered having them back home—"

"It was the chicken pox you had, my dear, not measles."

"And Joe?"

"Joe, too," her mother answered. She placed her hand on Maureen's forehead. "Perhaps it's time to come home."

Maureen's stomach roiled. Home? She knew her father would never allow it.

"Father said I'm not welcome. And besides—"

She lifted her skirt and stretched out her leg to get a good look at her purple ankle. "I really would prefer to stay here," she said. "I don't know if I can be of any help until my ankle heals."

"Good lord, Maureen," her mother exclaimed. "What happened?"

"I don't remember." Maureen shook her head.

"It must have happened when you ran outside last night." Patricia stooped down and examined it. "That looks like a mighty bad sprain. I don't think it's broken."

Patricia went about wrapping Maureen's swollen ankle in liniment-soaked bandages. "You can't walk on that for a couple of weeks."

"Then it's settled," said Maureen's mother. "You come home and rest it." She must have seen the panic in Maureen's face. "And then, if you want, and Miss Patricia needs you, maybe you can come back to Smoketown."

Maureen was grateful for her mother's support, even though she was afraid to go home and face her father. She knew if she left, she might never come back. And she was worried that by the time she was able to return, there might no longer be a place for her in Smoketown. If she stayed, she knew she would have to face that man again. That was something she couldn't do.

CHAPTER 17
HOME AGAIN

When her father saw Maureen limp in the door with her mother, he paused for only a moment, a look of concern on his face. Then with a fierce glare at his wife, he stormed out of the house. "I'm going to see Raymond. I'll be back when your daughter is no longer in residence."

Maureen was alarmed by her father's appearance. He didn't look well. Although his leg was stronger and he moved about with barely a limp, his hair had lost its luster. Deep lines crossed his pale forehead and cheeks. One thing hadn't changed. Her father's eyes still smoldered. They had lost none of their dark fire.

The house was unusually quiet during Maureen's convalescence. For the first few days, she stayed in her room most of the time. Then little by little, as the swelling and pain in her ankle subsided, she began to take over some of the household chores.

Her mother objected in the beginning, but it didn't take too much for Maureen to convince her she was well enough to peel potatoes or set the table.

Maureen felt like herself again once she could tend to the hens. She looked forward to greeting her hungry chickens each morning. They probably didn't miss her, even though she was glad to be needed again.

There was no denying it: The house seemed empty without her father there. True to his word, he left early in the morning before she rose and was gone until late at night.

One morning, the first day Maureen's ankle was strong enough to take her full weight, she woke to hear the door slam and a kitchen chair scrape across the wood floor. The smell of eggs frying in butter made her stomach rumble but she didn't dare move.

The voices she heard voices in the kitchen were low at first, and then the whispers got louder and louder until they sounded like hissing.

When curiosity got the best of her Maureen opened her bedroom door only a crack to see her mother standing over Father seated at the head of the table. She was tearing into him with a furor Maureen had never seen. She strained to hear what they were talking about, sure it was an argument.

It was a scene rarely observed in their household, although when they occurred, they were fierce. She feared she had come between her mother and father. What else except her return home could prompt such division?

Maureen gently pulled the door shut and sat on her bed, waiting for the discussion to end. It seemed to take hours, and Maureen held her breath to be sure she heard every word of it.

"What do you hope to accomplish, Daniel? That's what I want to know," her mother demanded.

"I came for my pipe, not to have an argument. That breakfast does smell good though."

"Here's your pipe. The breakfast is Maureen's, poor girl."

Maureen heard a chair scrape again.

"Where do you think you're going?" her mother asked. "Sit yourself down and stay there. You'll listen to me today."

The conversation was a little one-sided. Maureen could hear her father grunt and begin to argue, and yet her mother kept control as she reminded her husband of their days in Galway—days Maureen had rarely heard her mother talk about. She spoke of her first days at the pub soon after she'd married Daniel.

"We were young and idealistic then. We had opened our pub to every partisan who thought he could put an end to the British occupation. Most of us, including me, knew what we were doing was dangerous. But we believed in the cause, Daniel."

"No, Kate, you believed." Maureen jumped when he slammed his hand on the table. "I thought the lot of them were damn fools. All that talk and for what? Is Ireland free now? Do you think all those drunks shouting in our pub could ever make it free?"

"And I suppose you think I was a damn fool, too," Kate answered.

"Yes, darling. I do. I know you meant well. I know you were thinking of Pegeen and your other friends who died in the famine. And Raymond and all our neighbors who left Ireland. I thought it was dangerous. I was afraid the day would come when you or I would be arrested and what would happen to our wee ones?"

"It didn't happen, did it?" Kate countered.

"No, we didn't go to prison. What did happen was that someone firebombed our pub, only moments after you and I took our sleeping babies to their beds. Someone wanted us out. Poor old Sadie. We almost lost that dumb dog, too, remember? I can't imagine if I'd lost you."

As the kitchen grew quiet, Maureen let the words she'd heard sink in. She was shocked. She'd never known why there was a fire at their pub. She hadn't known what her mother thought. She had always believed her father supported independence for Ireland. It was her mother all along.

"I know you were willing to give your life for Ireland. I didn't like it, but I tried to support you—at least until someone tried to hurt us. I wonder every day if I should have told everyone to go home and ordered you to keep your views to yourself. Maybe then we'd still be in Ireland with our friends, the pub…"

So you blame yourself then, Daniel?" her mother asked.

There was silence before her father continued again. "Now, in this new country, I see how you have taught your children your same devotion. If we weren't in the middle of this damn war, I'd say it was commendable."

Her mother's tone was sharp. "How kind of you, Daniel. But look where you have led us. Our Joe is far away—we don't know where. We never got to say goodbye. I yearn to hold my boy in my arms one last time if only to give him my blessing. You made that impossible with your stubborn words. Now you've forbidden your only daughter from entering the house. Never mind that I brought her home sick and in pain. You get on your high horse and storm out, refusing to return until she's gone. And she doesn't even understand why you say the things you say."

"I won't relive those days for my children. What's past is past."

135

"You need to tell Maureen about what happened that night in our pub. You need to tell her about Raymond and Pegeen. And you need to forgive her."

Maureen could hear the growing anger in her mother's voice.

What about Raymond and Pegeen? Pegeen who?

The front door squeaked open. Maureen expected it to slam shut at any moment. She sat perched on the edge of her bed, wondering if she should interrupt her parents.

And then her father sighed and spoke again.

"I won't change my mind. Our children have turned their backs on us. They have chosen paths I knew were dangerous. They have defied me for the last time. Joe is gone, and I can't do anything about that. I will not be under the same roof as that girl. Not while she brazenly defies me by going to that damnable hospital."

"You stubborn man. If you won't tell her, I will."

"Tell her if you like. It won't make me change my mind."

"Get out, Daniel." Maureen heard the tone her mother used when she was furious: soft but steely. "We could have withstood anything as a family, but you have decided to tear it all apart. Get out. I don't care where you go. Our daughter needs us—me. I say she stays."

Maureen waited for her father to object. Instead, there was only silence until the door creaked again.

"Goodbye, my love. I'm sorry you see it this way." They were the last words Maureen heard before the door slammed shut.

Maureen sat frozen in her room. Her parents were divided over her. She'd never heard a conversation like that. She'd never heard an argument so painful between her parents.

Maureen put her hands to her feverish face, surprised by the dampness on her hot cheeks.

She wanted to run to her mother and beg her to call Father back.

Where will he go? Maybe I shouldn't be here?

The kitchen was quiet for only a moment before Maureen heard the sizzle and clatter of her mother making breakfast.

Maureen hardly knew what to think. And then it suddenly

dawned on her. Her mother had taken a stand. Like Joe. Like Maureen herself. And her loyalties weren't with her husband. They were with her children.

CHAPTER 18
A LETTER

Maureen couldn't take her eyes from the elegant carriage that stopped in front of the church. Among its passengers was Patrick. She watched him jump from the carriage and reach up to take the hand of the pretty girl first and then her mother as they stepped down. He entwined his arm in the girl's and escorted her to a pew across the aisle from Maureen's. He never looked Maureen's way. The pang of jealousy that jolted Maureen was painful.

She tried to focus on the minister leading the service. She studied her missal and sang the hymns with unusual vigor—anything to keep her eyes from straying to Patrick. Nothing helped. She couldn't help looking his way. She knew she was going to have to face him.

Patrick looked as uncomfortable as she felt as he emerged into the gray morning. When he saw Maureen standing outside with her mother, he dropped the girl's arm and fidgeted with his hat.

"Morning, Maureen." His voice was monotone, and his smile looked forced.

Maureen put on her own smile, greeted him and then turned to the girl. "Barbara Lee, so good to see you again."

"Yes." Barbara Lee flashed a weak smile as her eyes swept over Maureen from head to toe. Maureen tried not to be self-conscious about what she was wearing. Her old green calico looked shabby next to Barbara's gown in a cornflower blue that matched those judgmental eyes.

"Good to see you home, Maureen." Patrick's words helped shake Maureen's self-doubts away.

"It won't be too much longer," she replied with as much cheeriness as she could muster. "My ankle is nearly healed, and I'll be heading back to Smoketown soon."

"You're not—" he started to say. Then Barbara interrupted, "Come, Patrick. My mother's giving me her look. We can't keep her waiting."

Maureen sighed with regret and relief as they walked away. She was sad to see he had already found a new sweetheart. She was glad to avoid another interrogation about her hospital work. She had no intention of arguing with Patrick in front of that silly girl, her mother and her church's congregation. One argument with an audience had been plenty.

Patrick. Why, Patrick?

As she walked home, Maureen got lost in her thoughts about the soldier who knew how to drive her crazy. She didn't like being him with that girl. Try as she might to be magnanimous, it wasn't possible. To Maureen's way of thinking, Patrick should offer his arm to only one girl. Besides his mother, of course. Never to a girl as lovely and charming as that Barbara Lee.

Face facts, Maureen, she said to herself. You don't measure up to a girl like that.

As her mood sank lower than Maureen thought possible, her mother interrupted her thoughts with a sigh.

Maureen had walked nearly the whole way home without a word to her mother.

"I haven't been very good company, Mother," she said.

Her mother nodded and patted her Maureen's arm. "Thinking about your Patrick, I suspect."

"How—"

"I was young and in love once." Her mother smiled a little smile. "Patrick's a good man. I hoped you'd come to see it one day."

"It doesn't look like he sees it that way," Maureen muttered.

"It's this damn war." The words were harsh to Maureen's ears, even though they were delivered in her mother's most soothing voice. "It will right itself one day. You keep on loving him, and he'll come to understand. I hope it's soon."

They walked on until the house was in view. Then her mother spoke again, her voice wistful. "I've missed having those boys running through the house, tracking mud and who knows what else through the kitchen I just swept. I miss sitting on the porch with you and Eliza, teaching you how to sew. I used to imagine those boys grown up. I pictured Joe bringing his wife to the house and you chasing after children as active as you used to be."

Maureen realized her mother was lonely. She'd always been surrounded by family, and now she was by herself quite a lot.

"I wish I could stay home. I wish I hadn't caused whatever has happened between Father and you. I heard you the other morning," Maureen admitted.

Her mother turned to her. "Your father believes it is my job to stand with him—even when he's wrong." Then she sighed and looked down the road. "I mean to do that as I always have—except this once."

"Your support means everything to me."

"I know you remember the night our pub burned down." Her mother was silent until Maureen nodded. "Your father wants to protect you—he's afraid for you—but I need to tell you. It wasn't your father who those men wanted to hurt that night. They were after me."

Maureen came to a sudden stop on the road. She had heard her mother's words, although they made no sense. "I thought Father—"

Her mother shook her head.

"Father supported me, not the cause," her mother said. "That is, he supported me until the pub burned down. I passed messages and went to meetings, that's all. It was enough. I had been threatened before, and I scoffed. Then when it came to it, I couldn't sacrifice my family's lives. When your father said he wanted to go to America, I agreed."

When her mother put her hand out to Maureen, she took it, still confused.

"All this while, I have thought it was Father…"

"I know. Your father is one of those Irish men who feel they need to keep a secret. I think he believes he was responsible for the fire. If he had stopped me…if he had refused to allow his neighbors to say those hateful things about the British…if only he had done something different. His guilt is terrible. It isn't his fault, but he blames himself. Daniel doesn't cry, though when he realized if he had stayed a moment later at the pub his family might have died, he cried like a baby. That night. And many nights after."

She stopped there.

"I don't understand, Mother. Why would he keep a secret like this? Shouldn't Joe and I know?"

Her mother shook her head. "It must be an Irish trait. I don't understand it. A great many people don't. But you must understand how ashamed your father is about the whole affair. Was he at fault? Certainly not. And yet his guilt is so great he cannot speak about it."

Maureen walked on in silence until they rounded the bend toward their farm.

"Then he's afraid for me in a way I didn't understand. And maybe don't understand still," she said.

"He's a stubborn, cranky man who'll cry like a baby if anything happens to his children."

"Well, he's doing it all the wrong way," Maureen blurted out.

"Perhaps. He's doing what he thinks he must."

"Do you think I should stay home, too, Mother?" Maureen asked as they stepped onto the front porch. She waited as her mother searched her face with her big, brown eyes.

"Are you really ready to go back?"

"You know I am," Maureen answered with a nod.

"Your ankle certainly seemed to give you no trouble on the walk to church."

"Still hurts a little but it'll be all right."

Her mother said nothing more though Maureen was sure she heard the tiniest of sighs as she held the door open for her.

"It's getting colder," her mother reminded her. "Pack your warm things."

Maureen nodded. "We have already had some very cold nights."

Wordlessly, her mother went into the pantry while Maureen tucked a few last items in her haversack. She returned to the kitchen table with three apples and her father's gun. She handed them to Maureen. "I hope you don't need this."

Maureen felt the cold hard weight of the gun as she took it.

"It can't be much longer, Mother," she said. "There hasn't been any fighting since Antietam, so maybe the war will end soon. Maybe I'll be home by Christmas. It's only a few weeks."

"I hope you are right, dear," her mother answered. "The house will be so empty without you."

Maureen was moved to hug her mother, a rare gesture between them. "We'll all be back together before you know it."

"Now isn't that a touching sight." Daniel leaned against the door frame, his arms crossed over his chest, his weight off his lame leg. His lips smiled, even though his eyes were cold. In his hands, he held a sheet of paper.

"It's a letter from Joe," he told his wife. She rushed to take the letter, looked at Daniel and trembled.

"He's in Virginia." She sank into her chair by the hearth and silently pored over the cramped handwriting. She shook her head. "His spelling…" she chuckled.

Maureen waited, anxious for Joe's news.

CHAPTER 19
WHERE I BELONG

"It looks like there will be another battle." Maureen could see the pain in her mother's eyes as she read from the letter.

Finally, her mother looked up at her father who knelt beside her to put his long arm around her thin shoulders. She pulled away. "He says there are thousands of soldiers in... Do you know where Fredericksburg is, Daniel?"

"Raymond says it's somewhere near Richmond."

"Oh, blessed saints preserve us." Her mother dropped the letter in her lap and put her hand to her cheek.

"May I see?" Maureen asked. Joe's handwriting was so bad she could hardly make out the words except for "Army of the Potomac," "General Burnside" and "Rappahannock."

The ending, however, was easy to read. "I should have said goodbye, Mother. I should have said goodbye. I miss you and Father and Maureen every day."

She searched the letter for a date but he had written none.

"So we don't know when he wrote this? Has there been a battle there?"

"None reported in the papers," her father answered her curtly.

At a moment like this, Maureen wondered why her father couldn't put aside his anger toward her.

Joe's letter almost convinced Maureen to stay home. There was no telling if Mother would need her if...if something were to happen.

As she finished packing for her return to Smoketown, she fought against an undeniable pull to stay with her parents. She was certain it was difficult for Mother to let her go. She was convinced this was no time to back down to her father's demands. Once she was gone, he would return home and that would be good. Mother needed Father more than either of them needed her, especially now.

After she tucked a bit of bread into her haversack, she spied Joe's letter lying on the table. She picked it up and ran her hand over his illegible handwriting. How she wanted to take it with her. What if it was the last…she put it back down on the kitchen table and closed her bag.

When she heard the kitchen door open and close she refused to turn around.

"Looks as if someone's going on a journey?" She sensed her father's gaze but said nothing and refused to look his way.

"Did nothing I say matter?" he asked simply.

Everything you say matters, Father.

Instead of saying that, Maureen faced her father and reiterated her reasons for going. Impatience crossed Daniel's face.

"As far as I'm concerned," he interrupted her, "None of that is important as a daughter's respect for her father."

Maureen wondered for a moment, if she saw something else in his eyes. Perhaps it was pain. Her mother's story about the pub helped her understand her father a little bit better. Now if only he would understand her. She sat down, narrowed her eyes and crossed her arms. Clearly, nothing she could say would move him.

"You're so proud of yourself, going off to save the Union Army. What about your mother? Have you considered how she might need you?" He leaned on the table and looked into her defiant eyes. "Family is what matters. Over everything else. High time you learned it, girl. It's not right for a young girl to be out and about in times like this. And as a nurse! Do you know what kind of women serve in hospitals? Certainly not proper young girls!" he shouted at her, his face red with a vein in his temple bulging.

And then he stooped beside his daughter's chair, startling her. "You may think you're all fancy out saving the world in that hospital. Well, you're not. You're only doing the work nobody else will do. Grunt work. The work of a slave."

She refused to allow him to see the hurt on her face. His hurtful word would not succeed in convincing her to stay home. She forced her voice to be even and strong. "It's where I belong."

Her father listened and nodded.

"If that's how you feel, go then." His tone was quiet, thoughtful. She could tell the words were designed to cut. "If that's where you belong, you don't belong here. There's no place for you here."

He shook his head, turned and left the house.

By the time Maureen gathered her things to leave, her father was nowhere to be found. Leaving this time was different. Now, she knew how her actions hurt her father. She understood why he forbid her going even if she couldn't figure out why he wouldn't explain it to her. As before, he had left angry. Once again he had refused to say goodbye. Once again she had been told she wasn't welcome in her own home.

She swung the strap over her shoulder.

What am I doing all this for?

Doubt filled her as she wondered if perhaps it was only sheer stubbornness that kept her going. She wasn't yet sure she believed what she was doing made any difference.

Boys still ended up in the graveyard, whether or not she spent hours feeding and cleaning them, making sure their wounds were dressed, and their medicines were doled out.

So far, it had cost her father's approbation. It had cost her Patrick's love. It looked as if it had even cost her family. And Joe.... Even though her actions did not affect him, she knew it was costly for her parents to worry about two children. She could see it in their careworn faces.

Maureen looked around their little cabin and then closed the door behind her. She had to go. She had promised to return. And she'd fought so hard for her work, she didn't want her father to think his arguments had changed her mind.

Had they?

She didn't know. She knew for sure she had never felt so alone. After long weeks working at Smoketown, Maureen didn't really know if she'd done anything good.

She remembered with anguish the death of Theodore. She saw image after image of minie ball wounds that threatened every day to take the life of another young man. She recalled endless plates of inedible food, dirt covered bedding, pain without relief.

Maureen walked on, four miles to Smoketown. Her pace was slow. Her ankle was still stiff.

As she walked, Maureen asked herself why she was going back.

She remembered the fierce loyalty for her adopted home that led her to volunteer at the Pry House. Now, she saw why she wanted to be a nurse in the face of every patient. To her, all of them were Joe. And Robert. Yes, and Patrick. She wanted all of them to get well and go home to their families.

Then as she arrived at Smoketown, Maureen remembered her father's harsh words. He didn't believe she belonged here. And she wondered if he was right?

Does what I do matter?

It looked as if the hospital had gone on without her. No one paid her any attention as she passed the mess tent. Patients were eating dinner when she arrived at camp.

She glanced around the tent flap, looking for the mean face of that man. She couldn't even say his name to herself. If there was ever a reason to feel unwelcome, it was that face. But she didn't see him.

She did see Eliza, her arms laden with steaming plates of boiled potatoes and something brown. Maureen waited for her friend to hand out the plates. She could tell every one of those men had fallen in love with the petite blond with the giggle. And, from the looks of it, she had fallen in love with every one of them.

Maureen thought of Patrick with Barbara at that moment, sad at the love she'd lost. She didn't know if she could feel worse.

"Maureen!" Eliza threw her arms around her friend.

"It's so good to be back," Maureen lied.

"I was so worried you weren't coming back." She looked down at Maureen's ankle. "So, are you properly healed?"

"I couldn't have made the journey here if I wasn't," Maureen said. Her ankle didn't hurt too much.

"Can you help me? I have a few more soldiers to serve, and then we can catch up."

Maureen dropped her bag and picked up plates to hand out

to the men. Another delicious dinner, she thought as she followed behind Eliza.

"So how's Patrick?" Eliza said as they made their way to the nurse's tent and sat on their cots. "Did you see him?"

Maureen couldn't believe Patrick was going to be the first thing they talked about. She dropped her haversack and nodded.

"I saw him at church. And that was just by chance."

"I thought he'd be by every day once he heard you were home," Eliza said.

"No, I'm afraid not. I told him off, don't you remember? Do you remember Barbara?" Maureen struggled to keep her face from crumpling; everything felt wrong.

"Barbara Lee? The doctor's daughter. Yes, of course," Eliza said. "We used to be friends in school until she went away to that academy in Frederick. Why?"

"Patrick is sweet on Barbara now," Maureen said. "I saw them at church together. They were with Mrs. Lee. Who goes to church with their beau?"

"Maybe he was just being gentlemanly," Eliza said. "You know Mrs. Toohey. She would expect her son to escort ladies whether he liked them or not."

"Not this time," Maureen said, shaking her head. "He had his arm wrapped tightly around hers, like he was afraid she'd get away."

"Oh, Maureen," Eliza said.

"There's other news, too," she said. "We got a letter from Joe."

Eliza gasped. "Is he all right?"

"For now," Maureen answered. She couldn't help but notice the color drain from her fair friend's face. Though Eliza said nothing, her quivering chin hinted at her anxiety.

"He's in Virginia."

"Why is he there?" Eliza asked.

"Joe says there's probably going to be fighting near there. He said he's seen Confederate troops across the river—oh, I forget its name."

"And Joe's going to be in it." Eliza knotted her trembling hands in her lap and stared at them for a moment. "Your parents must be so worried," she said. She laid a cold, damp hand on Maureen's.

"I believe Mother has doubled up on her rosaries," Maureen said, adding, "He'll be fine. Joe never saw a fight he couldn't win. He'll be fine."

The silence between them grew heavy. Maureen peeled off her bonnet and smoothed her hair. She saw the doleful look on Eliza who slumped with the weight of worry on her shoulders.

"It will be fine," Maureen repeated, hoping it was true. "I'm glad we'll be here to wait for news together. In the meantime, we have a lot of work to do."

"Yes, we do," Eliza said, her voice flat. "I'm so glad you're back."

"Me too. I missed you. And everybody. I'm back where I belong. This is what's important now."

She'd given up a lot to be here, and even if she wasn't sure how important it all was, she hoped it was true.

Was it so important?

She missed Joe. She missed Mother and Father. She missed Patrick. She hadn't missed the filth, the smells, the bugs. She had given up comfort, family, even love, to be here, she hoped it was very important.

Chapter 20
BATTLE IN VIRGINIA

The moment Maureen put her clean white pinafore on, she grew more convinced she had returned home. She was still tying the sash, when Angela and Patricia rushed into the nurse's tent to throw their arms around the young woman.

Angela ordered Maureen to sit so she could examine her ankle while Patricia chattered on with the latest news. She listed soldiers who had recovered and returned to their units or who had gone home.

And then with her eyes downcast, she told her the names of soldiers they hadn't been able to save. "There are too many of them," she whispered.

"Your ankle looks good as new." Patricia tucked Maureen's skirt down around her foot. "It's time you got back to work, young lady."

"About time." Miss Hall entered the tent and smiled. "I was beginning to wonder when you would grace us with your presence again, Maureen."

She also asked to see Maureen's ankle and pronounced it fit for service. "If you feel any pain or get too tired, I expect you to sit down. We have enough patients."

I am home, Maureen thought, surrounded by the people who understand what I want to do. And best of all, they believe in me.

Maureen spent the rest of the afternoon visiting patients. Her measles patients had all returned to their regular tents, so she went looking for them. Like her, they were glad that ordeal was over.

None of the men seemed happier than Rusty.

"I missed you, ma'am." He rose from his bench under a sapling near his tent and tipped his cap. "I wasn't sure you was ever coming back."

"Not everybody wanted me to come back," she admitted. "My

father ordered me to stay home. But as you see, I wasn't a very obedient daughter."

"Lucky for us." Rusty grinned, and then his face turned serious as he told her he was about to be discharged. His arms were out of their casts at last, and his head wound had closed. Auburn hair was starting to sprout around the remaining scar.

"Are you returning to your regiment or going home?" Maureen asked.

"I ain't going home, ma'am," he said. "At least, not now. I'll return to my regiment pretty soon."

Maureen sat beside him, thankful to rest her ankle. "I'm glad you're well again."

Then he startled Maureen by taking her hand. "I wanted to tell you how grateful I was that you got my medical records fixed. Turns out someone at home was worried about me."

Rusty looked down at the ground, a little bashful. Then he pulled a letter from his pocket. "Turns out a girl I know had been praying for me since she heard the news I was missing in action. I didn't even know I was missing. Can you beat that?"

"That's wonderful," Maureen said.

Rusty handed the letter to her, as a flush rose to his freckled cheeks. "Her name's Jessica. Her father runs the post office. She wrote to me."

"This is so sweet," Maureen answered.

"Aw, don't read it. It's pretty mushy. She said my being here is a miracle."

"And it is, Rusty. Or, I guess, I should call you Allan now. Your sweetheart calls you Allan."

Rusty's blush darkened. "She ain't my sweetheart, Miss Maureen. I don't want you to think that."

"Why ever not?"

"Well, I, well, you know," he stammered.

Maureen caught on. The young soldier didn't have to blush anymore.

She spoke gently to him. "I will always be glad I met you, Rus—I mean Allan. You were my very first patient."

"And your favorite?" A blush rose again to his face.

Maureen demurred. "I can't say I have a favorite."

"I guess that wouldn't be right, now would it?" Rusty grinned again. "If you could, though, I bet it would be me."

"Go ahead and think that." Maureen handed back the letter. "And you write to this nice girl from Vermont. I think she's sweet on you."

Rusty blushed again, this time as a wide joyous grin lit up his face. He looked down at Jessica's letter again and nodded.

Maureen had to admit Rusty—Allan—was her favorite. He and other soldiers like him were reason enough to come back to Smoketown. She liked to think she made a difference in their lives.

She rose to leave. From the corner of her eye, she saw a familiar and unwelcome face. Harvey. She froze, hoping he didn't see her as he passed.

"Goodness, Maureen," Rusty said. "You look like you've seen a ghost."

Maureen forced a smile, waiting until the man was out of earshot to speak.

"Sometimes, it feels like I have, Allan," she said. She continued her rounds, remaining vigilant. She dreaded the moment when she and Harvey might meet.

Doing her job and keeping a lookout for that man was exhausting, and yet Maureen knew she had to keep her guard up. I don't know what will happen if I run into him, she thought. I can't even imagine what I'll do. Or, worse, what he will do once he knows who I am?

As days turned into weeks, she fell into her old routine. Her misgivings faded, shut out by long hours of work. But at every moment, she kept her eye out for Harvey. She stayed away from his corner of the camp, always listening for his voice or his coarse laugh.

And then, it didn't matter where he was or what would happen. Not once she got the letter from her mother.

It was supper time, and she was urging a feverish soldier to try a bit of soup. Eliza raced into the candlelit tent, tripped over a bedstead and fell at Maureen's feet. When Maureen saw the worried look on her friend's face, she dropped the soldier's bowl.

"It's from your mother," Eliza said. She handed Maureen the envelope before she even got back on her feet.

Maureen gasped and tore open the letter. Her eyes scanned the letter, and her face went white.

"It's Joe," she said.

Eliza dropped onto an empty bed as a look of dread crossed her face.

"He's dead?"

Maureen nodded. "At the battle that just happened in Fredericksburg. Mother says they found his effects on a body that couldn't be identified."

"Oh, dear Lord." Eliza raised her hands to her cheeks. "How horrible."

Maureen tried not to think about her brother's handsome face. Yet it came to her all the same. His laughing eyes, the dimples in his cheeks, the nose he broke falling from an apple tree. She stared at the letter. It was only a tiny piece of paper marked with simple words in her mother's childish scrawl. The words, however, were earth shattering.

"Please come home," it said. "We need you. It's Joe."

The rest of the note explained where he died. It didn't matter. Maureen ran her hand over the paper, smudged and marked with the faint "O" of a dried tear droplet. Maureen thought of her mother struggling to put words together as her heart broke. And her own heart raced as she labored to breathe.

The canvas walls of the tent seemed to close in on her until the edges of her vision grew black and blurry. The patient and his soup forgotten, she ran from the tent toward the nurse's tent into the darkening evening. She heard her friend following behind her, but she didn't look. She could hardly see through her blinding grief.

So, when Harvey came around the side of the tent, she didn't see him.

But he saw her. And he stepped into her path.

"Well, lookee who it is," he said with mock glee in his voice. Maureen tried to push past him, and he came closer than was polite.

"Who do you think you're pushing?" he said angrily.

Maureen didn't answer as she continued on her path, as if she was completely unaware of his presence.

The man grabbed at her arm and whipped her around so that his hand was at her neck, a knife's edge tearing at the tender skin of her throat.

Maureen shoved against his arm to get away, crumpling the letter and screaming in terror. He held her all the tighter. "Shut up!" he commanded her as he pushed the blade into her throat.

A thin trickle of blood wound its way down toward the lace trim of her collar. A spot of red soaked into the white of the pinafore. Rage rose in Harvey's face as he shoved her to the ground.

Her mother's letter fluttered to the ground, and Maureen tried to pull away from her attacker to retrieve it.

Harvey grabbed her and slapped her across her cheek. "You thought I didn't know you were here," he roared, grasping her elbows. "You little brat. Creeping around corners when I came near, slipping into tents. You thought you were so smart. I saw you all the same. I knew who you were."

He leaned over her, his knife glinting in the firelight. Maureen could smell sweat and alcohol, his sour breath and then the metal tang of blood as he ran the blade across her throat. She struggled to escape from him.

As he raised the knife to wound her again, a shot rang out. Harvey dropped his knife and jumped to his feet.

"What the hel—You!" he shouted.

Eliza stood at the entrance of the nurses' tent. The gun in her hands was pointed toward the sky. Her eyes were filled with steely strength.

Harvey lunged at Eliza before she could shoot again. She fell backward as he shoved her with both hands. The gun flew through the air. Eliza tussled with the enraged man for the gun, which lay out of reach.

Maureen scampered toward it, picked it up and pointed it at Harvey. He froze seeing her holding that gun over him again.

Eliza took advantage of his terror and jammed her shoulder into his body to push him to the ground.

By the time help came, Eliza was sitting on his chest with Maureen holding her gun.

A crowd of soldiers who gathered to watch Maureen and Eliza overcome their knife-wielding attacker cheered loudly. And that brought Miss Hall from her tent. She gently eased the gun from Maureen's hand. Weak and dizzy, Maureen slipped to the ground, her eyes trained on Harvey. Her heart pounded in her chest, and she shook violently. Even so, she wouldn't look away.

Harvey cursed her as soldiers came to arrest him for assaulting her and Eliza. Still, Maureen wouldn't look away until he was out of sight. Her eyes would focus only on his cruel face. She looked at him with contempt. This was even better than killing him in that cornfield. He'd suffered at her hands, and now he'd go to prison. She thought of Ernestine and was glad she'd faced him again. She hoped for justice for the evils he inflicted on them.

Maureen shook as Miss Hall stooped beside her. The beautiful nurse's eyes were full of kindness and concern. Angela knelt to examine to the cruel red stripe across Maureen's throat. Though it was shallow and thin, it stretched across her pale skin.

Then Maureen remembered Eliza. Eliza had saved her life. Where is she? Maureen thought. There by the tent, Maureen could see her friend, shaking. And she could also see her friend's triumphant smile shining in the light of a lantern. Maureen returned the smile. Thank you, she whispered.

"What happened?" Miss Hall asked.

"It's a long story," Maureen said.

"I'll make the time."

CHAPTER 21
A TIME TO MOURN

The story of Ernestine and Harvey spilled out. Maureen sat on her cot, Eliza beside her. Surrounding them were Miss Hall, Patricia and Angela. They leaned forward on tiny stools as Maureen talked. Miss Hall held Maureen's hands in hers. As she talked, Maureen could hardly look at Patricia and Angela. She had never told them the full story about Ernestine. Confessing to shooting that man took every ounce of bravery she could muster.

"I've prayed for forgiveness for my sin every day since." Maureen looked from Eliza to Miss Hall and finally to the sisters. She was afraid of what they'd say. No one spoke. On every face, all she saw was compassion.

Eliza finally broke the silence. "We have to go home, Miss Hall."

"It's my brother, Joe." Maureen held out the crumpled letter.

Miss Hall looked from one girl to the other and then read the letter.

"Fredericksburg," she said. "This on top of that terrible attack? You poor girl. I'm so sorry, girls. Of course, by all means, you must go. But it's much too late now. I can't let you go now that it's dark."

"First thing tomorrow then. Thank you, Miss Hall." Maureen tucked the letter back into the pocket of her apron.

"Maureen? Eliza?" Miss Hall said as she rose to her tall, beautiful height.

"I can't let you go without a word of thanks," she said, a smile on her gentle face. "You have been dedicated workers. I've watched you grow, learn new skills and become invaluable to our work here."

She paused for a moment. "I know you have to be with your family now. I do hope when the time is right, you'll consider returning to us. We all hope to see the war over soon and all these fine soldiers

155

back in their own homes. It is possible we'll be here after the new year. And if we are…"

Maureen nodded. "Yes, of course, Miss Hall. I know I want to come back. If I am able."

Once she and Eliza were left alone, Maureen collapsed onto her cot.

"I can't go home, Eliza."

"What do you mean you can't go home? The letter—"

"My father told me that under no circumstances was I welcome there."

"Maureen, he didn't know Joe was going to…" Eliza's legs buckled as she spoke. "Oh Joe," she wailed.

Maureen rushed to console her weeping friend as she collapsed onto her cot. "Eliza? I'm so sorry."

"Thank you, Maureen. I'm sorry I took so long to tell you about Joe and me. I am in love with your brother. I mean I was in love with your brother. I hoped we would be married after—" Eliza stopped and corrected herself. "I'm still in love with him. And always will be."

She threw herself across her bed. Maureen leaned over her, put her cheek on her friend's shoulder which convulsed with every sob. She patted her back. "Joe was a lucky man. We would have been sisters."

Eliza cried even harder.

Maureen fell back on her cot. The cut on her throat throbbed. The pain in her head blurred her vision, and her thoughts were a jumble.

Everything I ever wanted has come apart. My family, my plans, my work here. Patrick. Joe—my brother and my dearest friend—is gone. He never even said goodbye.

At last, the tent grew quiet. Eliza fell asleep, exhausted by the news, her grief and the commotion after the attack on Maureen.

Maureen watched shadows from the firelight dance across the canvas of their tent. She could hardly move, weighed down by the sadness that enveloped her. Her arms wouldn't move. Her neck seemed too weak to pick up her head. She didn't know how she could ever return home. What would Father say now? His worst fears had come true. She couldn't sleep. Or think. Or cry.

As night deepened, she lay there lost in her despair.

It grew cold, icy cold. The chill numbed her fingers and toes and reached into her chest. Shivering, she pulled the rough wool blanket up to her chin. Still dressed in her apron and heavy boots, she didn't have the strength to take them off. All the pins remained in her hair, poking her as she lay on her cot. It didn't matter. The discomfort from the cold and her hairpins was nothing compared to the black grief that enveloped her.

Maureen longed to be home. She wanted her mother's arms wrapped warmly around her. She wanted to hear her father laugh his great roar of a laugh and she wanted Joe to call her Moe one more time. When he called her Moe, she knew he was treating her like his best friend. He always called her that as they raced through the woods, or fished in Antietam Creek or watched thunderclouds roll through the valley on the darkest of nights.

As wretched as she was, Maureen couldn't wring even a single tear from her eyes. She waited for the dawn. It arrived only as the dismal pale light of a winter's morning. Silent, dismal. A rustling near her tent was the first thing she heard.

"I'm looking for Maureen O'Neill." Hearing a familiar voice, Maureen took in a deep breath.

"Patrick?" she whispered. *I must be dreaming. Why would he come?*

Maureen heard Miss Angela hush him. "We have two ailing nurses in here. Would you please keep your voice down?"

"I've got to see her, ma'am."

Maureen heard the desperation in his voice and jumped out of bed. As she reached for a shawl to wrap around her shoulders, she was surprised to see she was still dressed in her calico and pinafore. Her shoes were still on her feet.

"Maureen?" Eliza rolled over. "Is it time to go home?" Her face was puffy, creased from sleep.

"Soon, Eliza. I think I heard Patrick."

"Then I'll get up." Eliza's voice was small.

Maureen pushed open the tent flap. She saw Patrick, standing tall and proud in his Union Army uniform. His fair, freckled face was as puffy as Eliza's.

Has he been crying, too? Maureen's heart went out to him. *Of course, he has. Joe was his best friend.*

"Maureen!" he called as he ran to her.

"Patrick? What are you doing here?"

"It's your brother."

"Yes, I know." Maureen's voice caught in her throat. "Mother wrote to me yesterday."

He nodded. "She sent me to get you. Your father collapsed when he heard the news; she needs you."

"Father?" Maureen repeated with a start. Before she could say anything else, Eliza emerged from the tent.

"Patrick…" she began, as sobs wracked her slender frame.

Patrick put his arms out, looking tenderly from one woman to the other. Maureen and Eliza welcomed the comfort of a friend as he wrapped his arms around them.

Tears finally came for Maureen. She let them come in giant sobs as her body shook against Patrick's. He smoothed her hair and laid his cheek against the top of her head.

They seemed oblivious to the hospital camp around them as they shared their heartache. Though it was but a moment, Maureen later remembered standing there in Patrick's arms for a long, long time.

CHAPTER 22
THE ROAD HOME

Eliza leaned her cheek against Maureen's shoulder and wept their entire trip home. Maureen held her close, joining her sorrow with Eliza's.

"Can't you hurry up your pony?" Maureen asked again. Patrick prodded the russet-colored mare but Amber couldn't be persuaded.

"The only time Amber gets a spring in her step is when she's scared," Patrick said. The horse kept on, nodding her head in time with her plodding steps. Anxious and impatient, Maureen could hardly stand the slow rhythm of the horse's gait. All she wanted was to be home.

Mother needs me; she kept thinking. Why doesn't anybody understand that and hurry?

Instead, she sighed constantly and tried to think of anything else. She didn't want to look at Patrick. She ached for him to hold her in his arms and comfort her until she remembered Barbara.

Much as she tried not to, Maureen found herself envying his new sweetheart. Barbara was so pretty with those big blue eyes and fashionable dress. She had more to offer Patrick than Maureen: charm and grace, a place in society, such as it was in Sharpsburg. Maureen didn't think her little spark could ever compare with such a bright light.

She focused on her hands, cracked and rough. Her nails were short and ragged. Her sunburned skin was fading back to its winter pallor. Hers were the hands of someone who worked hard. They reminded her of the countless hours she had spent changing bandages, soothing feverish faces, spooning bowls of porridge. She wondered if her work at Smoketown—nearly four months—was now done.

Her mother needed her; her father—how was her father? "Patrick,

159

did you see Father?" she asked soon after the carriage passed the bullet-riddled Dunker Church.

"No, your mother said she put him to bed after he fell."

"Did she say how he was?"

Patrick looked at her with soft eyes and a serious expression. "Your mother told me Doctor Lee came to see him. She said he was overcome by the news. I think if it was bad, she'd have told me. I'm sure he will be fine, Maureen."

Maureen nodded. "Yes, I hope so."

The rest of the journey passed in silence. The only sounds were the wheels grinding against the hard ground and the pony's slow steps. Maureen was sure they all were suffering from the same sense of loss. For Maureen, thinking of Joe being gone left an ache deep in her heart. The dullness in Patrick's eyes betrayed his sadness.

Eliza never moved from Maureen's shoulder except to sigh. Maureen would have liked her to stir at least long enough to have a moment to stretch. Even so, she didn't dare disturb her friend, so deep in her grief.

The passing scenery had lost its color. Little copses of trees, only a few weeks ago a blaze of red, yellow and orange, were dull. She ignored them, remembering how they had hidden dangers just beyond. She paid no attention to the cornfields. Some of them were brown and black or flattened, reminders of the horrible battle. Tired to the point of aching, Maureen yielded to the rhythm of the carriage as it rounded wide curves and climbed gentle slopes. She closed her eyes and gave in to the comfort of the motion.

When she opened her eyes, Patrick had turned the carriage off the road onto the sloping lane that led to Eliza's house. He stopped the pony at the front porch and jumped out to help the two young women from their perch.

Maureen climbed down, and as she turned to pick up Eliza's valise, a mouse skittered past her feet. It ran under the hooves of the little pony which neighed in alarm and reared up. The carriage wobbled on two wheels for a heart-stopping moment. And then as it slammed back down in its proper place, Eliza was shaken from her seat and thrown to the ground.

Patrick turned and grabbed the horse's halter to calm her as Maureen rushed to her friend. She panicked to see Eliza unconscious on the ground. Her cheek was scraped and bloody. Her left arm was bent under her limp body at an angle that made Maureen worry it might be broken.

She wrung her hands, afraid to touch the injured girl. "Eliza! Eliza!" Her voice was edged with alarm. "Please wake up."

"Maureen, do something," Patrick urged her.

Yes, of course. She tried to calm herself down as she called on lessons learned during her long days of taking care of broken bodies. She wiped the dirt off Eliza's scraped cheek, checked her arms and legs for breaks and other injuries.

Maureen's Uncle Raymond came to the door to see what was causing all the commotion. When he saw his daughter crumpled under the carriage, he gasped and came running. Cradling Eliza's head, Maureen barked out orders to both men.

"Patrick, go for Doctor Lee. Tell him Eliza's arm may be broken." Then she thought better of it. "No, don't go yet. Uncle Raymond, do you have some smelling salts? And I need a length of clean cloth for Eliza's arm, a towel and water. Both hot and cold. Patrick, help my uncle get those things together. Oh, and bring me a blanket. Now be quick about it."

After she watched them rush into the house, Maureen sat on the cold ground and turned her attention to Eliza. She talked quietly to her friend, offering reassurances even though she wasn't sure Eliza could hear her. She took the smelling salts from Uncle Raymond and waved them under Eliza's nose.

"Oh, my head." She came to with a moan.

"Shhh," Maureen ordered. "Don't get up. You've fallen from the carriage. Can you move your arm?"

Eliza moved her right arm. "How about the other one?"

Eliza moaned again as she tried to move it. Maureen touched it gently. "It doesn't seem to be broken. You did fall hard on it, so the doctor will have to look at it. In the meantime, I'll put a sling around it, so you don't move it and hurt it more."

Then Maureen took the towels and basin of warm water Patrick brought her. She wiped blood and grit from the scrapes across Eliza's cheek. "It looks like you're going to have a black eye." She dipped a clean cloth into the basin of cold water and handed it to Eliza to put against her eye.

"No, the other one," she ordered and then, worried if Eliza was disoriented, she asked, "Can you see all right?"

Eliza nodded. Maureen wrapped her friend in the crocheted throw usually folded over the back of the parlor rocking chair. She asked Patrick to carry Eliza into the house. "Then will you go for the doctor, please?"

While they waited for the doctor, Uncle Raymond told Maureen Aunt Priscilla had gone to help her mother and father after they got the news about Joe. Hearing it again caused Eliza to weep quietly.

Moved by her distress, Eliza's father sat beside her on the divan and enfolded her in his arms. Maureen felt the cold sting of envy as she watched her uncle tenderly stroke his daughter's blonde hair and whisper to her. She missed the comfort her father had once lavished on her.

"What have we got here?" said Doctor Lee, bursting through the front door with Patrick. He leaned over the girl as he set his leather bag beside the sofa. He looked at Eliza's face and arm and tapped the blanket.

"Looks like you don't need me today." He looked at Maureen. "Is this your work?"

Worried she'd done something wrong, she nodded.

The doctor smiled at her. "You've done a fine job, Maureen."

Even in her grief, Maureen treasured the doctor's praise.

Doctor Lee examined Eliza's arm. "It's going to be sore for a while. You'll have to rest and keep wearing this sling. You've had a shock and need to recover. In a few days, you'll be fine."

"I saw your father this morning, Maureen," the doctor said as he prepared to leave.

"Yes?" Maureen was anxious for what he had to say.

"He collapsed at the news, and so your mother sent for me. He's fine, but he's taking it hard." The doctor was quiet for a moment. "You have my condolences. So many of our boys ... you've done good work, my dear. You've learned quite a bit. I'm impressed. I hope you'll be able to go back to the hospital in a few weeks or so."

"I hope so." Maureen rose, said goodbye and rushed to leave. Before she could reach the front door, Patrick stood in her way.

What now? Her impatience was growing unbearable.

CHAPTER 23
STRONG AND GENTLE

"I know I said I didn't want you to work in that hospital," Patrick said.

"Patrick—" Maureen didn't want to argue. She didn't have the strength.

"No, listen," he interrupted her. He hesitantly took a step forward and then, as if he thought better of it, stopped. "I really did think it was a terrible idea for a girl until I saw you take care of Eliza. I should have known you were so capable; I'd seen your work often enough. Now I understand why you would want to work there. And I see why you should. I'm sorry…"

He looked at her with that gentle expression he had the day he finally kissed her. His eyes were clear and direct. A hint of a smile played at his lips. And he looked so uncomfortable, standing across the room from her. He shifted from foot to foot and clutched his cap like it might get away.

"Really?" she said. Poor Eliza had to fall out of a carriage for him finally to understand. I must thank her later.

"Maureen," Patrick looked at her shyly. "I've missed you." He came across the room and started to take her hand, and then she pulled it away.

"What about Barbara?" she said.

"Barbara wasn't interested in me. Our mothers thought we'd make a nice couple, so we took a few carriage rides. Finally, she told me she had already set her heart on someone else. That day you saw us she had just told me she didn't care one bit for me."

She placed her hand in his. "Oh, I'm so sorry."

He looked down at her hand and back at her face, surprised. "You are?"

"Shouldn't I be? Aren't you?"

164

"No. She wasn't you." Patrick's words, low and soft, sounded like a song to Maureen. He squeezed her hand as her heart leaped in her chest. Much as she longed to fall into his arms, she wasn't sure she wanted to risk more heartache. She needed to sort out what she thought, how she felt. And she couldn't do that now, certainly not now.

"Patrick, I'd love to stay here and talk with you. But I can't. I have to go home. My mother is waiting for me. I have to see my father."

"Then let me come with you." His eyes were soft and full of love. His hand was warm and strong enough to hold her up. "Please, Maureen."

She shook her head and opened her mouth to speak. Instead, she slipped her hand from Patrick's and disappeared out the door before he could say another word.

Maureen turned down the well-worn path under the apple trees that stretched between Eliza's house and hers. She was surprised to see the last red apples hanging high among a few tattered gold leaves. They were too high for her to reach. She remembered another late autumn day when she was still little. It was a golden afternoon when her brother taught her to climb the tree to reach the last apples. He made sure she wouldn't fall. He made sure she was safe.

Come on, Moe. Reach up to that branch and lift yourself up!

It's so high, Joe.

Here, let me show you.

The memory set her to crying again.

Who will keep me safe now, Joe? Who will show me how?

Maureen ran from the path into the house. She passed her beloved chickens without a look. Blind from tears, she wanted only her mother. She needed her mother's gentleness and strength.

"Mother!" She looked around the empty house. "Mother!" She ran to her parents' room, expecting to find her tending to her stricken father. It was empty. She looked inside her room and then climbed into the loft that had been Joe's room. She returned to the kitchen to look in the pantry and peer into the back yard. Even the fireplace was dark and cold. The house was empty, quiet.

Maureen collapsed onto the rough wooden floor. She rolled onto her side, closed her eyes and wrapped her arms around herself. She cried, then, each teardrop hot and stinging. She didn't care. She cried until pain coursed through her temples. She wiped her cheeks on her sleeve again and again until the fabric was damp. And, finally, she was cried out. Exhaustion wracked her body, already frail from a sleepless night. She stared at the unlit fireplace and shivered.

Then, at last, she slept.

Maureen thought she was dreaming as strong arms wrapped around her and lifted her from the cold floor. She thought she could smell the peat of the hearth that warmed their pub in Galway. Her father whispered to her as he did when she was little. He had always soothed her with his soft words.

"Such a tiny slip of a girl," she heard him say as he held her close.

She thought she heard him call Mother and Joe as they entered the house. A cool breeze made her shiver, and her father hugged her just a little more tightly.

"There, there, precious angel, we'll get you in your warm bed soon enough," he whispered.

Maureen caught a whiff of malt on his warm breath. She loved the scent of the black stout her father served in their little pub. It was the scent of home, and she felt comforted.

She sighed as a drop of rain fell onto her cheek. No, it couldn't be rain, she thought. I'm inside the house.

She opened her eyes to see a tear stain on her father's cheek. Father was carrying her.

Why is he crying? Where are we going?

Maureen closed her eyes again. She remembered Joe. He wasn't with Mother. No, he was with God. He was gone forever. That's why her father wept.

"I'm sorry I couldn't keep you safe," he whispered to Maureen as he lay her on her bed. She didn't understand.

Safe from what?

Father's weeping had turned into sobbing. "I couldn't keep the two of you safe that night in Galway. And now, I couldn't keep Joe and you safe here."

Maureen wanted to reach her arms around her father's neck, but she couldn't make them move.

Am I dreaming? Her eyes wouldn't open even as she felt the weight of her father leaning over to kiss her.

"I'm so sorry, Maureen," he whispered.

"Joe," she mumbled.

Yes, he's talking about Joe.

Her eyes fluttered open.

"Joe," she repeated. Her father caressed her cheek.

"There, there, girl," he said. "I'll leave you here to rest. Your mother has been anxious to see you, but she wants you to rest for the moment. Hush. Don't say a word."

She nodded obediently, as she had done as a child. He caressed her hair as he had done when she was little and then without another word, he left the room.

Maureen watched her father go. His care and protection comforted her in a way she hadn't seen in a long time. She remembered how as a little girl, she was so easily charmed by her father. As the silence closed in, the comfort dissipated. Maureen rolled over and cried into her pillow until, exhausted, she slept.

The afternoon sun was streaming through the little window over her bed when Maureen awoke. She jumped up, alarmed to be in bed so long. Rare was the day when she was in bed in the afternoon. That happened only the few times she had been sick.

She thought for a moment about her dream and relished the sweet feeling of being carried like a child into her room. Then she realized, it wasn't a dream. She had been carried into this room. She smoothed back her hair and pulled open the door. Her father was in his usual chair. Her mother was sitting at the table, her hands around her tea cup. Neither spoke. They looked up as Maureen approached. Maureen could see the shadow of sadness in her mother's eyes and her father's puffy cheeks and red nose.

Her mother rose from her chair to straighten a place at the table

167

for Maureen. She poured Maureen a cup of tea and brought her some bread and apple butter.

"There's not much to eat, I'm afraid," her mother said. "I just haven't had the energy today."

Maureen hesitated. *What do I say? What do I do?*

"Please sit down, Maureen," her father said. His voice sounded hoarse and much too soft. She did as she was told.

The table was littered with Joe's things.

"Those were in Joe's pockets," her mother said. "His regiment sent them, along with the letter to tell us he was gone."

Maureen forced herself to drink her tea, warm and aromatic, as she looked over each item. The things he carried on his last day. Some were things she expected: his well-worn prayer book, a set of black rosary beads, his pocket book. Some things surprised her. A crumpled letter looked like it had been read again and again. Maureen could tell by the round loops of the handwriting it was from Eliza.

The handkerchief he had carried wasn't his. It was hers: a fine linen cloth stitched with lace from her grandmother and a pale pink "M" Maureen had embroidered herself. Maureen had looked everywhere for that handkerchief. It choked her up to see it spent the past few months in her brother's pocket.

She reached for it, eager to touch something he cherished.

"Did they tell you what happened?" Maureen asked.

"They found him on the battlefield in Fredericksburg." Her father's voice was colorless, not a hint of sadness nor pride. "They only knew who he was by the things in his pockets, those things. His whole battalion was shot down during the fighting at a place called Marye's Heights."

"We can't have a funeral, of course," her mother said. "Father Murphy said we could have a memorial service." A sob caught in her voice and she turned away, squeezed shut her eyes and held her hand to her mouth. She struggled to regain her composure. "That will be on Saturday. Your Aunt Priscilla suggested having people back to her house afterward. I told her no, it should be here."

It's all real, then. We're talking about Joe as if he's gone.

168

She pushed away the bread which tasted like sawdust in her mouth. She couldn't bear the sweetness of the apple butter. Not when it came from the trees where she and Joe had played.

"We thought about having pallbearers even if there isn't a casket," her mother said. "We don't need all six, I wouldn't think. Your Uncle Raymond, of course. Doctor Lee and Mr. Toohey. Most of his friends are gone because of the war. Patrick's here, and I think he should…"

"Kate," her father said. "There's nothing for the pallbearers to do. Don't trouble yourself thinking about this. Just the service will be enough for our Joe. Raymond and Patrick have both said they will give the eulogy."

"Yes, but I have to do something," she said. Her chin quivered, and she laid her head down on her hands. Maureen's heart ached for her mother.

Her father struggled from his chair to get on his feet. He took his wife in his arms and held her close. It had been a long time since she'd seen this. Her tiny mother was gathered into the powerful arms of her father who stood more than a foot above her. Maureen felt out of place as her parents lost themselves in their grief. She'd never seen her parents, always so strong, look so fragile.

CHAPTER 24
DAMN WAR

"Damn war." Maureen heard her mother mutter as she emerged from the parish church. Such language usually didn't come from her mother, but this wasn't an ordinary day. Maureen wanted to put her arm around her mother's narrow shoulders even though she knew better. Her mother handled intense moments better on her own.

The day was too splendid for a funeral. After an unseasonably cold night, the sun had risen in a cerulean sky, bright and warm. The maple trees planted beside the tall white church had held onto to the last of their crimson leaves. A gentle breeze swept across the lawn and tugged some of their leaves off the branches.

Father Murphy, still in his silver-trimmed black chasuble, greeted the family on the church lawn.

"Thank you for a lovely service," her father said politely to the rector. It was filled with uplifting songs, plenty of sniffles and a sermon that paid tribute to Joe and his service to his country. In their eulogies, Raymond and Patrick remembered the energetic Irish lad who had fallen in love with America.

"I've been officiating at far too many of these services," Father Murphy said. "I've had much too much practice."

Funerals at Sharpsburg churches were usually community affairs. Everyone came. Maureen and her family had attended funerals for ancient patriarchs, women in childbirth, a child felled by influenza. They thought everyone would attend Joe's funeral, too. But war brought change. In recent months, not everyone came for boys killed in battle. Even Sharpsburg was sharply divided in their loyalty to President Lincoln and President Davis. So, some pews remained empty. Maureen noticed who was missing. Joe's friends, of course, whether they had joined the Union Army or crossed the Potomac to join General Lee. Some of their parents, feeling the divisions too

170

keenly and missing their sons too keenly, stayed away, too.

Maureen was surprised to see how such divided loyalties could continue into death. Even so, she understood. Some families perceived it as disloyal to attend the funeral of an enemy soldier—even if the boy was one they'd known since birth. Some were dead, and still, the divisions remained—even as these boys were united in death.

Tom Henderson's mother was a rare exception. With her head held high and a lace-trimmed handkerchief crushed in her gloved hand, Mrs. Henderson came up to Maureen and her mother as they stood by the church door. She nodded at her mother and whispered her condolences. Then she kissed Maureen. Maureen hadn't seen the elegant woman since before she helped Tom in this very church right after the battle.

"Thank you for what you did for my Tom," Mrs. Henderson added, her voice cracking. On that horrible day, Maureen had been so ashamed because she had helped the enemy. Now, looking at that proud, sad mother, Maureen's shame and guilt faded away. The wounded men in that church weren't evil. They were sons who were loved and now lost.

"I wish I could have done more, Mrs. Henderson," Maureen said. "Tom was thinking of you and Zack the whole time I was with him. He wanted you to know he was brave."

Mrs. Henderson squeezed Maureen's hand. She held her face firm, her lips pressed together. She said nothing more, nodding as she turned away.

Maureen couldn't help but hear the sob that escaped Mrs. Henderson's throat as she walked away.

She started to go to her, until her mother held her back. "I should go."

Maureen turned to see the two mothers leaning on each other for support, sharing words of comfort.

Though their children had been on opposite sides of the war, the mothers were united in grief, mourning young men they would never see again.

By the time the family arrived home, a crowd was gathered. Early that morning, when she had seen the day would be unseasonably

171

warm, Maureen's mother and she carried the kitchen table out to the front lawn. Aunt Priscilla sent over plates of sandwiches, bowls of pickled vegetables, stewed tomatoes and a platter of sliced pound cake. Neighbors brought their favorite dishes until there was enough to feed the whole town. It wasn't long before their farm was filled with friends. Patrick came with his mother. Except for a polite nod at the church, he had stayed away from Maureen. Maureen kept looking for Eliza. She hadn't seen her at the church or now at the house.

Feeling more alone than ever, Maureen kept busy helping at the buffet table. She was unable to eat, unable to add anything to a conversation. When she was sure everyone had a plate of food, and she knew her mother wouldn't be calling her, she wandered across the road to walk beside Antietam Creek.

Beside a crook in the stream, she found Eliza sitting alone, staring at the damp handkerchief she twisted in her hands. Her eye had indeed been bruised in the fall, and now it was also red from weeping. Maureen sat beside her, and without a word, they gazed into the creek. With so little rain, the water level was low. Maureen and Eliza listened to the creek spill over a cluster of rocks. The pretty scene brought no peace to Maureen. When she asked Eliza to come back to the house, Eliza only shook her head.

"This was our meeting place," she whispered. "I want to stay here."

Eliza ran her hand through the rough grass beside her. Maureen kissed her friend's tear-stained cheek and sat quietly beside her for a few minutes.

Once she was convinced Eliza would be all right alone, Maureen returned to the yard to feed the chickens. The noisy black hens scurried at her feet happy with an unexpected—and unnecessary—spread of seed.

It was only then Maureen realized she missed them and the routines of everyday life. It seemed as if years had passed since the last time she had fed them.

Maureen tossed one more handful of seed and leaned against the split rail fence to see who got the last bite. After the hens lost interest and wandered off, Maureen kept her gaze on the bit of dusty land where they had been.

She recalled the day she was old enough to feed them. Joe kept an eye on her to be sure she did it right. He showed her how much to feed and water them and how to separate the noisy birds when they got out of hand.

Joe had taught her many things. Things everybody needed to know how to do: feed chickens, build a fire, pick apples. And things he wanted to teach a little brother. He taught her to release a fish from a hook and how to skip stones on the creek. It was he who had taught her to shoot a gun. They hiked the nearby hills when they had a free summer afternoon and swam in the river.

She remembered the first time he called her Moe. She was only five and didn't like it—until she realized it rhymed with Joe. That made her laugh.

No one else ever called her anything but Maureen.

Now no one would ever call her Moe again, she thought with a lump in her throat.

Sounds of conversation and even laughter woke her from her reverie. It was time to get back. The buffet table might need restocking. And she worried about leaving her mother alone too much longer. She wasn't holding up well these last few days.

Maureen was wiping the dust kicked up by the hens from her skirts when she saw a man approaching. For a moment, she thought it was Joe and her heart leaped—and then, like a punch in the gut, she remembered Joe was dead.

"What do you want, Patrick?" she asked with some irritation and thought, I haven't got time for ye.

Even if he did look offended, Maureen didn't care. She'd had enough of his newly-forged bullying, and she wasn't going to listen to him on this day or any other.

"I am only here to see how you are faring," he said. "If you'd rather I leave, then—"

"No, no." She sighed. "You're welcome to stay, It's been a difficult morning, and I couldn't smile at another person."

"I was worried about both you and Eliza. I thought she might be

173

here with you," Patrick said. "She looks bad."

"She is taking Joe's death pretty hard." Maureen leaned her back against the fence.

"Joe thought the world of Eliza." He nodded before leaning beside her and crossing his arms across his chest. "He told me he was hoping the war would be over soon so they could get married."

"I can't understand why they kept the fact they were courting so secret," Maureen said.

"Some things Joe kept close to the vest, you know," Patrick said.

"I wonder what else I don't know."

"You know he thought you were the best 'little brother' in the world. I remember correcting him and saying he meant 'little sister,' and he said, 'No, I meant little brother.' You had to be his little brother because you were always going to be good friends."

Patrick's soft tone and kind words soothed Maureen. "We went fishing one day this past summer, and he told me about bringing you when you were just old enough to be out without your mother. He remembered how thrilled you were bringing in your first croaker."

Maureen nodded. "He used to call me 'Moe.' We did have some fun as children."

She grew quiet, her eyes fixed on the ground as memories flooded her thoughts. As she recalled adventures with Joe and the neighborhood children, she suddenly realized Patrick had often been with them.

Funny, she thought, how she had never given Patrick the time of day and yet he had been a faithful friend all her life.

He might have taken to acting like a protective mother bear in the last few months, but he cared about her. And here he was on one of the saddest days of her life, trying to be the friend she needed.

"I can't for the life of me understand how he went off to war without telling me," Maureen said.

"I wish he had. When I left, he said he didn't like long, sad goodbyes," Patrick responded.

A painful silence fell between them. Even though Maureen knew he was trying to be nice, she didn't know what to say.

"Can I get you anything? How about a piece of cake? My mother

174

scraped together enough sugar to make her spice cake. Would you like some?" Patrick asked.

"No thanks, Patrick," she answered with a polite smile. "I'll go back now. Mother may need help."

"If you need anything at all, I'm here."

"Thanks, Patrick. That's a comfort."

CHAPTER 25
DARK DAYS

Maureen awoke on a Thursday morning, nearly a week after Joe's memorial service. It was cold and drab like any other winter day. She rose to stoke the fire and put on a kettle to boil. The day seemed colder than usual, lonelier too. And she knew why.

The day was Christmas Day.

The holiday was usually a quiet one for the O'Neills. There was no time or money for fancy decorations or special foods. Instead, it was a day for church, the exchange of a few handmade presents, and a cup of hot cider to toast the day. Mostly, it was a day for laughing and singing.

Maureen knew she should be getting ready for the cold walk to church, but she didn't quite know how to celebrate the birth of the newborn king today. There were no presents. Not even a jug of cider to heat over the fire now crackling in the hearth. Maureen went about the business of making the usual breakfast.

While she hoped her mother might take at least a few bites of her oatmeal, Maureen knew she would likely remain in her bed, silent, her face turned to the wall. Maureen ached for her mother, as her mother ached for her lost boy.

Maureen sank onto a chair once her preparations were done. Perhaps because it was Christmas, her sadness seemed more profound than ever. She'd pushed away her grief to help her mother who was laid low by her own mourning. Mother had gone to bed after the funeral and stayed there. She'd stopped eating. Maureen couldn't tell whether she was angry or grief-stricken. Maybe it was both.

A creaking floorboard alerted Maureen that her father was awake. She poured tea for three and retrieved the crock of butter from the pantry. She was slicing bread when her father appeared.

"Morning, Maureen," he said. "Happy Christmas."

Maureen smiled though she didn't feel it in her heart. It couldn't be a happy Christmas this year. He stopped before he reached for the cup he would take to his wife. To Maureen's surprise, he came up to her and wrapped his arms around her.

"I know it's not the same," he said to her. He laid his cheek on the top of her head, and she breathed in the warm earthy smell of her father. "Without you here, the day would be so terrible."

He kissed the top of her head and then took a cup to her mother. It had become a ritual. Father took in the cup. It got cold before her mother ever took a sip. Then he left and didn't return for the rest of the day.

He turned as he crushed his hat on his head and gave her a gentle look. It was an expression far different from the scowls of the previous few months. Maureen treasured these rare moments of gratitude.

Maureen wasn't sure where her father went but knew it couldn't be far. Although his strength was returning, he still wasn't well enough to walk more than a mile or two. She suspected his walks led him to Uncle Raymond. Father was mourning in his own way, she decided.

Today would be no different from other days of late. Maureen stirred the oatmeal and added a generous dab of butter. The steam warmed her cold cheeks as she carried a bowl for her mother into her parents' bedroom. She hoped the aroma of melting butter and sweet oatmeal would entice her mother. Yet, she barely moved when Maureen entered the room. She was awake, staring at the ceiling. Her eyes were framed by dark circles. Her frail hands clutched the black beads of her rosary.

"Mother," Maureen whispered. "I brought you some oatmeal."

"Thank you, Maureen," her mother answered.

When she made no move to accept it, Maureen laid the bowl next to the untouched tea.

"Would you like anything?" she asked.

"Yes." Her mother pointed to the chest across the room.

Maureen opened the chest, a trunk that had brought all their worldly possessions from Galway. Inside were two knitted scarves.

Maureen touched the ivory colored wool and looked at her mother.

"One of them is your Christmas present," she said. "The other one…"

Maureen picked up the top one and rushed over to her mother. "Mother," was all she could say. She embraced her mother, and the two of them sat quietly together.

A slight movement signaled to Maureen it was time to let her mother be. Maureen would have loved to talk to her mother. It had been so long since they had a conversation. Instead, her mother turned away and heaved a sigh. Maureen crushed the soft wool to her chest and retreated from the room.

The scarf was lovely. Knitted in the traditional knots and braids of Ireland, she thought it was the prettiest thing she had ever seen. She knew her mother had spent long days knitting two of them for the children she missed. The thought took Maureen's breath away. She sank into her mother's chair by the fire, closed her eyes and held her Christmas gift close.

Prayer hadn't come easily for her as she had grown used to suffering and pain, especially now that Joe was gone. Today, it was the only way she could mark the day.

Days faded into weeks as Maureen, left alone, continued to handle the household chores. She swept and cleaned, tended the fire and cooked food no one would eat.

As quiet as the days were, the nights were full of bitterness and grief. Maureen found herself waking up to the sound of angry words. She's lay awake, listening to her mother and father tormented each other. Maureen didn't understand what was happening between her parents. This was more than mourning. They had always been happy together. From the words she could piece together, Maureen realized her mother resented how her father had treated Joe and her. She heard her mother cry out that she'd never had a chance to say goodbye and it was all his fault.

Then one morning, after one especially long argument, Maureen summoned her courage to speak to her father.

"I need to talk to you, Father," she said as she handed her father his morning tea.

"Yes?" He looked up from his coffee cup, a look of innocence on his face.

"What is happening here? I can't help but hear the arguments night after night——" She didn't know how to continue.

"Nothing for you to worry about," he said.

Maureen, however, wasn't about to be brushed off. "I don't believe that."

Her father glowered at her and rose from the table. "Now don't you be starting, too." Then he stormed out the front door.

Maureen turned to the dish pan, hurt and confused. With her arms deep in dishwater, she found herself feeling sorry for herself. She missed Joe. She missed Eliza, wishing she was sitting at the table, filling her in on the latest gossip. She missed her life. The life she had given up here. The life she had taken on at Smoketown.

Will I ever get another chance to go back to nursing? Maureen wondered as she began yet another in an endless series of the farmhouse's daily routines.

With no one to talk to, she kept herself busy. She had filled the pantry shelves with apple butter, pickled eggs, and corn three different ways. She'd shined their few copper pots, reorganized the shelves and learned how to make a pie in hopes it might entice her parents to eat, maybe even eat together. She'd packed away Joe's things, except for his rosary and prayer book and the handkerchief he'd carried on his last day. She tucked the handkerchief in her pocket. The other things she arranged on the mantelpiece with the few mementos the family brought from Ireland.

In the evenings, she studied a little primer Angela and Patricia had given her while she was sick with the measles. She'd mastered long and short vowels and now recognized many more words without sounding them out. She read them aloud and wrote them down, growing more proficient every day.

It still stung when she remembered how she had to refuse soldiers who asked her to read letters from home. Now she was confident she could read to them.

Every night, Maureen went to bed tired and achy. Despite all she did, nothing seemed to matter to her mother and father. Their late night arguments continued unabated. She mourned as if she had lost her whole family.

Finally, a week later, Mother spoke. Maureen slipped silently into her parents' room to find her mother asleep.

It was mid-day, an hour when her mother normally would have been her busiest. Instead, she was motionless. Only the tiniest movement of the bed sheets signaled to Maureen that her mother was alive. Her mother had grown so pale and gaunt in the past month. Her hair, spread out over the pillow, was grayer now. Instead of her usual rosy complexion, she had dark circles under her eyes and hollow cheeks.

Maureen pulled open the curtain, hoping a little sunshine might raise her mother's spirits. Truth be told, nearly every day had been cloudy since the funeral. Today, however, a ray of sun had broken through. She was relieved when her mother's eyes fluttered open.

"My arms hurt so," she said. She struggled to raise them off the coverlet, and Maureen rushed to her side. "They've ached since the day…" She closed her eyes and shook her head. Then she looked at Maureen. "I've wanted to hold my boy since the day he didn't come for dinner. He was such a strong boy, wiry like my father, filled with energy. I wanted to hold him again. At least once. I shouldn't have let him go."

Her face crumpled as tears streamed down her cheeks.

Maureen pulled her handkerchief from her pocket. The handkerchief Joe had carried. She gave it to her mother who dabbed at her face.

Although she couldn't imagine what words would comfort her mother, she knew her presence could offer at least a little solace. She'd learned that at Smoketown. The most grievously injured soldier found a little peace in the presence of someone who cared. Sometimes it was all she could do.

And now, kneeling beside her mother, her strong, rough hands covered her mother's frail, thin ones. She wished she could do more. Nothing she could say or do would dull the ache that her mother suffered.

Her mother slept again. Maureen attempted to take her hands

from her mother's, but she stirred and cried out. Maureen shifted her aching knees though she didn't move.

The sun's rays filled the room with afternoon light and warmth that soothed Maureen. Though she had spent much of the past four months amid the worst physical pain she'd ever witnessed, none of it had touched her as her mother's had. She feared for her strong mother.

Her mother opened her eyes, keeping her gaze on the ceiling.

"It's not Daniel's fault," she mumbled. "I can't blame him. He didn't shoot our Joe, did he?"

"Mother?"

Maureen waited a few minutes for her mother to answer. Her mother's eyes searched the space before her. She sighed deeply and closed her eyes.

What was troubling her mother? Maureen sat quietly and wondered. Her parents had always been devoted to each other. Theirs was the kind of love Maureen hoped to have. Until now, Mother and Father thought and acted as one. At least that's the way Maureen had always seen it. But now she saw division. Was it caused by the war? Or had she and Joe caused it? Or had it always been there, another thing parents kept from the children?

What do I know? Maureen asked herself. Who is this woman?

Maureen had heard the stories of how her parents had met. She'd come around to her father's pub with a friend and her sweetheart.

Her mother noticed the handsome publican right away. Though he was nearly ten years older and a bit gruff, she had taken a shine to him. He was a hard worker, tending to his farm by day and keeping bar at night.

It was only a few months later that they married and moved into the thatched cottage beside the pub. They brought two children into the world. It was a happy life.

Maureen had no memories of ever being hungry or even hearing he parents worry about making ends meet. Then again, what child remembers such things? Although she knew about the famine, she had no memory of it touching her life.

Maureen put her hand over her mother's. "You always took care of me. You never let on if there was any worry. Now it's my turn."

She turned in the direction of her daughter's voice, filled with determination. She smiled a little and looked away. Maureen wasn't sure her mother understood.

Maureen sat by her mother who slept fitfully through the rest of the day. When darkness came, she slipped out of the room, exhausted. The rest of the house was quiet and cold. The fire in the hearth, unattended all day, had gone out.

She sat in her father's empty chair. Loneliness closed in. This had always been the warmest spot in the house. Her father delighted in his family from this place. When she was younger, she had clambered up to sit on his knee. Joe would lean on the back of Father's chair when he needed advice. And beside him in everything was their mother.

"What happened?" Maureen said aloud, staring into the dark fireplace.

"Maureen?" It was her mother, looking ghostly in the darkness. "Is that you?"

Maureen quickly lit a candle and held it up. "Yes, Mother. Is there something you need?"

She barely recognized her mother. Always petite, she looked smaller and frailer standing by her door. "Come sit here." Maureen jumped from the chair. "I'll get the fire lit."

Her mother said nothing more until the fire burned brightly. Then she folded her hands before her and looked at Maureen.

"I need to tell you something." Her voice was gentle. It was a trick she said she'd learned from her mother. Whenever she spoke softly, her children paid attention. It had worked since Joe and Maureen were wee toddlers in Galway. Even Maureen's father listened whenever his wife spoke in her quiet way.

Maureen sat down again and waited.

"Do you remember Ireland?"

"What a question, Mother. How could I forget home?"

"I meant no harm." Her voice was raspy. "I am glad you still think of Ireland as home. You were so little when we left. I don't believe you know how desperate the times were…the neighbors and friends who left Ireland when they could no longer feed their families…the troubles that started because the Irish felt so helpless…the farm…"

"We were never hungry," Maureen said. "I never remember being hungry."

Her mother smiled. "Your father and I went without food many a night so you and Joe would have full bellies. It was hard. The pub helped. The men needed their pints and their conversation. If they didn't have the money, they paid in bread or turnips."

"I loved that place. All our friends were there and remember Sadie? I wonder if the Mulligans still have her," Maureen said. "Joe and I used to sit by the hearth listening to the men tell all their stories."

Her mother nodded. "It was often a convivial spot. And yet, there was a dark side, too. Men who gathered late at night arguing how to get the British out of Ireland. I don't think you know I welcomed them into the pub even after your father objected. I thought they had the country's best interests at heart."

"I thought Father…"

"No, he thought the lot of them were fools. He was afraid for the two of you. I don't suppose you remember the fire?"

"Oh, but I do. We were so afraid when we heard Sadie barking in the pub," Maureen said.

"Poor dog. She'd gotten left behind. We were lucky to get her out. The pub was a total loss." Her mother took a deep breath. "I need to tell you what happened. Even though your father has forbidden me from telling you."

Maureen leaned forward. Her mother hadn't spoken in days. She had talked in her sleep, confusing words, troubling words. She longed to know what was in her mother's heart.

Her mother filled in details of a story Maureen knew. She remembered the pub well enough. And she remembered the fire. She woke up in her father's arms when she heard the smashing of glass and then saw a bright light. Her father held her tighter as he rushed into the house and tucked her into bed. She remembered the horror she felt when she saw the roof of the pub bright with fire.

"The fire was started on purpose," her mother said. "It almost cost us our lives."

"Why would anyone hurt us?" Horror chilled Maureen.

"We never knew for sure who set the fire," her mother said. "What we did know was that we had to go. We knew it was a warning. And it wasn't the first."

The front door slammed open, and her father filled the doorway. "Am I correct in saying I just heard you talking about the fire with our daughter?"

"She needs to know, Daniel." Maureen watched as her parents eyed one another. Her father stood firm with his fists on his hips. Her tiny mother looked up at him with a steely gaze. "And in a minute, I'm going to tell her the other story."

Maureen waited for the shouting that was sure to come. She could see the anger rising in her father's face.

"Or you could tell her," her mother said quietly.

"Tell her? Tell me what?" Maureen asked. She looked from mother to father.

"Daniel." Her mother's voice was soft as her eyes narrowed when she looked at her husband.

Maureen's father grunted and sat in the chair next to her.

He sat quietly for a moment, leaning his elbows on his knees as he gazed at the fire. Then he suddenly turned to Maureen.

"I know you think you're doing a great thing, getting yourself involved in this war. I know you think your brother Joe is—was a hero. Robert, too. And your friend, Patrick, no doubt."

Maureen nodded. "That I do."

"Yes," he said, "I'm sure you do."

"And don't you, Father?" she asked.

"It's hard to say," he said. "Rebellion is a terrible thing for a country. Maybe it's necessary. Maybe it's not. One thing I know for sure, it divides families and breaks many a mother's heart." He paused for a moment. "Fathers' hearts, too."

"Yes, but," Maureen began. Her father put his hand up.

"Hear me out, girl," he said. "I've had a bit of experience with

184

rebellion, you see. Eliza's father, your great Uncle Raymond, has suffered greatly because of it twice now."

"Uncle Raymond?"

"Aye, I heard your mother was telling tales about her activity. Now you need to know about the uncle you never knew in Galway," he said.

During the Great Famine, Uncle Raymond had gone to work in Ballingarry, a town more than a hundred miles from their farm. The crop had failed again, and his family was starving. "He had a wife and a son," Maureen's father said quietly. "They died while he was gone."

Maureen gasped, shocked she had never heard about them before. Her mother nodded. "She was a lovely woman. Pegeen was her name," she said. "She was my best friend. She was the girl who introduced me to your father."

Maureen struggled to understand the connections as she looked from her mother to her father as he continued his story.

"Pegeen was also my father's cousin, even though she was younger than I. You weren't more than a toddler when she died. Though we refer to Raymond as your uncle, he's only my cousin by marriage. He took the death of their son Seamus very hard. The little boy had been the light in his daddy's eye."

"One thing led to another after Raymond learned the news. He was still in Ballingarry, and when he got drunk in a pub, he shouted all sorts of anti-British slogans. Even if that kind of talk is tolerated in the pubs on a usual evening, it wasn't that night. There had been a rebellion in the town that same day. The police started looking for him. He went into hiding and then shipped off to Philadelphia. We never saw him again," her father said.

"Until we came here," Maureen said.

"Until we came here," he echoed. "At your Uncle Raymond's invitation, I might add."

"You've never mentioned Uncle Raymond's first wife and baby before. I know I don't remember them," Maureen said.

"We don't know if your Aunt Priscilla knows," her mother said.

"Raymond blames himself, you know. He thinks if he'd been

185

home his family would have lived," her father said. "Now he can't bear to hear poor Pegeen's name."

Maureen wanted to ask why her father blamed himself. Instead, she asked,

"And was he part of the rebellion in Ballingarry?"

"Ah," her father said. "That's something else we don't know. I don't know if he'll ever tell us."

Maureen was silent. She was surprised by her family's well-kept secrets. She thought everybody knew everybody else's business in her close-knit family. More importantly, now she understood her father's unfathomable pain a little better.

"I remember how hard he took Pegeen's and Seamus's deaths. He still does. And so now maybe you see why I opposed your going to that hospital and didn't want Joe to join the Army," her father said. "Family is more important than anything else."

Maureen nodded. She knew he expected another argument, though none came. Maybe it was time to stop. She saw the old familiar light in her mother's eyes as she looked at her husband. Maureen understood her parents' connection a little better now. Daniel nodded at his wife.

"I can't believe that story about Uncle Raymond is true," Maureen finally said.

"It is, every word of it," her mother said. "They were dark days, dark as these."

CHAPTER 26
WILL YOU WAIT?

"Eliza's doing quite well." Maureen's father bustled into the house one cold January morning and gave her a pointed look.

"I've missed her so much." Maureen sighed as she replaced the lid on the steaming pot.

She'd been so busy in the weeks since the funeral. Mother and the house needed her attention and she had been to see Eliza only a few times.

"I should go see her."

"Why, yes, you should indeed." Her father nodded and struggled into his chair, grimacing at the pain that continued to nag him. "Patrick had just arrived when I was leaving. He's grown into a fine man, Patrick has."

"Patrick?"

"He was at the house." Her father acted casual as he filled his pipe. "You could go now if you like. I'll watch the fire. What's in the pot?"

Maureen hardly heard him as she thought about her hair and smoothed the curly tendrils by her face. She untied the apron that protected her favorite green calico dress.

"Maureen? The pot?" her father repeated.

"Hmm? Oh! A bit of soup."

"And here under this towel?" He leaned over to peek under it.

"Soda bread. Don't you be eating that until supper," she scolded as he unwrapped the rustic round loaf.

"Why Maureen Regina O'Neill." He smiled. "I do believe you've become a regular Irish homemaker."

Maureen stopped what she was doing when she saw that smile. She had pleased him.

Then she made a face at him. "Why wouldn't I be able to make a simple loaf? I've had a wonderful teacher. I've helped Mother plenty of times."

"I always said she'd make someone a wonderful wife one day," her mother said matter-of-factly.

She had quietly entered through the back door and put a basket of eggs on the table. "Are you going somewhere, Maureen?"

"I suggested she stop what she's doing and go visit Eliza," her father said. "Her arm is fully healed. Patrick was visiting, and he asked about our girl."

Maureen turned abruptly, surprised by her father's words. "You didn't tell me that."

"Didn't I?" He casually busied himself again with his pipe.

"Go on then," her mother said. "We can manage on our own for a little while."

Maureen's heart raced as she ran from the house and under the apple trees, now bare of leaves and fruit. She skipped up the steps of the front porch of the grand house. When she knocked on the wide whitewashed door, she heard laughter. She knew Eliza's exuberant chuckle right away.

Eliza still had a wide smile on her face as she threw open the door and greeted her friend.

"She's finally come, Patrick," Eliza called back to the parlor.

Maureen hugged her friend, happy to see her happy again. She looked thin, though the bruise on her face was long gone. She held her arm stiffly, a sign to Maureen that it was still troubling her. Eliza led her into the parlor where she spied Patrick. He was obviously uncomfortable, holding himself stiffly as he politely spoke to Aunt Priscilla and Uncle Raymond.

He tapped one foot and nervously handled the cup of milky tea on his knee. He was listening attentively and answering questions about the hospital.

"Yes sir, there's still a fair number of men—"

When he saw Maureen, he nearly tipped over his cup of milky tea as he jumped up. With a quick movement, he grabbed the cup and saucer before they crashed to the carpet. And then he stepped onto the cake plate at his feet. He blushed and sighed deeply, standing there with icing on his boot and tea glistening on his arm. Then he smiled at her with delight. Maureen had to admit it: she was thrilled even as the heat of her blush rose to her cheeks.

Maureen couldn't help but laugh at the sight. Eliza rushed over with a napkin to wipe the drops of spilled tea on Patrick's sleeve.

"I'm so sorry, Eliza."

"No harm done," she said. "Except to your cake."

"Oh, my," Patrick lifted his boot to see the crushed cake under the toe.

He drew out his handkerchief and wiped the shoe.

"Give that plate to me, Patrick." Eliza took the dish and motioned to Maureen. "Sit down, the both of you."

Maureen accepted the dainty cup Aunt Priscilla offered and took a seat beside Patrick. She sipped the tea and glanced at Patrick, hoping he would look at her. When he didn't, she looked around the parlor, trying to think of something to say. She admired the fashionable furnishings, the thick draperies and colorful carpet. It was so different from the rustic cabin her family called home. Maureen loved to come here, for its warmth as well as for the kindness of the close-knit family who lived here. The mood was pleasant, although Eliza's black dress reminded her of her friend's grief.

"And how are Robert and Amy? Still in Baltimore?"

Aunt Priscilla filled them in on the couple. They were coming home any day. Robert planned to move into his family's house and hoped to offer piano and singing lessons to some of the local children.

"Will he go back to the college?" Patrick asked.

"Not at present," Uncle Raymond said. "Too many steps to manage."

"And a wife who needs him very much," Aunt Priscilla added. "She's not been well, poor lamb. I couldn't leave her in Baltimore until her mother came. Once she arrived, I had to come straight home for Eliza. I never did have a chance to thank you, Maureen. Doctor Lee said you looked after my Eliza as well as he could have."

Maureen loved hearing that.

"We're expecting him any minute," Eliza said. "He wants to

check my arm. It hardly hurts at all anymore."

When there was another knock on the door, Patrick stood up. "Looks like you might need this seat. I best be going back."

"You just got here. And I know Maureen wanted to see you as much as she wanted to see me." Eliza's comment made Patrick blush again. He sat down and smiled stiffly.

Doctor Lee bustled into the room, peppering Eliza with questions about her health. He stopped when he saw Maureen to greet her. After inquiring about her parents, he told her Smoketown was short-staffed now that two of the finest nurses he knew were no longer there. "As you well know, the place was always short-staffed," he added.

Maureen avoided Patrick's eye, hoping to avoid yet another confrontation. "I miss the work. For now, though, my place is here."

"Understandable, considering all that's happened. I do hope when your parents are up to it, you'll be going back." Then without waiting for an answer, the doctor turned to Eliza. "Let me look at that arm."

"I really must be going." Patrick jumped up again.

"Patrick—" Eliza looked up, disappointment on her face.

"It's been very nice visiting, and I'm glad to see you looking so well." He turned and looked down at Maureen. He extended his hand toward her and asked softly, "May I walk you home?"

Maureen looked up at Patrick and then over at Eliza, who was nodding at her, a smile on her face. Then they said their goodbyes and Maureen promised to visit again soon.

Patrick was quiet as they walked down the front steps and turned toward the path under the apple trees.

"I've missed talking with you," he began suddenly. "I thought about stopping at your house a couple of times though I didn't know if I would be welcome."

"Whatever do you mean?" Maureen asked.

He looked straight ahead, not at her, as they continued toward her house. He didn't offer his arm. He didn't take her hand. Maureen missed the warmth of his touch.

190

"Our last meeting was less than I'd hoped for." He still wouldn't look at her. Finally, Maureen stopped on the path and tugged on his arm.

"Patrick, our last meeting came at the darkest hour of my life. You don't know the half of what happened."

"Of course, I do," he interrupted. "I lost my best friend. You lost your brother. Your best friend fell out of a carriage. You'd been sick. You'd worked yourself to exhaustion."

Then he looked at her. "I thought you might need a friend."

"I did," she whispered. "I wasn't thinking straight. It had been two days of one horrible thing after another. And you don't know everything that happened. I could only think of getting home to Mother and Father. I didn't understand what you were trying to tell me. I still don't."

She thought of how he haunted her thoughts and dreams.

He took her hand and held it against his chest. "All I want is you, Maureen."

She felt the beating of his heart as he continued in a soft voice. "I want you to love me as I love you. I want you to need me as I need you. I want you as my wife. I want to go into the next battle knowing you are at home waiting for me."

"Battle? Are you leaving the hospital?" She pulled her hand away and ran it through her hair. A familiar terror rose in her heart. His words weren't making any sense.

"Are you listening to me?" Patrick shoved his hands in his pockets as Maureen heard the exasperation in his voice. "I expect to be called back to my regiment soon. I'm fully recovered. The hospital is closing, and I must go back. The war is far from over, Maureen."

Maureen cried out in anguish. "Oh no, Patrick. Not you too."

She threw herself against his chest, and he wrapped his arms around her and held her tight until she quieted down. Then he held her far enough away to look into her red-rimmed eyes.

"Maureen." Patrick's voice was soft. She looked up at him and sniffed. "It's my duty to go. Just as it was Joe's. And all the boys we know. You know I have to go, don't you?"

She nodded. "Of course. I understand—"

191

"Will you at least think about it?" he asked.

"Think about what?" she asked.

"Will you think about marrying me? I won't rush you. But I would go gladly into battle if I have your promise in my heart."

It was the wrong thing to say. Maureen began to cry again. She shook her head. "No, no, no," she cried out between sobs as she ran away through the orchard. She heard him follow and then stop. She was glad. She couldn't bear the thought of saying goodbye again.

CHAPTER 27
NEW HOPE

"How could you, Maureen?" Eliza frowned at her friend.

Maureen hadn't slept after her conversation with Patrick the previous day. She'd paced the floor and stared into the last embers of the kitchen fire. By the time her parents were awake, the chickens had been fed, the fire was blazing and the water boiled on its hob. After breakfast, she had hurried over to tell Eliza what had happened.

"What do you mean?" Maureen said.

"He was asking you to marry him. Even I knew that's what he was fixing to do all afternoon."

"That didn't even sink in at the time." Maureen paced around her friend's parlor. "All I could think of was waving goodbye to my dear old Patrick and then getting a letter like the one my mother got. 'We regret to inform you...'"

"It doesn't have to be that way. And you, of all people, understand his duty to serve his country." Eliza frowned as Maureen crossed the room again and again.

Maureen saw sadness turn down the corners of her friend's mouth. "You're right. I'm sorry, Lizzie," she said. She sat on the divan, on the very spot where she sat with Patrick the previous day. She ran her hand over the silky fabric.

Had she lost him? Maureen didn't even realize she could have him.

She told Eliza about her endless night. She had suffered through emotions ranging from loss to regret to fear.

When dawn came, she realized that what really mattered was love. Patrick's love for her, and yes, she finally realized, her love for Patrick.

"He's been so stubborn, and I have been too mad at him to think about loving him." She knew Eliza was rooting for her. For both of them. Just as she had been since those early days in the Pry House hospital.

"He's going to come back to you. He always does." Eliza's voice was soft, soothing. "You are all he thinks about. He comes to visit me, and we talk about you."

"I'm sorry, Eliza," Maureen apologized.

Eliza smiled. "No need for that. It's sweet to see someone so completely in love."

"He's still dead set against my going back to Smoketown, isn't he?"

"I think so," Eliza said frankly. "I also believe he will respect whatever you decide to do while he is away."

"At war. He's going to be away at war. More Antietams and Fredericksburgs. Oh, Eliza, I can't sit around waiting for bad news." Maureen looked out the window, her feelings so raw she could hardly bear them.

"You won't be sitting around. You'll be tending to other women's Joes and Patricks. Keeping them alive, helping them get well. He'll understand that. Look at how impressed he was with the way you took care of me," Eliza said.

"Do you really think so?" Maureen sensed a flicker of hope kindling in her heart.

While they were speaking, Eliza's mother answered a knock at the door.

"We meet again." Patrick entered the parlor and bowed to both young women.

Maureen shot a glance at her friend. She could see Eliza holding back a smile.

"Good afternoon, Patrick." Eliza invited him to sit down and gestured to Maureen to sit beside him. "Now let me go see about some refreshments. Maureen, you stay and entertain our guest. I'll be back presently."

Off she went. Patrick put his Union cap on the glossy mahogany piano and sat beside Maureen.

"I'm sorry about yesterday, Patrick."

Patrick took her hand in his. His look was solemn. "No need to be. I suppose I was clumsy. I didn't mean to alarm you. I only meant to tell you how much you mean to me. How much I love you."

"Yes, Patrick." Maureen's heart leaped to her throat, and she took a deep breath.

This is it.

"And I love you."

"You do?" He looked surprised. And Maureen was taken aback by his response.

"Yes. I really do."

"Then why is this so hard?" He smiled at her, went down on one knee and took her hand. "Maureen Regina O'Neill, may I have the honor of asking for your hand in marriage?"

"Well, Patrick—I don't know your middle name—Toohey, I believe that the answer is…yes," she said and then added quickly, "And yet we have to have an understanding on some things."

Maureen watched the sudden delight on Patrick's face dim a little.

"I will happily marry you as long as you agree to my continuing as a nurse for as long as they will have me. And I'll want to continue making my home with my parents for as long as you are gone. I don't think my parents could bear to lose both of their children in the same year."

"I knew you would want to go back to Smoketown. I don't want you to go—"

"And I don't want you to go back to your regiment."

"I was going to say, we both have our duties to perform. It won't be forever. The war can't go on too much longer, can it? And then we'll be together and can raise a family and live happily every after." He slipped her hand in both of his and raised it to his lips.

"You make it sound like a fairy tale." Maureen delighted in his sweet kiss until a hint of reality made her pause. "You know we could have a sad ending."

"Don't let's think about that," Patrick said. "Let's enjoy this moment."

"Shouldn't you ask my father?"

"Already taken care of." Patrick smiled. "Yesterday."

Maureen wanted to kiss her new fiancé more than anything, but before she was able, Eliza returned with a tray. Maureen could tell by the sparkle in her eye that she knew everything. She had probably listened in the hall, waiting for the right moment to interrupt their tete-a-tete.

"It looks like you have some good news to share." She placed the tray on a small table and sat across from them, an expectant look on her face.

"Indeed, we have," Patrick said, a flush rising to his freckled cheeks. He took a cup of coffee from Eliza and handed it to Maureen. "Here, dear. Eliza, you are the first to know Maureen has agreed to be my wife."

Eliza jumped from her chair, shouted with glee and rushed to hug the two of them.

As she listened to Patrick announce their engagement, Maureen couldn't believe she had just agreed to spend the rest of her life with this man. She hadn't expected such a giddy kind of joy. So soon after she felt like she'd fallen into the abyss.

She knew Joe would have teased her mercilessly about falling for his best friend. She hoped, as a lump formed her throat, that he would approve.

"Maureen, are you feeling unwell?" Eliza looked anxiously at her friend.

"Yes, of course, I'm thrilled." Maureen forced a smile and then added with some hesitation, "I suddenly thought of Joe."

The little celebration grew quiet for the moment.

Patrick broke the sad moment. "Joe loved you both, you now. You, Moe, his sister, and you Eliza. He told me his one regret after joining the army was leaving you behind. He said he has always loved you."

His words were bittersweet. Maureen was thrilled to hear Joe's nickname for her and happily surprised by what he said to Eliza. As he spoke, Eliza dropped back into her chair and buried her face in her hands. She found it all difficult to hear.

Maureen flew to her side, pushed the extra embroidered pillows out of the way so she could squeeze into the chair with Eliza. She wrapped her arms around her friend and wept with her.

"I was expecting a celebration, but it looks more like a wake," Uncle Raymond said as he entered the room. "Lizzie, whatever's the matter, child?"

She looked up at her father with tears streaming down her pale cheeks. She wiped them away. "We were talking about Joe." Then she looked at her friends and her father. "I'm spoiling the fun, aren't I? I'm sorry, Maureen, Patrick. I miss him so much. I keep hoping one day he'll walk in."

Eliza struggled to smile and then hugged Maureen. "I'm so glad for you. You know I am."

Maureen nodded. She squeezed her friend, and Eliza trembled. As elated as she was about her engagement to Patrick, she understood Eliza's pain. She was thinking of Joe, too. And missing him.

Chapter 28
New Orders

Maureen's father came in from the yard, and much to her surprise, kissed her cheek. His tender gesture was far different from all the previous times she had packed up her haversack and headed out the front door. This time, he leaned on the table as she put in an extra petticoat and shawl and packed her Christmas presents. There was a book of poetry from Eliza and the scarf her mother knitted.

"I never thought I'd forgive you for going to that hospital," her father said.

"Neither did I," Maureen answered. "I believe I have my mother to thank for that."

"Will you be needing my gun, girl?"

Maureen looked up from her bag in alarm.

"Your mother told me. And she told me you had to use it. The only thing she didn't say was who you used it on. Did you kill anyone, Maureen?" He lowered himself carefully into his chair by the fire and stretched out his sore leg.

Maureen shook her head. "I thought I killed a man, a very bad man. It turns out I didn't. I found him wounded and alive at Smoketown."

"Gracious, girl! Did he know it was you who shot him?"

Maureen sat beside her father and reluctantly told him what happened and how Harvey had attacked her in the camp. She finished by crediting Eliza with saving her life.

"I must admit you girls have a lot of spirit. Where'd you learn to handle a gun? I don't remember letting you use mine."

"Joe taught me how to shoot the rifle. I had never shot a pistol before that day. And I've never shot one since. I was just lucky."

Maureen's father laughed heartily. And then stopped. "Are you going back to that hospital knowing that man is there waiting for you?"

"He's gone," Maureen said. "After he attacked me he was taken away."

Her father shook his head. "I've said it before, and I'll say it again. I still don't want you going there. I think you're putting your life in danger. It's one thing for a young man and quite another for my daughter."

"Father," Maureen began. She knew he meant what he said even though he had become resigned to her work. For that she was grateful.

"You're planning to defy me again, aren't you, girl?" Maureen knew by his tone he already knew the answer.

"Ya know that I am, Father," she said. "There's nothing you can say to stop me from going."

"I told you, Daniel." Her mother closed the back door, wiped her hands on her apron and sat down beside her husband. "There's no stopping your daughter when she's set her mind on something. We just have to let her go and hope for the best."

"Thank you, Mother," Maureen valued her mother's support. She could see the love in her mother's eyes. Even more, she could see the sadness that had settled there. Maureen wondered if her mother would ever smile again.

"I won't go if you need me here," Maureen added.

"No, I wouldn't keep you here." She shook her head and turned to her husband. "We'll be fine, your father and me, won't we, Daniel?"

"Indeed we will, Kate."

Maureen hoped they would be fine. They were in much better shape than the day she returned home. She still worried about her father's leg. Even though he was mostly recovered from his fall, he sometimes still struggled and refused to allow anyone to help him.

Losing Joe had been such a shock to them all. Now, however, Maureen understood better than ever how much her father cherished his wife and daughter. He had shaken off his bitterness to take care of his grief-stricken family.

Maureen's mother was improving, too. Once she had forced her husband to mend the rift between himself and their daughter, she had gone back to her old routine. She still spoke only when necessary. She worked without a word. She had little patience for small talk or, even worse, gossip. If she spoke, Maureen knew it was important, and she listened.

Maureen was grateful for the support she had finally received from her parents, especially her father. At last, they saw her as mature enough to take on adult responsibilities. Perhaps they still worried about her return to Smoketown and to nursing. Of one thing she was certain: they were thrilled at her coming marriage to Patrick.

As she finished packing, Maureen realized she was anxious to return. She had gained confidence in her abilities—and that was something that came from within herself, not from the approval of others. Not even her parents or Patrick. What was important as she said her goodbyes was something she knew she had all along, their love.

Smoketown looked different from the day she and Eliza left it more than a month before. The trees were finally stripped of their last leaves. Haze from the many fires wreathed the tents. But their warmth was no match for the frigid winter temperatures. Not only was it cold, the ground was slippery from the previous night's sleet. A gusty wind whistled through the branches of the trees and tugged at the tents.

Maureen pulled her shawl tighter as the wind wrestled to take it away. The cold crept through her heavy boots, making her last steps painful. Eliza shivered and held onto her friend.

At first glance, the camp looked deserted. The usual clusters of patients had given up their outdoor gathering spots on this chilly morning. Then Miss Patricia hurried by.

"As I live and breathe! Maureen and Eliza have returned." Patricia turned away from her planned destination to hug the new arrivals. She squeezed Eliza's hand and then examined Maureen, checked the scar on her throat and shook her head.

"What's wrong?" Maureen asked her.

"I hoped the two of you would have fattened up a little with some home cooking. We've all gotten thinner trying to eat the poison they serve us every day here. I was imagining you eating real meat, unspoiled potatoes, maybe a glass of fresh milk or … I get carried away." Patricia's frown turned into a quick laugh. "Gracious! We've missed you."

The noisy reunion brought Miss Hall out of her office tent.

"We're so happy to have you here with us again." She hugged Maureen and Eliza. Then as always, Miss Hall wore a smile as she doled out her crisp orders. "Ladies, we have an awful lot of work to do. Perhaps we should return to our duties and let Miss Maureen and Miss Eliza get settled. Make yourself at home, and we'll talk at dinner." Miss Hall smiled and returned to her desk.

"We have our orders," Miss Patricia whispered. "See you at noontime."

Maureen and Eliza fell into their old routines, putting away the few belongings they brought before sitting on their cots for a moment's rest.

Eliza pulled a crumpled letter from her pocket. When she sighed and sniffed, Maureen rushed to sit beside her.

"Has something happened?" she asked, looking at the letter.

"This? Oh, this is a letter from Amy." Eliza shook her head. "They're on their way home. Robert's doing well, all things considered, and Amy's morning sickness has gone away. She says she is getting bigger every day. Mama and Papa will be so glad to have them home again. I guess I'm feeling a little envious. Everybody is getting settled except me." Eliza sighed again. "I miss him, Maureen."

"I know you do. I do, too." Maureen wrapped her arm around her friend.

"Sometimes I dream he walks in through the hospital gates looking for me." Eliza stopped and blew her nose. "It could happen. We don't know for sure that was Joe's body they found in Virginia. Maybe he's alive somewhere. Haven't you wondered?"

Maureen nodded. "It's only wishful thinking. Look at all the women who have had to accept the death of their loved ones without seeing their faces ever again. I would have liked to see Joe one more time—even if it was after he died. We all would, I suppose. It would make it all final in a way it isn't now."

Eliza was silent. She stared straight ahead though she didn't seem to be looking at anything at all.

"I'm not ready to believe he's really gone," Eliza said. She smiled a brave little smile.

Maureen wound her arm in Eliza's. "It's hard, I admit. And yet, we must keep going. All these young men need us. You have your work. We have our work. We'll be partners until our work is done."

"You mean until you get married."

"I'm not going anywhere. Patrick and I have agreed not to marry until the war is over and he is home to stay." Maureen stood up. "Now wash your face and find a smile for the soldiers out there who need it so desperately. Let's find ourselves a couple of pinafores. Then we can go visiting until dinner when Miss Hall wants to see us."

Miss Angela smiled broadly as she rushed in. "Patricia just told me you'd arrived, Maureen."

They caught up on Joe's memorial service, how the family was faring and Maureen's engagement. Miss Angela listed all the soldiers who were no longer at Smoketown.

"I didn't hear you mention Rusty," Maureen said.

"He's still here. Now he's working as a nurse. After Doc took off his casts, he decided Rusty, I mean Allan, still wasn't strong enough for battle. So, he put him to work here in the camp. He'll move on when the camp closes."

"It's true then. It's closing?" Maureen's thoughts of Rusty vanished.

"It won't be for some time. We're discharging men every day. We still need the two of you here, dear." Angela patted the young woman's shoulder as she prepared to leave. "Other nurses have been transferred to other hospitals where the need is much greater. I'll let you get settled, and then there's work to be done."

Maureen was rooting through her haversack when she thought she heard Patrick's voice. Eliza stopped tying on her pinafore and looked at her friend.

"What's Patrick doing here?"

"I'm sure I don't know."

Maureen ran her fingers over her curly head, despairing over its unruliness. She brushed the dust from her favorite dress. Patrick had seen her green calico so often by now he probably thought it was the only dress she had. At least it was newly scrubbed so that the usually dingy lace collar was a bright white.

Then, unwilling to wait a second longer, she bolted from the tent and rushed into Patrick's arms. With his eye patch and his blue uniform, he cut a fine appearance.

Ignoring the proper etiquette of the moment, he pulled her close and kissed her, warmly, gently, and then a little more fervently. "I—"

He kissed her again, and Maureen was sure this was a kiss she would remember forever.

"I've got my orders. I have to go tomorrow. Sooner than I expected."

"Much sooner," she said.

"The army moves in its own way. I'm sorry, Maureen, I thought we might have more time. I hoped we would."

She looked at him carefully. The experiences of battle, his wounds and his long hours in the hospital had etched fine lines and shadows on his freckled face. His boyish look had faded.

"Then we have today. Let me talk to Miss Hall. I'm sure under the circumstances…" Something in Patrick's face made her stop. "We don't have even today, do we?"

He shook his head. "I have the usual army bureaucracy to attend to at the hospital, and my bag to pack and my mother has things for me to do. I'm sorry, Maureen. I only have a few minutes. Take a ride in my carriage with me. Unless you think it's too cold."

Even if it was snowing, Maureen wouldn't turn Patrick down. This would be the last time she saw him for … how long? They only had a few minutes, so she planned to cherish every one of them.

Patrick turned the carriage down the road toward Sharpsburg. They rode in silence, along a wooded path filled with memories of Ernestine and that man whose name she still couldn't say.

Patrick pulled off at a clearing that overlooked the rolling brown fields. He enfolded Maureen in his arms and sighed.

"I haven't even begun to get accustomed to this."

"Accustomed to what?" Maureen asked.

"Holding you in my arms. I dreamed of it for so long. And now here you are, and it's the last time."

"Don't say that, Patrick. It will only be a little while, and then you'll be home."

"We may not have time for a wedding, but I made time to bring you a proper wedding ring," Patrick said. "I want you to have it now as a sign of our promise."

He pulled a small gold ring from his pocket. A pebble-sized sapphire glittered from its filigree setting. "It was my grandmother's. My father's mother. Before she died a few years ago, she gave it to my mother and said I should give it to the woman I wanted to marry. Mama said she hoped it would remind us that love can last a lifetime. My Mom-mom and Pop-pop always seemed happy together."

"It's beautiful, Patrick." He slipped it on her finger, only a smidgen too big. "I'll wrap thread around the back and it will be perfect," she said.

Maureen loved the pretty blue stone. It was a grand ring, like nothing she had ever expected. She thought of her mother's thin gold band, a ring she'd never removed since her wedding day.

"It looks good on your tiny hand." His lips grazed her knuckles before he pulled her hand around his neck to kiss her cheek, her throat, her mouth.

Then he buried his face in her shoulder. "I will miss you so much."

"Me, too," was all Maureen could say.

They might have remained in their embrace for hours if not for the impatience of Patrick's pony. She was getting restless and shifted enough to move the carriage.

"Amber has had enough of our farewells, I'm afraid. I suppose I must take you back." Patrick sighed, picked up the reins and signaled the horse to move.

On the way back, Patrick asked Maureen about Smoketown.

"It's closing in a few weeks. Some of the nurses have already moved on to other hospitals. Miss Patricia said she and Miss Angela are staying until it closes."

"Most of the hospitals around here have closed. I think Smoketown is about the last one. What will you do then?"

"Maybe I'll go to a new hospital. I'll find another way to help. I'll keep busy. And I'll miss you."

"Will you write to me?" he asked as he pulled her close to him.

"I promise I will. I've gotten much better with my penmanship. My spelling still needs work, but I have been studying."

The ride back ended too quickly. Maureen hated to get out of Patrick's carriage. He jumped out ahead of her to help her down and to wrap his arms around her again. As they kissed again, she pulled him closer to feel his body warm against hers.

"I must go," he whispered at last.

She nodded and took his hand for one last moment.

"Stay safe," Maureen asked him.

"Stay out of the wards with catching diseases," he answered her.

Then he climbed in the carriage and urged his horse down the road.

Maureen watched him go, waiting to see if he would turn one last time. Just before he passed through the gate, he did. He waved his Union cap, and she savored the look of love in Patrick's eyes.

CHAPTER 29
NEW ARRIVAL

"Wake up, dreamer," Eliza said in a sing-song voice as Maureen stood in the middle of the camp.

"What? Oh, I guess I was, a little." Maureen turned her gaze to the ring around her finger. "Look what Patrick just gave me."

Eliza grabbed her friend's hand to have a good look at the sapphire ring and then stared at Maureen, wide-eyed. "It's beautiful! Aren't you a lucky girl?"

Maureen nodded with a joyful smile. "Aren't I, though? It was his grandmother's, a gift from her husband. Now it's mine."

As she admired the sapphire's sparkle, she told Eliza about their short carriage ride, about his orders to report to his regiment, about the ring.

Patricia was bustling by when she saw the two staring at Maureen's hand. "Miss Patricia!" Eliza called. "Maureen has gotten a present."

She held up Maureen's left hand. "Isn't it beautiful?"

"What's this?" Patricia asked.

"A gift from Patrick. We're getting married...someday."

"Well, goodness gracious, all the best wishes to a fine young woman and her intended." Patricia threw her arms around Maureen. "Was that your young man that I saw whisking you away a while ago?"

Maureen blushed.

"Yes, it was," Eliza answered. "Patrick Toohey. He's a local boy. One of the heroes of the Battle of Antietam."

"A soldier," Patricia said.

"An old friend," Maureen said, her blush deepening.

"I'm so happy for—" Patricia started to say until the rattle of carriage wheels racing up Smoketown Road interrupted her.

206

The three women turned as it clattered into the space ambulances usually used.

A small dark-skinned girl jumped out before the horse even stopped.

"Help me!" she cried.

"Ernestine!" Maureen ran to her. "Ernestine! What's the matter? Are you hurt?"

Terror was etched in the teenager's face.

"No, not me. I was walking along the road behind a soldier." Ernestine wrung her hands and pointed to the wagon. "He collapsed right in front of me. By the time I got to him, he was barely conscious, and the cut on his face was bleeding. I gave him some water from my jug here and wiped the blood from his face."

Ernestine's eyes shone with concern. Her white shirtwaist was soiled, a smear of blood across the front.

"Where's the soldier now?" Maureen asked.

Ernestine grabbed Maureen's hand and pulled her toward the carriage. "I had helped him up and was trying to bring him here. He needs a doctor."

Ernestine looked up at the man holding the reins. "This man helped me. He carried both of us here."

It was Patrick.

"Patrick?" Maureen had just watched him leave, and here he was again.

"Can you help him?" he asked, his eyes slipping toward the back of his wagon.

"This soldier stopped when I called to him," Ernestine continued. "Please, please, I called, and he stopped right away. He helped me pick up the man and put him in the carriage."

Maureen, Eliza and Patricia climbed to find a soldier, bloodied and ragged, lying on the floor of the carriage. It wasn't long before a crowd of curious soldiers had surrounded the carriage. Angela came running to see what all the commotion was.

"Please, allow us room to work," Angela commanded. "You there," she pointed at two of the strongest-looking men. "Help us carry him into that tent."

DIVIDED LOYALTIES

The man they carried weighed about as much as petite Ernestine. He groaned as they moved him. He was gaunt and appeared to have had nothing to eat for days. His face was blackened by the dust on the road. A long thin scar down his cheek had traces of fresh blood. A thick dirty bandage was wrapped around his left arm.

His uniform was frayed at every seam, and the color was neither blue nor gray. It was more of a dirty brown. And it didn't fit his wiry frame at all. He wore no shoes and from the look of the calluses on his heels he had gone without shoes for some time. His eyes never opened but his breathing was regular.

Maureen held onto Ernestine's hand as they went into the tent. Patrick followed silently behind them.

After he was settled on the cot, Angela went through his pockets looking for identification. All of them were empty. Eliza brought a clean, damp cloth, and gently dabbed at his face.

"His face is so cold," she murmured as the man's features emerged from layers of dirt and blood.

"Maureen…" Eliza looked up with surprise and wonder. Her eyes grew to an enormous size, and she beamed a joyous smile.

"What is it?" Maureen looked at Eliza and then at the soldier.

"It's our Joe," Eliza exclaimed.

"Joe!" Maureen breathed. She rushed to Eliza's side and stooped beside her. "It can't be. Our eyes are deceiving us."

"Oh, Maureen, it is, isn't it? It's Joe!"

Maureen recoiled and shook her head, as if she was looking at a ghost. "No," she repeated over and over. Her head throbbed, and her hands grew cold as ice. She stared at the motionless face which bore little trace of the brother she loved and missed. She began to cry.

Patrick crouched down beside her and gathered her in his arms. "It's all right, Maureen," he whispered.

Maureen buried her hot, wet face in the scratchy wool of his coat. Yes, she wanted it to be Joe. But Joe was dead. He was gone forever. No amount of wishing would bring him back. When she was quiet, when she could force herself to breathe regularly, she turned to look at the soldier again. She held onto Patrick's arm with such force she was afraid she would hurt him. How she needed his strength.

Eliza's gaze was trained on the wounded man. She held his hand as if she was afraid to let it go.

"It really is Joe."

Maureen couldn't believe it. This man couldn't be her brother. She looked at him, his high forehead, his pronounced cheekbones, his thin lips. She didn't dare believe. Sure, he had the map of Ireland on his face same as she did. Yet, she still didn't believe. This wasn't Joe.

"Eliza," she began to say when the man's eyes fluttered open.

"'Liza." His voice was raspy.

"I'm here, Joe," Eliza whispered, delight coloring her words. "Maureen and Patrick are here, too."

The man turned and looked around, a look of confusion in his eyes until they rested on Maureen. "Moe," he murmured.

Maureen's heart swelled, and she gasped at hearing her brother's name for her. Even though her eyes still didn't recognize the man on the pallet, only Joe had ever called her "Moe."

Eliza called to her and Maureen obeyed.

"I'm here, Joe," Maureen forced the words from her lips. He turned and looked at her again.

"At last." He sighed and closed his eyes.

"Joe!" Maureen cried in alarm. She feared he was dead and then his eyes slowly opened again.

"I'm so tired." A weak smile formed on his lips.

Eliza brushed the hair from his forehead and leaned to place a kiss gently over his right eye and then on his lips. "Yes, Joe. You need your rest. We'll talk when you wake up."

And then she added, unselfconsciously, "I'm so glad you're here, my love."

Maureen marveled at Eliza's composure at a moment so strange and unexpected. Though she was still reeling from the possibility that this stranger might be her brother, Eliza's faith was complete.

Angela and Patricia gestured for the three of them to withdraw from the tent while they peeled off his tattered coat and the rags packed under them for warmth and bathed him.

DIVIDED LOYALTIES

Once outside, Eliza could no longer contain her joy. She raised her hands over her head and shouted amid the crowd of patients gathered to hear the news about the stranger. The men, in return, cheered. Even if they didn't know exactly what was going on, they clapped each other on the back and shook Eliza's hand.

Maureen wanted to feel their infectious joy, and yet her heart wasn't ready for any disappointment that still might come. She wasn't sure the newcomer was her brother.

"Wishes do come true. He's come back to me, Maureen, he's come back," Eliza shouted as she flew into Maureen's arms.

Then she swung her friend around and laughed a grand laugh.

"You are certain, then?" Maureen was breathless.

"With all my heart, Maureen. I know that's my Joe."

"The Army said——"

"The Army was wrong, Maureen. Some other man is dead, not Joe."

Maureen wanted to believe, but the pain of her grief, of the grief of her parents had gouged such a deep gash into her heart.

Eliza, her eyes aglow and her smile beatific, danced over to Ernestine and hugged her.

"Thank you, thank you, my dear new friend," Eliza said to her. "You've saved my love!"

She raced over to Patrick and hugged him, laughing. "Joe's come back to us."

Eliza's faith gave Maureen a wisp of hope. Maybe Eliza was right. Maybe the man Angela and Patricia were tending to really was her brother.

"Do you think it's really Joe?" she asked Patrick. She looked up at him, and he silently nodded.

She held onto him as her strength left her. His hold on her tightened, and she gave in to his support. Her breath quickened as the impossible became the possible.

Miss Hall emerged from her tent, filled with questions about the crowd that hovered.

"Miss Hall! It's my Joe." Eliza giggled as she announced her good news.

"Joe?" Miss Hall looked from girl to girl, waiting for an answer.

Maureen stepped forward. Even if she wasn't convinced, Miss Hall was owed an explanation. "My brother. My fiancé Patrick and my friend Ernestine have brought a soldier to the hospital. It's my brother Joe. I feel like the father in the story of the Prodigal Son. He was dead, but now he's alive. Miss Angela and Miss Patricia are inside right now, tending to my brother Joe."

Miss Hall told the men to disperse before turning to Maureen and Eliza. "Now ladies, while Angela and Patricia tend to this young man's wounds I need you to do a few things." She turned to Eliza. "Eliza, would you be so kind as to call the doctor? He's somewhere around here. You'll have to look for him." Eliza nodded, and Miss Hall turned to Maureen.

"Maureen, why don't you take your guests to the mess tent? Let them warm up a little by the stove, get some coffee, and we'll call you after the doctor has seen the patient. I can't imagine it will take too long."

Eliza danced away, while Maureen led Patrick and Ernestine toward the mess tent.

"You know this girl?" he whispered, nodding in Ernestine's direction.

"Yes, I do. We had a long and difficult day together once upon a time. Let me tell you about it some day. Would you like some coffee, Ernestine? You must be so cold."

"I don't think I should." Ernestine tucked her package under her arm and wore a frown on her face. "I really must be going. I was already in a hurry when I came across this man."

"Please stay at least for a moment. I'd love to hear how you've been faring." Maureen led her toward a table. If that man was indeed Joe, Maureen knew she owed Ernestine an inestimable debt. Perhaps she had saved Joe's life. Maureen still wasn't ready to accept that this new patient was her brother. She didn't know how she could face a new round of grief if it wasn't.

"How come I haven't seen you around here?" she asked Ernestine after she handed out cups of coffee.

"I try to stay away from this road since, well, you know. Today

211

though, I was running an errand for my mama, and this was the quickest route." Ernestine showed a parcel wrapped in brown paper. "I was hoping to get back home before the snow. Mama's going to worry. She worries about me a lot, you know."

Then Ernestine rose to leave. "I thank you for the coffee. And I'm grateful this man—I'm sorry I don't know your name," she said to Patrick.

Where are my manners? Maureen thought as she wound her hands around Patrick's arm.

"This man is my fiancé, Patrick. Patrick, this is Ernestine. We became friends after the fighting in September. Would you like Patrick to take you home?"

Ernestine shook her head. "It's not far to go, and now I must hurry." She rushed out of the tent and Maureen followed her.

"How has your hand healed?" she asked.

Ernestine held her hand up and wiggled her fingers. Her deep brown, slender hand bore an ugly scar. The little finger curled in an unnatural way and didn't move with the others. "Almost back to normal."

She looked from her hand to Maureen. "I was lucky. I can sew and knit almost as well as I could before. Didn't really slow me down none."

She stopped, and a troubled look crossed her pretty coffee-colored face.

"What is it?"

"Mama and me, we're heading to Buffalo once spring comes."

"Buffalo? Why so far?" Maureen said.

"Mama has people living up there. They say it's safer for us. Mama wanted to go when she first heard what happened to me. She says this ain't no place for us no more."

Ernestine shifted from one foot to the other. "She worries someone else will come after me, so she keeps me in her sights most of the time. She wanted to go before now, but there's already too much snow up north."

Then she paused for a moment. "You know I ran into that man. I saw him right after you and I met. He was all bandaged up at this very hospital. He was sitting in a chair near the road and smoking a cigar, like he was somebody."

Maureen started. "Did he see you?"

"Yes, ma'am, he did, but you know sometimes it's good to be invisible. Folks like me is invisible a lot. I was invisible to him that day. He looked right at me and then through me with nary a hint of recognition. Just to be safe, I never walked past here again until today," she said.

"I'm so glad you walked past here today."

"I guess it turned out to be lucky."

"And, Ernestine? That man was arrested. He attacked me when he realized who I was."

"Then he got what was due him. He don't belong out with proper people. I hope they throw away the key," Ernestine began to turn away. "And now I best be going."

With a nod, Ernestine pulled her heavy shawl tighter around her thin shoulders and marched down the road.

Maureen ran out after her.

"Patrick will take you. You shouldn't be going out if there's going to be snow."

Ernestine shook her head. "I got to go now. My mama won't be happy if I don't get this package delivered. It looked to me like your man ain't quite ready to say goodbye yet. But I got to go."

She stopped for a minute. Maureen waited for Ernestine to decide what she wanted to say. "I'm happy things are turning out so well for you. He seems like a mighty fine man. If you don't mind my saying so."

Maureen hugged her tightly. "I'm so glad you're well, and I wish you all the best as you move north."

Ernestine nodded and hurried away.

Maureen returned to Patrick, her heart full of joy. Maureen didn't know if she'd ever seen so many good things all at once.

She smiled at her fiancé.

"So what was that all about?" he asked.

"What?"

"That girl, Ernestine."

"Yes, Ernestine. We met on the road the very first time I came to Smoketown." Maureen decided to omit any mention of how the two of them met. A smile played on her lips as she realized the burden of mortal sin, of thinking herself a murderer, could be put to rest. If she had felt like bursting before, now she was giddy.

"Is there something you're not telling me? You look as if you have something on your mind."

Maureen shook her head. She didn't think she needed to tell Patrick the whole story. It was over and done with. She was glad that she hadn't committed a grievous sin. She was even glad that awful man wasn't dead; she hadn't killed him after all. She was glad that Ernestine had not only survived, but she had also thrived. Maureen was glad she had seen her again.

"No, we met on the road near here and spent an evening together with the sisters." She avoided his gaze.

"Maureen." He turned and looked at her. "We shouldn't have secrets between us. Did something happen? Is there something you are afraid to tell me?"

Maureen looked straight ahead and shook her head. "No, Patrick. It's nothing important. Maybe someday it'll be a story worth telling."

"Very well." From his look, Maureen could tell he was none too pleased. "If you decide you want to tell me what you're keeping from me, I promise you needn't worry about what I'll say. You know you can trust me."

She smiled at him, wavering for a moment in her decision. "That's good to know."

CHAPTER 30
LOOKING INTO THE FUTURE

It seemed like a dream. Maureen could hardly shake the feeling she was asleep and having the most wonderful dream. Even if it was all real, she couldn't believe it. And it was all real.

She was still waving to Ernestine when Miss Patricia beckoned her and Patrick to see Joe. Maureen could hardly feel her feet touch the ground as she stepped inside the tent. Eliza was already sitting beside him, her hand firmly clasped in his.

"Moe!" Joe called to her with a hoarse, weak voice.

She stooped down beside him and took his free hand. "We thought you were dead."

"Did you now? I'm happy to tell you that you were wrong." A hint of a smile played on his lips.

Such hollow cheeks, almost like a skeleton, Maureen thought.

"Eliza filled me in. She said the service was very sad but beautiful."

Maureen's heart felt like it would burst as she drank in the sight of her brother. It really was Joe.

Once strong and vibrant, he had clearly fought to live. It wasn't just his cheeks. His bony shoulders poked through the thin white cotton of the nightshirt he now wore. His eyes were sunken. Usually clean shaven, a shaggy dark beard fringed his razor sharp jaw. The hand she held was scarred and rough. Wherever he had been, it had been harsh.

And yet here he was, she thought, her heart full of gratitude that he had returned home. She had thought he was gone forever.

"Where have you been all this time? Why did your regiment think you were dead?" she asked.

Joe looked at her and joy lit his eyes. "To tell you the truth I was left for dead. I wasn't no goner. No sir. I have to give the credit to

215

a big dark man who took me in and nursed me. Never did hear his name. He didn't talk much, you see."

Maureen leaned in as Joe's voice got quieter. He stopped for a moment. Then he continued his story.

"I'd been walking for days. Since I got separated from my regiment, I'd been trying to catch up to them, you see. I don't want you to think I'm a deserter or anything like that, Maureen. I'm no coward."

Joe's eyes searched Maureen's and then Eliza's. "I wanted to fight from the minute I left the farm. I met up with Union soldiers on my way into town and then there were plenty of Rebs all over Sharpsburg. They'd taken over the town. Hundreds of them, thousands of them. I never saw so many men in my life. They were everywhere."

Joe went on to tell his sister, Eliza and Patrick how he started on his way to Hagerstown to enlist. He was part way to the place where he would sign up when a farmer on his way to Gettysburg stopped to give him a ride. "He figured it might be safer at his sister's farm up in Pennsylvania. I don't know what happened to him. I guess he made it fine."

Joe's travels took him from the enlistment office in Hagerstown to a training camp somewhere in Pennsylvania called Camp Curtin. From there he joined the Army of the Potomac just as it was marching into Virginia. "I only had one chance to write. Did you get my letter?"

Maureen nodded.

"I hoped to get leave but couldn't work it out. And I hoped to write more. With all the marching and drilling I was always dead tired by supper time. I would've thought farm work would have made me fit for a soldier, but I never marched so much in my life."

Joe stopped as a cough wracked his chest. When he recovered, he began again. "Then I got sick with something that kept me in bed for weeks. The field hospital was filled with people even before they took one shot at a Reb."

Joe's eyes glittered as he recalled his days of learning to be a soldier, getting to know people from all over the country, and long hours when he wondered if he would ever see battle.

Eliza laid her hand on his shoulder when he paused.

"I finally did, Patrick, I finally did see battle." He looked at his old friend and nodded as he recalled the days near Fredericksburg. "George Washington grew up in Fredericksburg."

Maureen heard the note of awe in his voice. She had always been amused by her brother's interest in his new country, now a country he had offered his life for. And which, she realized with a hitch in her breath, he had not had to give.

"We set up camp on a hill near a river in Virginia with a long twisty name I can't ever remember. And then we waited. We must've been there a month. I lost track. Every day was the same. Bad food and lots of drilling. I wondered what I was there for. We couldn't get across the river for about three weeks. The Rebs knew we were there. When we crossed the river, the Rebs were lined up right on the other side shooting at us."

"Well, it looked good at first, except for all that shooting. We took over the town of Fredericksburg, a mighty pretty place, I thought. Then the Confederates turned the tables and beat us out of town. It was a terrible battle, and it went on for days. There was this place called Marye's Heights that we kept fighting for. When it was over, we had been whipped."

Joe was silent. Maureen thought his frail shoulders quivered as if he was stopping a sob. She knew she wanted to sob.

"Burnside, he was our general, he finally gave up and led us, or what was left of us, back to the other side," Joe continued.

"And you weren't hurt?" Maureen asked.

"Oh no, some Reb got me as we retreated." He raised his arm, now covered with a fresh bandage. "I fell and slid down that hill before I could cross with the general. I finally stopped when I hit a corpse. By then I was dizzy and disoriented. I thought I was going to die just like the guy next to me."

Joe didn't remember how long he lay there. He didn't have the strength to move.

He didn't have a gun to fight with anymore either. He lost it as he slid. Finally, he blacked out from the loss of blood.

When he woke up, he was in a tiny cabin with a dirt floor. A man

DIVIDED LOYALTIES

found him still alive on the battlefield and carried him to his house. There he took care of Joe until he woke up.

"That nice colored man—you should have seen him, so big he didn't look like he could fit inside—was sitting beside me, wiping my face with cool water," Joe said.

When the man saw Joe was awake, he brought him food and then put him on his horse to take him to an army field hospital. The hospital was really a house, overcrowded with injured men.

"He probably saved my life, and I don't even remember his name," Joe said.

Joe told them about the awful conditions at the hospital. He remembered the chaos and the noise as dozens of injured soldiers cried out in pain and fear. He saw men whose legs and arms had been amputated and worried about the fate of his injured arm.

"I guess they thought I was going to die and there wasn't any reason to chop mine off," he said. "I didn't die, but I wanted to. That hospital was an awful flea-bitten place, full of bugs. And it smelled to high heaven."

A place like here, Maureen realized. She nodded. She could certainly picture it.

Then he got a fever as infection set in his arm. He said there was a long time he couldn't even remember because he was either unconscious or deranged.

Then one day he woke up as a nurse was wiping his brow. "I got better after that."

Once he was recovered, he was sent back to his regiment. "I got separated somewhere near the Potomac River. I knew if I followed the river, I'd find home and then I could find out where I ought to be going."

"We were told you were dead. Mother and Father... Oh, Joe. We have to get word to Mother and Father."

Patricia who was hovering nearby patted her shoulder. "We've already taken care of that." Maureen smiled with gratitude.

"We have your rosary and your pocket book at home. How could we...?"

Joe laughed. "Heaven plays funny tricks on us now and again.

Some guy, from I don't even remember where, stole my good coat. All my money, my rosary and my letter from Eliza were in that coat. I wasn't wearing it at the time; it was too hot. Then when I went to get it—I'd hung it on a branch to keep it looking nice—my buddy said this guy had picked it up for me. That was a lie. I went looking for him and when I confronted him, he said he didn't know what I was talking about. And he was wearing my coat."

"So he's the one that's dead?" Eliza asked.

"I would suppose so."

Patrick, who had remained quiet, spoke up. "I'm sorry that fellow's dead but I'm thrilled for my friend and these two lovely ladies. I've been taking good care of them while you were away."

"And, what, may I ask, have you been doing so close to home with a war on? I suppose it has something to do with that eye patch," Joe asked his friend.

Patrick nodded. "I discovered eyeballs and bayonets do not mix."

"Were you at Antietam, Pat?"

"I was. And so was Robert. He's on his way home from Baltimore." After a pause, he said, "I suppose I ought to tell you Tommy's dead. Zack too."

"Oh, no." Joe was silent for a moment. "Poor Tom. Wouldn't kill a fly if it bit him. Damn war."

"That's what Mother said right after your funeral," Maureen said.

"There's good news," Patrick added. "Maureen and I are engaged to be married."

"Moe! Patrick finally wore you down," Joe teased. Patrick blushed. "He's been sweet on you a long time."

"Look at us," Eliza said. "All together again. I feel like dancing."

"I wish I could join you." Joe looked at her with a smile. "Today isn't a good day for me to be dancing."

Maureen saw a light in her brother's eyes she had never noticed before. Thrilled for them, she took Patrick's hand and squeezed it.

Maureen had never known a happier moment, nor one so

filled with hope. Someday—soon, she hoped—she'd marry the shopkeeper's son. Eliza would marry Joe and become her sister. Maybe one day, they would gather around them a flock of youngsters in their little town by Antietam Creek.

"Patrick," she whispered.

"Yes, Maureen?"

"I needed you all to myself just for a moment." She drew him outside to a quiet place in the sunshine.

Patrick smiled and took her in his arms. He was warm and strong. He smelled of wool, horse and bay rum. Maureen drank it all in. He lifted her chin to kiss her softly.

"Come home to me," she whispered.

"I will," he promised.

Maureen knew better than to feel her life was set. All she dreamed for was here: her love, her work, her family. Yet the war still raged. Patrick would soon be far away. And she had work to do.

She kissed Patrick again. She hoped the war would end soon. Until then, she was willing to pray, serve as a nurse and wait for peace.

EPILOGUE

Dear Mother and Father,

We are on our way. When we pulled out of the station today, I thought of you. I wondered if I felt as you did the day the ship left the docks in Ireland. I'm excited but I'm scared, too. Patrick takes my hand and promises it will be good for us.

Did you feel such hope and despair? I am so hopeful for our future out West. But I am despondent of leaving you and the farm and Sharpsburg behind, especially knowing I may never return. I am hopeful, too, that we will meet again. And soon.

Tell Eliza her namesake is a fussy baby. She reminds me of my dear friend. Her eyes are so bright. Her hair—yes, I see hair finally making its appearance! Her hair is as blond as Eliza's. I hope she and Joe are as excited about their new arrival as we are with ours. I know her time draws near.

Patrick claims I am spoiling baby Eliza and then he holds her all evening until she falls asleep in her Papa's arms.

We are well, Father. Please don't worry about us. Patrick says we'll be on the road for a several weeks until we arrive in the Colorado Territory. Patrick's Army buddy has already moved to Golden and said the growing town is sorely in need of a shopkeeper. Patrick can't wait to get there.

As for me, I'm enjoying the scenery as we pass through this big country of ours. Since we crossed the Alleghenies, we have passed through farms as wide and long as the great blue sky. Acres and acres of grain. I thought I'd seen enough cornfields to last a lifetime but I never saw anything like this.

Already we see a big city in the distance. I think it's St. Louis though the buildings are only tiny specks on the horizon so far.

I pointed them out to Patrick but he can't see them, of course. His sight in his injured eye isn't improving and I worry that he strains his good eye.

DIVIDED LOYALTIES

He can see me well enough to tell me I look pretty. Old married people and he still tells me that.

Little Lizzie is getting restless. I better see to her dinner. Next letter, I'll tell you more.

All my love,
Maureen

ACKNOWLEDGEMENTS

I have so many people to thank for helping me turn an idea into this story.

I want to thank my family, particularly my husband Raymond Truitt, my children Gina, Sean and Brigid, and my father William Tilghman, for all their encouragement and patience. I know I talked their ears off as I researched and wrote this story.

I am so grateful for the honesty and support of my critique group, wonderful writers in their own right: Kimberly Butler, Margaret Bates, Alexa Jacobs, Nellie Jane Romance, Patty Lacey and Kristie Wolf.

I am thankful for the careful editing of my work by Amy Donnelly of Alchemy and Words, LLC, for the professional advice of Jamie Bischoff and for the delightful cover artwork by Megan Tilghman.

I counted on a lot of experts to get historical details right: the librarians at the Maryland Historical Society's H. Furlong Baldwin Library who found all sorts of treasures about the Battle of Antietam and Civil War nurses in their collection including a 1910 pamphlet in honor of the National Association of Civil War Army Nurses.

Also, Terry Reimer, director of research at the National Museum of Civil War Medicine in Frederick, Stephanie Gray, curator at Antietam National Battlefield, Allison Seyler, archivist at the B&O Railroad Museum, and John Banks who writes a Civil War blog.

And finally, thanks to the authors whose books help me understand various aspects of life after the Battle of Antietam. These include Ross Kelbaugh, who wrote the 2012 *Maryland's Civil War Photographs: The Sesquicentennial Collection;* Kathleen A. Ernst, author of *Too Afraid to Cry: Maryland Civilians in the Antietam Campaign*; Terry Reimer, author of *One Vast Hospital: The Civil War Hospital Sites in Frederick, Maryland, after Antietam,*

Also, Charles J. Stille, who in 1866 published *History of the United*

States Sanitary Commission being The General Report of Its Work During the War of the Rebellion.

Thanks to everyone who read *Divided Loyalties.* I hope you love my brave nurse and her friends and family as much as I do.

For more information and news for my upcoming books, go to MaryKTilghmanWrites.com.

COMING IN JULY 2019
The prequel to *DIVIDED LOYALTIES*

Love Letters & Gingerbread

WHAT IS LOVE? For Patsy, it's the passion burning in her heart for faithless Vincent who fails to write after he goes away. For practical Angela, love is the tasks that fill her day taking care of her grieving mother and little sister.

Life has changed for the Harris family since the death of their father. Their house is sold and they plan to move to the outskirts of Annapolis to live with their mother's brother Max.

While eighteen-year-old Patsy pines for Vincent, William, their new neighbor, showers her with kindnesses. Angela finds unexpected emotions rising in her heart when she catches the eye of Gordon, a student who lives in Williamsburg.

With the approach of Christmas and, more importantly for Patsy, the Winter Ball, Patsy finds her heart rent in two over a man who has forgotten her and one so close and so kind. Angela, who considers herself a spinster, resists giving her heart to Gordon—but can't help the fears that rise up when a visiting Virginian hints that she is in love with a student at home.

This novella set in 1831 Annapolis, a prequel to Divided Loyalties inspired by the stories of Jane Austen, tells the love stories of two of the Civil War nurses, Angela and Patricia back when they were young.

Chapter 1
Letters

"Patsy, you have a letter!" Angela called from her usual seat at her desk in the drawing room. Patsy skipped merrily down the steps to pluck the small white square her sister held aloft.

Angela's pile of mail was always serious, filled with all the correspondence and bills she had taken over since Father's death.

If a letter was addressed to Patsy, it was happy news, often a message from her beloved Vincent. This one, as she hoped, was from her beau. She instantly recognized the big loops and decorative capitals of his penmanship.

She giggled as she clutched it to her bosom and ran to the sun-warmed window seat in a corner of the room. Her constant companion, a little brown and white pup named Timmy, danced beside her.

She gathered him up and stroked his head as she sat for a moment to study the pages that so recently were in Vincent's hands. She relished the idea that he had thought of her, dreamed of meeting her again, longed to be by her side. Then, as she felt the heat of a pink blush rush up her face, she tore open the letter.

Though Vincent Stewart only lived four doors away, the romantic young man thrilled Patricia with these tiny declarations of love several times a week.

But this one was different. She knew immediately. It was short, addressed only to Dear Patricia. Why didn't it say "Dearest?" she wanted to know.

She quickly scanned the few lines he had written and gasped. None of it made sense. He was leaving? For Frederick? Until the New Year?

"Oh Vincent, how could you!" Patsy's voice was filled with

1

despair. Little Timmy hopped up and stared at her, his tail wagging.

"What is it, dear?" Angela looked up from her correspondence. Even if she was sure her sister couldn't possibly understand, Patsy needed to tell someone.

"Vincent is going away. He'll be gone until the New Year." She sighed heavily and looked back at the letter. "And I've been knitting the perfect Christmas present for him. His mother's family invited them to spend the winter in Frederick." Her mood became blacker as soon as she realized something terrible. "He won't be here for the Winter Ball."

"Oh, Patsy. Your first dance and he won't be there."

Patricia appreciated her sister's sympathy, even though it wouldn't help.

"I can't imagine why they're going away now." She wiped her damp eyes and stood up as she folded the letter and put it in her pocket. "At least he promises to write while he is gone. That is something."

"Won't you see him before he leaves?"

Patsy shook her head. "He's leaving tomorrow. He says his parents have him running around as they get everything packed for the journey. So our carriage ride with his mother yesterday was the last time I'll see him in 1831. It will be 1832 before I see him again."

"It's only three months," Angela said.

"Nearly a hundred days. That's a long time without the love of my life." She sighed again. "I better go write a farewell note." She trudged out of the drawing room, every step heavy as she climbed the stairs. Timmy raced after her, his paws clicking on wood floors.

A knock on the front door stopped Patricia in her tracks. Perhaps Vincent had come. Perhaps he was coming to say goodbye in person.

She flew down the steps and swung open the door. A brisk autumn gust tore the note from her hand as she came face to face with its author.

"Mr. Stewart!" Patricia was breathless as she took in the sight of the young man. He stood there with his broad-brimmed tan hat in his hand. And he was wearing her favorite tailcoat in a beautiful shade of dove gray.

"May I come in? It's quite cold today." If his tone was sharp, Patricia didn't notice. Her dog, who stood nearby, growled and ran for his pillow in the drawing room.

She was overwhelmed to see him so soon after receiving his letter. She took his hat, thrilled to see the curly brown hair and fiery dark eyes she loved so much.

Recalling Angela was busy with the bills, Patricia wrapped her arm around his and suggested he accompany her to the kitchen. "It's much warmer there. Perhaps you'd like a cup of tea?"

Once she had put down his hat on the kitchen table and put the tea kettle on to boil, Vincent gathered her up in his arms. "I'm so sad to be leaving you, dearest Patsy."

Patricia nearly swooned in his embrace, to hear him use her given name, to feel his warm arms about her. "So am I, Mr.—" She giggled a little and blushed. "So am I, Vincent. You won't be here for Christmas or New Year's. Or for so many things. Not even the Winter Ball."

When the water began to boil she invited him to take the chair by the fire while she filled the teapot.

Instead, Vincent waited only until she moved the kettle off the heat before he captured her hand in his and pulled her to him. The tea forgotten, Patricia ignored the rules of propriety and threw her arms around him. "I'm going to miss you." She whispered the hot words into his neck. Vincent turned his head to kiss her cheek. "Will you write?"

She nodded. "Every day." Then she pulled away with a look of worry. "But I don't know where to send the letters."

"I thought of that," he responded with a slight smile. From the tiny pocket of his waistcoat he retrieved a small square of paper. "My aunt and uncle's address is here."

Patricia crushed the paper in her fist and hugged her beau

3

again. "Getting a letter from you every day won't be the same as having you here, but it will help."

When he didn't respond, Patricia concluded he must be overcome with emotion. She allowed them to remain entwined in silence for as long as she could. The sound of footsteps forced her to step away.

"Patsy, who was at the door?" Angela stopped at the entrance to the spacious kitchen when she saw Vincent. "Oh, hello, Vincent," she said. "I understand you are spending the holidays in Frederick. We'll miss having you around here, won't we, Patsy?"

Patricia blushed. "Mr.— Vincent gave me his address in Frederick. I told him I would write." She smiled and cocked her head at her beau. He took her hand.

"I really must be going now." He bowed slightly to Angela. "Mother has a thousand errands for me to run before we leave in the morning."

"Oh, no. So soon?" Patricia was crestfallen.

"Mother thinks I'm on my way to the market. That will take half the afternoon so I knew I could fit in a few minutes with you."

"I'm so glad you did." Patricia smiled again, though she held back tears that burned her eyes. She didn't want Vincent to see her as anything but happy and completely in love with him. She hoped for some tender word of affection from him. But she knew Vincent wouldn't chance such a thing in the presence of her sister.

"Did you want something?" she asked Angela. "I just made some tea."

"Yes, I could do with a—"

"Oh, well, then. Let us get out of your way. I'll walk Vincent to the door." Hoping her sister would keep busy in the kitchen for a few minutes, Patricia picked up Vincent's hat and put her hand in his.

One tear slipped down her cheek as they reached the entrance hall. She leaned against his strong arm and let the warm, soft wool of his coat soothe her face. How would she be able to bear so long a time without him near? She almost asked him until a noise from the kitchen made her stop.

"The holidays won't be the same without you," she said instead. "I was so looking forward to the Winter Ball. I've been dreaming of dancing every dance with you."

"I'm sorry, Patsy." Vincent's dark eyes looked directly into hers and she was sure she could see disappointment there. "But now I must go."

He eased his hat out of her grip, letting his hand rest on hers a little too long. "Farewell, my dearest." He rushed down the front steps.

"Dearest." She echoed Vincent's last word in the faintest of whispers as he hurried away.

Little Timmy stood at her feet, looking up with his liquid brown eyes.

She stooped down to pick him up and nuzzle his sweet head. "Are you my dearest?" she cooed. "Of course you are. Would you like to come help me write my letter? You would?"

Then with a giggle, Patricia gathered her skirts and her dog and swept up to her bedroom. She had to write this very instant. She wanted her love to have a letter waiting for him when he arrived in Frederick. She would miss him terribly all through the winter, but she was determined that he never forget her.

With Timmy resting at her feet she put her pen into the ink pot. Her hand shook as a a sudden thought troubled her: There might be distractions in Frederick that Vincent wouldn't find at home. Her letters would be more important than ever.

She had to be sure he remembered his one true love waited for him, patiently in Annapolis.

From LOVE LETTERS & GINGERBREAD
To be released July 2019
Find it at Amazon.com